JUL   2007

DEMCO

Finding Anna

**Center Point
Large Print**

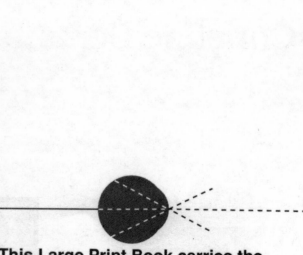

**This Large Print Book carries the
Seal of Approval of N.A.V.H.**

FINDING ANNA

Christine Schaub

CENTER POINT PUBLISHING
THORNDIKE, MAINE

Schaub
Christine

This Center Point Large Print edition
is published in the year 2007 by arrangement with
Bethany House Publishers, a division of Baker Publishing Group

Copyright © 2005 by Christine Schaub.

The text of this Large Print edition is unabridged. In other
aspects, this book may vary from the original edition. Printed in
Thailand. Set in 16-point Times New Roman type.

ISBN-10: 1-58547-995-0
ISBN-13: 978-1-58547-995-5

Library of Congress Cataloging-in-Publication Data

Schaub, Christine.
    Finding Anna / Christine Schaub.--Center Point large print ed.
        p. cm.
    Summary: "An historical drama based on the story behind the hymn 'It Is Well With My
Soul.' When tragedy strikes, Horatio Spafford writes a poem on the back of a telegram--words that
have become a hymn of hope for millions facing sorrow"--Provided by publisher.
    ISBN-13: 978-1-58547-995-5 (lib. bdg. : alk. paper)
    1. Spafford, Horatio Gates, 1828-1888--Fiction. 2. Hymns--Authorship--Fiction.
3. Chicago (Ill.)--Fiction. 4. Hymn writers--Fiction. 5. Large type books. I. Title.

PS3619.C333F56 2007
813'.6--dc22

2007000303

Finding Anna

for Ilah Lucinda Zimmerman Schaub
beloved grandmother and tireless storyteller
Oh, how I miss you . . .

ACKNOWLEDGEMENTS

I will have to begin at the beginning, more than ten years ago, when Steve Williamson (then music minister at East Side Church of God in Anderson, Indiana) asked me, "Do you know the story behind the writing of 'It Is Well With My Soul'?" I answered, much like you would, "I think so."

"You know, it would make a great drama," he told me, the church dramatist. So I researched the story a little, developed it into a drama, and began a "hymn story" franchise that included dramatic tellings of the writings of more than ten great hymns.

Then two years ago I sat in a Nashville Starbucks with Steve Brallier, friend and agent, discussing writing concepts, and I asked him the same question about the hymn. He gave me the same answer. I gave him the short version, and he said, "You know, that would make a great made-for-television movie." And so I developed that hymn and three others into teleplays.

Enter Randall Dennis—a Bethany House author—about a year ago. Brallier and I laid out our movie proposal to Randall, hoping he might interest his publisher in the film production. He listened very patiently, and then said, "You know, these would make great historical novels."

And voilá—you hold my first hymn-story-as-novel in your hands . . . just ten years and three idea-meddlers later. Thanks, guys.

The Research

History rarely reveals itself in an orderly fashion.

I, like many researchers, began with current and out-of-print books, newspaper microfiche, and the Internet. When those were exhausted, I turned to experts for the details, experts like Debbie and the staff at the Chicago Historical Society; Barry Smith, historian for Lincoln Park Presbyterian Church; Mary Pelzer-Cabrera, lawyer and research librarian at the South Street Seaport Museum; Karsten Tveit, Norwegian journalist and author of *Annas Hus* (The House of Anna); Mike Thornton, volunteer research librarian at the New York Public Library; Gary Wollenhaupt, brilliant writer and tireless fact-checker; and Hank Workman, the inspiration for getting started, the "what-if" plotter, the personality profiler. Many, many thanks.

The Writing

I am not a poet. For the original lines of lyrical thought in this book, I must thank David T. Sanders, my own personal bard.

As the research became an outline and the outline became prose, I turned to my small group of tireless readers: Barbara Smith, Pam Clanton, Cory Ridenhour, and my mom, Sondra Schaub. This savvy group gave their fair share of compliments. But, more importantly, they provided invaluable critiques. Bless you.

Many family members and friends cheered me on through this new adventure. You know who you are . . . much love to you.

Finally, heartfelt appreciation goes to the staff at Bethany House Publishers—especially Carol Johnson, Charlene Patterson, and Sharon Asmus—for championing, acquiring, and editing the book to completion. A story like this can only be published when someone believes in you. Thank you, ladies.

FROM THE AUTHOR

"Don't let a few facts get in the way of a good story." That's what my editor told me when the facts suddenly interfered with my narrative timeline late in the writing of this novel. And it is also a wonderful definition of "historical fiction."

Most writers of this genre will exhaust every possible resource to determine the facts of their books' characters and eras—setting, language, dress, culture, attitudes. This is the historical part that intrigues part-time history buffs—something just shy of footnotes and heavy documentation, something close to a biography.

But then comes the fiction part—characters thinking, saying, and doing . . . the intimate details of lives and loves that cannot be found in any public records or newspaper accounts. This is where the writing process becomes really exciting. This is where the story comes alive.

The MUSIC OF THE HEART series marries the history—the known facts behind the writers of our most famous hymns—with the fiction—the imagination of their everyday encounters. If I did my job and convincingly wove those two elements together, if I presented you with a really exciting, plausible story, you won't get caught up in the details, wondering, *Did that really happen?* You'll just believe it.

Read on and then tell me. I'd love to hear from you.

I wonder which grief weighs heavier—
  longing for what you have never had, never known,
or losing what you have *had, what you* have *known.*
  I don't know the answer.
But I do know the weight of each.
                    —THE ROAD TO EDEN'S RIDGE
                 M. L. Rose

PROLOGUE

Atlantic Ocean
December 13, 1873

He stared down at the captain's hand on the chart and suddenly, shamelessly, wanted to smash it, as if crushing the finger pointing to the coordinates would dispel the tragedy and life would return to . . . to what? Exhaustion? Indecision?

O dear God, he prayed. *What have I become? What have I become?*

The captain's finger tapped the chart, just once, and the man tried to focus—47 degrees latitude, 35 degrees longitude.

". . . three miles deep . . ." the captain was saying in his gruff Italian accent.

He continued to stare at the captain's rough hand, the wool sleeve ending just above the cuff of his poplin shirt, shockingly crisp and white against tanned and weathered skin. Four shiny brass buttons stood at attention on the blue fabric, and he could see in them a reflection of himself—distorted, like the reality of the past fortnight.

Was it truly just two Wednesdays hence that he'd closed one of the largest real estate transactions of his professional life? Could he have known amidst handshakes all around that what he cared for most in the world would be lost forever?

15

He'd worked into the night. He'd dined with friends. His days and nights were as they always had been—full of professional and social responsibility.

And then the news report. The paralysis. The inability to make simple decisions—when to eat, how to dress, what to say.

The captain cleared his throat, lifted his hand from the chart, and rested it on his guest's shoulder. He opened his mouth to speak, hesitated, and tried again. "I am deeply sorry for your . . . *enorme* loss."

The man looked up into the captain's deep brown eyes and saw in them an emotion beyond sympathy, an empathy that moved him.

"I know *Capitano* Surmonte," said the Italian, his gaze steady. "He is a good man. And a good friend."

The man nodded and braced himself for the inevitable questions about his own misfortune. But the captain surprised him. "You are a man of God, no?"

He felt his head nod, even though his heart was unsure. Guilt was a relentless and crippling force.

"What say you," demanded the captain, "to a God who gives and takes at will? Who grants mercy and judgment at His pleasure? What say you?"

The man thought about the last two years and had no response.

The captain tightened his grip. "I say, what good is life without Him?"

Horatio Gates Spafford looked again at the map. He knew the answer to that question. And it mattered not.

PART I

Joy and sorrow are inseparable . . .
    Together they come and when one sits
alone with you . . . remember that
    the other is asleep upon your bed.
    —KAHLIL GIBRAN

CHAPTER 1

Chicago
Sunday, October 8, 1871

Spafford stood with a thousand other spectators on the east bank of the Chicago River and simply stared. What he saw was breathtaking in its awful beauty.

For half a mile real estate on the west side of the river glowed orange. Flames danced across the night sky, reflecting off the water, bathing everyone and everything on the riverbank in the warmth of fire-light. A wind blew, carrying across the fire's *crackle-pop* and smell of burning pine. It had all the elements of an early winter evening beside the hearth.

The night was full of sound as steam pumpers clattered down the street, horses' hooves pounding over the Madison Street Bridge, fire marshals and engine foremen shouting orders through their brass-speaking trumpets. The crowd reacted with "oohs" and "ahhs" when the first spray of water doused the burning wood and sent up great clouds of steam, as if from a giant teakettle. The observers pointed and exclaimed, speculation passing in and out of the crowd. "That Irishman, Patrick O'Leary . . ." ". . . firemen into the whiskey . . ." ". . . flames out of control . . ."

And because no one had Tuesday's hindsight, because the madness and weeping had not even

19

begun, because no one had the premonition of disaster, the mood was light and festive.

On this side of the river.

A gust of wind suddenly rushed through the crowd, sending hats and hairpins flying and coattails flapping. Spafford made an expert catch of his own hat as it lifted off his head and settled it precisely back into place.

Everything about the man was precise. He stood exactly six feet with a stalwart frame toned by a preference for walking the rambling route between his law office, the business district, and his vast real estate holdings. His features were strictly patrician and set at perfect angles—the square jaw and sculpted lips, the linear Roman nose, the spike-lashed eyes below arched brows.

He had even aged with perfection. His coal black hair showed gray only at the temples, and tiny lines fanned out from intelligent black eyes set in a perpetually tanned complexion.

He was as meticulous about his appearance as he was his business dealings. His suits were pressed, boots shined, nails trimmed, beard clean-shaven. His stance was both erect and skillfully passive, with no telltale signs of his state of mind.

His precision created an air of excellence and wisdom that inspired men to treat him with respect. His clients and business partners considered him a fair man, and he appreciated that. They also were a bit afraid of the furrowed brow, stubborn jaw, and piercing stare when he was displeased. And that suited him.

At the moment, his lips pursed in silent concern. While the crowd pointed and bantered with no sign of disbursing at such a late hour, the fire seemed to grow. It looked to him to be every bit as big as last night's blaze that had destroyed five square blocks and required sixteen hours of diligent fire fighting.

He squinted at his watch in the glow of the fire-light—close to midnight. Nearly an hour and a half had passed since he'd stepped outside the Opera House and followed the crowd to the riverbank. He really should go home. He stole a last glance across the water, then watched in morbid fascination as the unthinkable happened.

The fire jumped the river.

In one dreadful moment, the wood on the great steeple of St. Paul's Church ignited, caught the wind, and rode to the east side in a terrific shower of sparks. The crowd gasped almost in unison, and shouts of "Across the river!" followed. Within minutes smoke began to choke the bystanders, and they backed en masse up Market Street and across Madison into the heart of downtown Chicago.

Spafford moved with the crowd and, like most of the hurrying people, kept turning to look behind him, surprised at the rolling clouds of smoke and ash caught up in the wind and moving ever faster with them. The night sky was lit with a strange dancing light that cast the familiar into curious shapes and angles. Almost without notice he was in the midst of a block of brick buildings, tall and serene and wholly unfamiliar. He turned about several times, searching for a landmark, and spied a statue of George Washington atop a fierce pawing stallion of the richest black. The president sat the saddle with complete confidence, shoulders back, pointing the way.

Ah, Washington Street, he mused and headed in that direction.

The whole commercial center was electric with hotel guests, businessmen, and late-night sightseers milling about the courthouse lawns, conversing over the clanging of the massive bell that signaled *fire.* The weeks of fall had been unspectacular in their dryness. The leaves did not change color as much as shrivel up like old paper bags, then hang dejectedly until a stale wind coaxed them to the ground to scuttle along the wooden streets. By October the drought-ridden city was averaging six fires a day, and a good blaze on a warm Sunday night kept the crowd outside and buzzing with excitement.

He stood gazing hypnotically at the colorful sky until it occurred to him that if he could catch a bridge across the river, he could watch the fire's progress from a safe distance and height . . . in his own office.

He turned up Clark Street and arrived at the river just in time to watch the iron swing bridge, loaded with people, halt in the middle of the river while ships of every size passed through to Lake Michigan—a curious sight for the middle of the night. He'd had the misfortune of being "bridged" for long stretches of time and considered the LaSalle Street Tunnel a better option.

Off he headed down Clark, turning west on Lake Street. At the corner he looked toward the Sherman House and was surprised to see that during his short trek the formerly passive crowd had turned anxious. The sidewalks were crammed full of people looking upward, shielding their eyes against the falling ash. Guests hung out of hotel windows, pointing and shouting, their words tossed into the wind. Spafford listened closely but could decipher nothing until it was passed down the street toward him. And then what he heard made his blood run cold.

The gasworks were on fire.

The explosions started soon after, and the already anxious crowd panicked. Spafford raced down the next block and turned on LaSalle. The tunnel—just opened in July—loomed ahead. The vehicles in the center passageways were moving in a calm and orderly fashion, both north and south, and the footway glowed under the lights, revealing pedestrians moving steadily.

Spafford stepped into the underground highway and walked quickly under the river. The air was moist and cool here, and he relaxed for the first time in an hour. He started devising a plan. He would go to his office, secure essential documents, then look for a cab that would take him north into Lake View. The hour must be excessively late. He reached for his pocket watch, trying to guess at the time when, without so much as a flicker, the gaslights went out. A moment of stunned silence was followed by the screams of horse and driver plunged into total blackness. *Fool!* He admonished himself. *You knew the gasworks were in flames.* Through the stone wall Spafford heard the unmistakable sounds of a mass of frightened humanity trapped underground with skittish horses.

People in the footway had come to an immediate halt. Seconds ticked by, then a murmuring began, followed by a slow jostling, then apologies all around as strangers collided in the darkness. And then, gridlock. Their side of the tunnel was remarkably quiet and composed while they waited for verbal direction passed down from either end. People stood amicably, breathing in and out. The scent of lavender drifted toward him, and he thought of his wife, abed several hours by now.

He pictured her there. Her golden hair would be tied with a ribbon to match the trim of her nightgown. She would be lying on her side, one hand tucked under her cheek, a child's pose that suited her delicate features. When he slid into bed, she would open her eyes and smile ever so briefly, revealing very white and even teeth. And then she would return to her slumber on the lavender-scented sheets, content that he was beside her.

Content was a word he used often with Anna. Her Norwegian heritage had instilled in her a realism and discipline that resulted in few surprises. She was nei-

24

ther dramatic nor excessive, like so many wives of his colleagues, and therefore rarely dissatisfied. She'd had certain simple expectations when she'd married him—a cheerful home filled with flowers and children, a dining room open to friends and strangers alike for long lively suppers, a parlor for entertainment round the piano.

And that's what he had given her. His business success had allowed him to give her more, but she'd never come to expect it. And her surprise and delight at each gift, at each thoughtful gesture, was Elysium to him.

A more intense jostling brought him back to the tunnel, and the word was passed: North. All pedestrians must travel north. There was an edge of urgency to the message, and Spafford wondered at it as the crowd shuffled along in the darkness, then gained a little space, then moved freely under the river.

At last he was out of the tunnel and onto the ramp, then on the wooden sidewalk, clattering along with the crowd now laughing with embarrassment and relief. And then in slow motion, it seemed, they all turned and looked behind them.

Across the Chicago River, as close as Washington Street, the business district was consumed with red tongues of light. It seemed impossible, as he had just come from there. He stared in wonder. The Chamber of Commerce, Brunswick Hall, and Methodist Church all seemed to be burning. That would have to mean Farwell Hall was destroyed, and the Reynolds Block and McVicker's Theatre. It looked to be a wall of flame for blocks behind those buildings. His spirit took a tremendous plunge.

He was ruined.

All the money he and his friends had invested just this spring in land—land to the north, land in the direction of an expanding city—was folly. Chicago would not expand. It might not even recover. His ears were ringing with alarm, and he shook his head to clear them.

The fire brigade pulled up and began pumping the chilly water directly from the river and throwing it onto the facing buildings. "Little Giant" was stamped across the engine's side, and indeed, it looked to be a David and Goliath moment. Spafford turned up LaSalle and prayed they could stop this violence.

Within moments he was standing outside his office building, torn between continuing on to Anna or gathering essential paperwork from his desk and safe.

Somewhere a bell tolled one.

Spafford looked up. The unmistakable glow of kerosene lamps lit the upper-floor windows with a soft, inviting light. He hung his head. McDaid was inside and must be told of their loss.

He dragged himself up the stairs, forming the words that would forever change his partner's life and livelihood. At the landing he scanned the brass nameplate:

SPAFFORD & McDAID
ESTABLISHED 1867

Five years they'd worked together, two with another partner, the last three comfortably paired in Rooms 4 and 5 at 147 LaSalle.

The office was open, and Spafford stood in the doorway watching his partner sort methodically through a mound of papers. He stepped into the room and clicked the door shut. McDaid looked up from the files just long enough to acknowledge him.

"The real estate paperwork is scattered. Truly, I thought it more organized."

Spafford grimaced. "Leave it."

McDaid ignored him. "I've managed to find the original investment with all signatures and the profit forecast—"

"Henry."

McDaid looked up, a wariness in his eyes.

"The business district is gone."

"Gone?"

"I stood at the river and watched it burn. The hotels, the banks, the theatres—all are gone."

Several emotions flashed across McDaid's face—confusion, disbelief, horror, and finally resignation. Spafford knew the same realization had struck his partner—that the bulk of their investment, land for enlarging parks and expanding a growing metropolis, was useless now. For who could think of such trivialities when an entire commercial city must be rebuilt? He noted how his partner's shoulders slumped, then squared as he carefully organized the paperwork and slid it into his valise anyway.

27

Spafford watched him work a few more moments. Theirs was an easy partnership. Where he was outspoken—even blunt—with clients, McDaid was reserved and cautious. His partner could sit through hours of meetings, taking meticulous notes, smiling at the animated bantering, and speak no more than five words. While he itched to be out, surveying new properties and soliciting clients, his partner was content to work complex financial equations and pore over tedious real estate law at his desk. Their personalities and skills were a true complement to each other. It was what made the law firm of Spafford & McDaid so successful.

But their partnership was more than that. McDaid was deceptively smart, driven, and a gentleman—in short, the brother Spafford had always wanted. He had never known a kinder, gentler man than Henry McDaid—a man no one hated, a man who would drop his jaw in astonishment to learn that his partner aspired to be more like him.

A gale-like wind shook the building, rattling the windows, and the men looked up and out in unison. Beyond the panes it looked as if a snowstorm was in full force . . . little flakes of ash stained with fire.

Spafford's hands hung at his sides like iron weights. The futility of it all overwhelmed him. He could not even bring himself to step into the adjoining law library with its leather-bound volumes of books—books on which he'd lavished so much money and pride. But McDaid's persistent sorting and storing provided a purpose and a glimmer of hope that they would recover from this, that all would not be lost. He moved to his desk and started to work.

No words passed between the two men as they saved and discarded papers pertinent to their corporate survival. Land leases, client histories, court judgments came and went.

When the glass on the windows facing the street cracked and the frames began to smoke, they worked faster. When their valises bulged, they removed large documents to the steel safe and became more selective.

When smoke crept into the room and hovered near the ceiling, Spafford consulted his watch—half past two. He moved to the window and peered out through the rolling fumes. In the distance, aglow like a warrior's torch, the courthouse's grand cupola blazed in majestic beauty. As he watched, the tower glowed even brighter, then crumbled inward, the massive bell still clanging until, with a resounding thud that shook the earth, the symbol of a thousand civic ceremonies and celebrations tolled no more.

He was surprised at the tears that sprang to his eyes. He wanted to weep at the destruction before him and bowed his head, schooling his emotions until the intense heat emanating from the cracked glass forced him to jerk back.

He looked toward the street, and what he saw and heard in that brief moment was enough to propel him into action. He grabbed his valise off his desk, fastened it, and turned to McDaid.

"We must go. Now."

McDaid never slowed. "Just a few more documents."

Spafford stopped him with a viselike grip on his upper arm. "The sidewalks are on fire and people are stampeding in the street. We are in danger here."

As if in emphasis, a ball of flame burst through the window, scattering little pockets of fire across the room, igniting stacks of papers. McDaid slammed and locked the safe, then grabbed his valise, and the two men dashed out the door and down the stairs.

At street level, the scene was pure chaos. The door had burst open and flames from the sidewalk licked at the frame. In the street, panic-stricken people pushed and shoved, screaming children crushed behind their parents, and everywhere cinders fell like snowflakes, lighting new fires.

Spafford took one look and pushed McDaid back into the hallway. He was shouting now, the street noise and roar of collapsing buildings deafening. "You must get to Anna if I cannot. And I will do the same with Dora. Lake View may be too close to the forest to be spared. Go to the north beach in Lincoln Park. Anna knows the place. I will find her there."

McDaid nodded. "God be with you." The partners and friends clasped hands and locked eyes now red from smoke. "And also with you."

Out the door they ran, leaping across the burning sidewalk and into the masses of stampeding people. It was futile to do anything but move with the crowd as it surged forward, the leaders searching for a street or alleyway not yet consumed by smoke and fire.

Barely one block west the crowd came to a bone-crushing halt, and Spafford turned his head, looked back, and watched as the law offices of Spafford & McDaid, against a backdrop of a lurid yellowish red, crumbled to the ground. The collapse made a tremendous roar and sent a storm cloud of dust and cinders rolling down the jammed street. And as he threw up his hand to shield his eyes, he instinctively thought of the biblical promise that in hell everyone will be salted with fire.

He clutched his valise to his chest and his hat to his head and determined he would not test that promise today.

He watched the destruction march toward him, masses of flames bounding from building to building, and could see that the pace of the fire would soon out-match that of the crowd. He cast about for McDaid, not finding him, then fought his way to the street's edge and leapt onto the elevated sidewalk, jumping over flaming wood and bundles, halting at the edge of Wells.

Here, the route was swarming with a rush of people streaming across the Wells Street Bridge on horseback, in carts, carriages, wheelbarrows, and every type of conveyance. Horses pranced and tore at their harnesses. Stray cows, dogs, and cats ran terrified through the people on foot. The din of screaming children and animals and shouts of "North! North!" was terrible.

He calculated his odds and decided to continue westward toward the north branch of the river. It was no more than four blocks away, and he could fling himself into the water if the heat and fumes became too great. A plan formed as he fought his way across the crowd. He would get to the river and cross at the railroad trestle on Kinzie. The area was nothing but iron track. Surely it would not burn.

But he underestimated the desperation of the fleeing crowd. He tried to push westward, and the people dragged him north. He watched a man on horseback force his way through, flinging a whip left and right, his horse trampling those who would not yield. He wanted to tear the brute from his saddle and watched in some satisfaction as many of those marked by the whip did just that.

And always they were just moments from being consumed by the fire.

They were surrounded now by near-constant explosions of stores of oil and other combustible material. Windows blew out, showering them with glass, tearing into their skin. Buildings fell with a force, their bricks, boards, and burning shingles picked up by a hurricane wind and flung over their heads, falling around them, setting their hair and clothing ablaze.

It was more horrific than any description of the bowels of hell.

At last, singed and bleeding, his hat still miraculously on his head, Spafford was on the other side and at an intersection he was sure was Wells and Ohio. He turned left and was suddenly, eerily, alone.

Buildings burned on both sides of the street, and the air was so full of dust that he could see no more than half a block ahead. He hesitated, glancing back at the mass of stampeding people. Should he go west when everyone else headed north? The wrong decision could cost him his life.

A sudden, terrific explosion pitched him forward and blew his waistcoat over his head. He tumbled like an oak leaf down the burning street, his valise clutched tightly against his chest, and slid to a halt against a stack of bricks.

His body numb and hearing muffled, he scooted to an upright position and tried to disentangle his coat from his head. Hot, sticky objects slapped against him, and he ducked down, deciding to leave the coat in place and peer out at his surroundings.

Truly the Day of Judgment had come.

The air was full of firebrands—little red and yellow devils that darted and swirled through the street, tugging burning planks and shingles along like kites. He watched in disbelief as a marble-topped dresser danced silently by, collecting embers in its open drawers. A man's shirt sailed close behind, sleeve outstretched, waving good-bye.

He shook his head. He felt as if he were in a dream—a nightmare with no sound and no escape. Yet he was awake and alive and still in command of his limbs.

The ground rumbled and the wall at his back collapsed inward, sending up and out a cloud of dust so thick he could see no more than a few feet around him.

He struggled to his feet, peeking out through the coat, hearing little. A curtain of embers fell in front of him and lit the street. The gale-force winds still blew but now were filled with particles that pinged against his torso like sewing needles. He turned and followed the wind, the needles at his back.

Monday, October 9, 1871

He woke with a yell and looked wildly about him. The children! Where were his children! He groped around for Bessie, reaching for her little arms still pudgy with baby fat. His hand connected with rough wood, and his surroundings came into slow focus.

He was on a pile of lumber, on a dock, on the edge of the river. It was daylight, but the sky was overcast and hazy with smoke, and as far as the eye could see north and south, across the river, Chicago was aflame. The Queen City of the West was no more. He stared at the sight, dry-eyed.

What time was it? He pulled his watch from his waistcoat, blinked down at it, then remembered. The crystal on his watch had shattered in the explosion, and the mechanism had stopped at three minutes after four o'clock this morning. He recalled fighting his way to the river, crossing at Kinzie Street, turning down Canal, and collapsing close to the water. He looked around and recognized his whereabouts as Avery's Lumberyard.

He lay back down, sick of the sight of burning buildings, sick of the running, desperate for a drink of cool water. He closed his eyes and immediately opened them as his nightmare returned. Anna was there, surrounded by Annie, Maggie, and Bessie, baby Tanetta in her arms. They were gathered in the parlor around the rosewood piano, holding quite still for a family photo. Except, he was not with them. He was standing in the hallway watching them smile, watching the picture start to burn around the edges, watching the flames move closer and closer, shouting at them to *run!* Watching in horror as they kept smiling, even while the flames licked at their faces.

Tears streamed down his cheeks, and he forced himself off the lumber pile with a sob. He had to keep moving. He had to find his family.

He turned north and followed the river, still clutching his battered valise. He trudged block after block, choked by the smoke, his throat screaming for moisture. Not a soul was on the streets, and he supposed they had fled west to the prairies when word came that this fire jumped rivers. But it hadn't crossed the river here. Not yet.

He finally reached Chicago Avenue and found a well where, mercifully, someone had left a tin cup. He pumped the handle and fresh water trickled out, just enough for a desperate man and a little cup. The feel of it on his tongue and throat was enough to move him to tears again. He choked them down, rested no more than ten minutes, and continued north.

By nightfall he came to North Avenue. He had spent precious time at each street crossing, turning east to the edge of the water, turning back from the flames, then finding a way across the river's north branch, then back to the canal. As dusk settled, he realized he'd walked all day and covered less than two miles.

A current of defeat coursed through him. He would never make it in time. He would die failing to protect his family. He leaned against a wooden fence, slid down to the ground, and wept like a child. The burning photo played over and over in his mind. He tried to think. He tried to pray. But all that came to his mind were snippets of verses about hell, being cast into hell . . . soul and body in hell . . . the rich man in hell.

He tried to think of better verses. He would recite the Twenty-third Psalm. But how did it go? Panic was taking over his mind. He couldn't think. He couldn't breathe. He was sick with worry.

And then he heard a voice—not his own—from deep within.

Pray.

He was trying to pray, but he could not remember the psalm! It had always been such a comfort to him, and now he could not even recall—David! King David wrote it. He was sure of that. But he wasn't always a king. He was a . . . a . . .

Speak to me . . . from your own heart.

His mind went blank. From his *own* heart? He couldn't. He didn't know where to begin. What could he say that could possibly be more eloquent, more worthy, than the words of a king?

Come to me . . .

He heard the voice and instantly his heart completed the phrase. *And I will give you rest.*

So he sat perfectly still somewhere on North Avenue, just yards from fallen walls and blackened trees, and for the first time in his forty-three years, he bared his soul and had a simple conversation with the Lord.

CHAPTER 2

Lincoln Park, Chicago
11:00 P.M.

She would not bury her children. Anna's mind registered the panic racing through the crowd, heard the repeated cries of "The fire is at the gates!" She felt the crush of bodies pressed close, breathed in the acrid smoke, and resolved: She would stand in the chilly water with her children even if the flames licked at their backs. But she would not bury them in the sand.

Perhaps the men who frantically dug the holes on the beach were smarter than she was. Perhaps the women and children climbing into those sandy graves

37

were braver, more trusting. But no matter what befell them this night, she would never be able to release the image of burying her children alive—even to escape the fire.

The park had been so calm, idyllic even, when they'd arrived—she, the children, the servants, and the McDaids. They were so certain of their safety here that they'd spread a blanket on the sand and enjoyed a picnic lunch.

But that had been twelve hours ago—twelve hours of, first, common concern, then speculation and worry when husbands returned for just moments to report on the fire's rapid advance, then real fear when burned and tattered refugees told morbid tales of devastation. Then anguish, the air filled with quiet weeping.

And as dusk fell and the sky was lit by the strange orange glow of the fire that raged throughout the city, she'd taken the baby and gone for a walk toward the front gates, hoping to find encouraging news. But there, among the empty graves of the old cemetery, she found people—possibly neighbors and friends—so grimy with dust and smoke, so strangely dressed in fragments of clothing, they were unrecognizable as male or female.

They said not a word, but sat with their precious bundles close to them, forlorn in every way, smarting with burns, the whites of their eyes in ghostly contrast to their blackened skin. They looked up only at sudden powerful gusts of wind that carried smoke from afar and scattered leaves, ready to flee, yet again, in an instant.

Anna was glad for the dust that filled her eyes, that forced her to turn away from the gate and disappear into the thickening crowd. She trudged through the park, trying every distraction her mind could invent to push away the image of Gates, blackened and burned, running from the flames.

She thought of him on the day he'd proposed to her, so tall and handsome, so overpoweringly masculine. She thought of the confident and optimistic look on his face as he'd taken the wedding vows and sealed them with a kiss. She thought of his joy when she'd told him of her pregnancy. She thought of the letters.

The letters. When Henry had come to their door this morning, exhausted and filthy from his trek north, and told her to pack what she most valued, she'd fled to her dressing room—not for jewels or money or artwork in gilded frames. Those she could replace. It was the letters Gates had written to her that were dear to her in a way that superseded financial value. For her husband hid from the world an extraordinary love and talent for sculpting words and phrases into literary masterpieces. She thought of his first poem penned to her when she was but seventeen and away at school.

Deep in my heart it grows
Yet only my God knows
An interest I concede
Has begun to overcome me.

39

She smiled at the recollection. Her husband could have easily become a novelist, an essayist, a poet—and enjoyed considerable vogue—if he'd been willing to share his gift with the world. But his willingness went only as far as to his own home, his own wife.

So Anna had collected her treasured letters, placed them with her Bible and her mother's watch in a waterproof satchel, and hurried below.

Dottie, efficient as ever, had already dressed the children in warm coats, hats, and gloves, even though the October weather was too mild for such attire. At the look on her mistress' face, the housemaid set her jaw and was dangerously close to a sass.

"I dun lived through Atlanta, ma'am. I knows what to do." And with that, she held out a coat and helped her missus into it.

Anna smiled now, reliving the moment and praising God for Dottie's foresight. They had, indeed, needed the coats to protect their skin from falling embers.

Nicolet had descended the stairs like the nobility her Huguenot family had been and every bit the example of French refinement in the face of peril. "*Volons, mes petits oiseaux,*" she had said to her young charges. *Let us fly, my little birds.* And they had grasped hands with their beloved governess, smiling up at her with complete confidence.

And then Anna praised God for Cook, who had thought to make an adventure of their escape by packing an impressive reserve of food and calling it a picnic.

It almost seemed an adventure when Henry returned to their door minutes later and loaded them into his wagon. He worked in a restrained hurry as he settled Annie, Maggie, and Nicolet amongst the trunks and placed Bessie on his wife's lap.

But when he reached for Anna's hand, she turned and looked at her house and saw the stone porch where she liked to take her first coffee, and the inlaid wood of the massive front doors, and the mums in grand planters flowering so peacefully in the late autumn. It seemed impossible to her that this house, with the intimacy of ten years of marriage and birth and childhood and all the books and pictures and relics of that time, could crumble and blow away in the southwest wind.

It seemed impossible that she was looking upon her home for the last time.

Henry squeezed her hand, and she clutched the baby to her chest, allowing him to pull her into the wagon. And off they flew down Clark Street. And nobody spoke at all.

The only thing that kept her sane after dusk was knowing that Henry had gone to find Gates. He'd kept his promise and delivered them to Lincoln Park, then unhitched the horse from the wagon, kissed his wife, and rode back into the city.

She looked over at Dora—hand-in-hand with Maggie, every bit the second child, the drama of it all more enticing than the danger, even for her brief seven years. Anna hoped she and Dora were not now widows. She searched for Dottie and found her knee-deep in water she could not swim in, humming softly to Bessie who clung to her neck, wide-eyed in three-year-old wonder. She tried to smile at Cook, then Nicolet, her arm around Annie—so wise for her nine years, obedient, confident, never questioning their circumstances. She looked down at Tanetta—just an infant, so reliant and trusting.

And now, with the fire at the gates, she thought she would go mad from the responsibility of it all.

So she did what she always did in times of trouble—she spoke to the Lord. Her lips never moved, but she poured out her heart. She asked Him to watch over Gates, to spare his life and comfort him if they should perish. She thanked Him for Henry and Dora, for their influence and their courage. She praised Him for His mercy.

As she prayed for the families around her, she looked down at her own glassy-eyed children, shivering in the frigid water, backs hunched to the wind, and cried out as she had a hundred times that day. *What shall I do? How shall I save my children?* And this time He answered her.

Sing.

And so she sang. At first, she sang children's songs designed to move their lips mechanically and keep their teeth from chattering. Then she tried little scripture verses set to music in Sunday school to engage their troubled minds. A smattering of childlike voices joined them on "Jesus Loves Me," and she was encouraged.

Finally, she began to sing the great hymns. The smoke swirled around them, and falling embers hissed when they touched the water. But many more voices joined her, and her own voice grew stronger as she sang, "Abide with me . . . help of the helpless, O abide with me!" When that song ended, she recalled hymn after hymn, singing, "Jesus, the very thought of thee with sweetness fills my breast."

Then an Irish tenor began "Rock of ages, cleft for me, let me hide myself in Thee." And the voice was so pure, so rich that a full verse passed before a single person dared to join in. But join they did. Soon a powerful chorus in four-part harmony filled the eastern bank, then the park, words of God's amazing grace and love ringing out across Lake Michigan. Song after song began anew—sometimes by a baritone, often a tenor.

And then, "Praise God from whom all blessings flow! Praise Him all creatures here below! Praise Him above, ye heav'nly host! Praise Father, Son, and Holy Ghost!"

As she lifted her face to sing the "Amen," she felt a cool substance strike her cheek. And then another, and another. And after a brief moment of complete silence, the park erupted in joy.

Rain.

There was no warning of its coming. No thunder, no lightning, no cooling breeze. It was as soft and unexpected as a summer shower from clear blue skies, refreshing and invigorating.

Almost immediately the sparks stopped flying. The leaves and trees stopped igniting. The wind still blew, but now it caressed their skin with moisture.

Shouts reverberated around the park. The rain that had eluded them for three long months finally, mysteriously, appeared and put out the fire. It was as if God stood at their gates, outstretched His mighty hand, and said, "No more."

Miraculous . . . miraculous.

CHAPTER 3

Lincoln Park
Dawn, October 10

Spafford stood at the charred and twisted gates to the old cemetery, refusing to believe that all might be lost to him, unwilling to enter the smoking ruins to confirm it. All along the once peaceful fence smoldered the remains of furniture and trees and shrubs. Blackened grave markers of those once resting here fumed around cracked marble vaults.

He stared at the wreckage and reeled with the knowledge that he'd sent his wife and children into hell. With the fire at the gate and the water behind them, they must have been faced with a terrible choice: to burn or to drown.

Oh, God! his heart cried. *Why did you save me for this?*

He swayed slightly as the sky lightened to a somber

gray and the ghosts of Chicago's dead moved silently through the rain. He watched, fascinated, as the specters slowly bent and straightened, interacting solemnly with one another, bowing heads, cradling children. He followed the movements of a particular spirit who glided through the debris, looking left and right, touching nothing until it stopped at the smoldering fence.

And then it spoke to him.

"Sir?"

Spafford opened his mouth but could not respond. The icy hand of death and fear and despair had gripped his heart and throat, tightening, squeezing until his eyes began to close and his mouth went slack.

But the spirit persisted. "Sir? Are you looking for someone?"

His eyes flew open. Yes! He inhaled a great gulp of damp air, clearing his mind, focusing. He took in the rain-soaked dress, the smoke-streaked skin, and realized he was facing a very real, very human, young woman. He struggled and found his voice.

"I'm looking for . . . my wife."

She nodded and gestured toward the sagging gates. "Do come into the park. We can help you."

He took one hesitant step, then another, then hurried past the smoking fence, the crumbling markers, and came to a halt at the sudden vista before him.

Thousands, no, *tens* of thousands of people huddled together in the rain as far as he could see through the haze. They crowded under trees—trees!—oaks and pines unmarred by flames. He wanted to laugh for the sheer pleasure of finding something living, something untouched by fire. He wanted to sink to his knees and give thanks for this remarkable refuge. He wanted to run to the beach and find his wife.

But he did none of those things because he was immediately surrounded by people eager for information. They all began talking at once—earnest, persistent, desperate.

"Sir, do you know about Trinity Church on Van Buren? My nephew went there."

"Sir, my parents were at the Tremont. Did it survive?"

"Were the hospitals saved, sir?"

"The YMCA—did it burn?"

He looked into the hopeful faces and could not bring himself to describe the scene of destruction, the stampedes to escape the very locations they mentioned. He searched his mind and found a response he trusted would ease their worry. For now.

"There was a tremendous exodus to the west . . . over the Randolph Street Bridge. Thousands were saved." He singled out one young man to whom he could give a forthright response. "The Tremont did not survive, but it was evacuated in time."

An elderly woman touched his sleeve, and he strained to hear her quivering voice. "Is it true, then? Is Chicago lost to us?"

The small crowd fell silent, blinking in the rain,

waiting for his proclamation. He felt the crushing responsibility of proffering inspiration when faced with defeat, and called upon his years as a lawyer and teacher to hearten these hurting people.

"The buildings may be gone, but the spirit of the city remains. Chicago will survive." And in his heart he believed it.

More people approached with more questions, and he felt the panic rise in him again. He wanted to help these people, but he needed to find Anna.

His anxiety must have shown because the young woman—a true negotiator—took pity on him and eased him away from the crowd, telling them of his mission.

"We must go, dear people. This man, like you, searches for his loved ones."

The crowd reluctantly parted.

No more than fifty yards away, she turned. "Do you wish me to call for her?"

He shook his head, her meaning eluding him. And then, with the blood no longer rushing through his ears, nor the panicky heartbeat pounding in his brain, he heard them—voices, male and female, young and old, echoing through the early morning hush. They called without decorum—no fashionable titles, no divisions of wealth or status. Just first and last names.

"Mary Hutcheson! Mary!"

"Jonas Barkley! Jonas Barkley!"

"Aurelia Thomas! Aurelia! Aurelia!"

They called, but no one answered. And it tore at his

47

soul to think of those lost, never to be found.

The woman gently touched his arm. "Where can I take you?"

"There is a place on the north beach. My wife . . . we both know it well."

He followed as she picked her way through the park, around families still asleep under trees, around makeshift tents. They passed by people in every class of life, lying in the rain, living out of doors—the rich and poor of yesterday divided only by their memories of what had been.

He tried to keep his mind blank as they trudged onward, not daring to hope his family had endured. But as he passed through the camps of survivors by the thousands, his step lightened. He knew in his heart that McDaid had reached them in time. He knew it.

At last they arrived at the northern shore. It was mostly deserted under the leaden sky, waves rolling onto the beach, giving the impression of tranquility even in a downpour. He saw what looked like shallow graves dug in the sand. He glanced away and asked no questions, for he did not want to know the horrors that transpired here.

He and the young woman spotted the lone figure at once. "Your wife?" He nodded, and she turned back toward the gate without a word. Another family restored.

He trod the final yards of his harrowing journey, watching his wife, now kneeling in the sand, praying—for him, he knew. Her clothes, drawn close around her, were wet and filthy, her hair matted to her head. But he had never found her more alluring, more appealing.

She knelt near the very spot where he had dropped to one knee ten years ago, her hand in his, and said to her what he had written and rewritten and rehearsed and remembered even to this day—"Miss Anna Larson, I am in need of more to my existence. I will that you would be my wife." He remembered the slow smile that had spread across her young face, how she'd dropped to his level and reached for his other hand and said, "But, of course."

He remembered all this and the following happy years in a flash. And for a moment, looking across at her still form, the horror of the past hours faded away.

But then she looked up, her eyes widened, and he watched her take it all in—his blackened face, his tattered, singed clothing, his mangled boots and twisted valise. He watched her assess the damage and conclude without asking that he'd survived a terrible ordeal. And they would never have to speak of it.

He stopped before her, reached out his filthy hand, and helped her to her feet. Slowly they came together in the rain—alive, united.

He knew he clung to her more than she to him. It had always been that way—his fierce possessiveness and drive matched against her emotional steadiness and acceptance. Sometimes, in a rare moment of introspection, he acknowledged the imbalance and marveled that it did not trouble him.

He rested his weary cheek on her head and looked out at the masses of people. Whole families gathered miserably in the rain—thousands of cold and weary women and children. His heart thudded. An uneasy feeling welled up and settled within him.

"Anna . . . the children . . " His head suddenly pounded as the image of children running lost and terrified through the burning streets played over and over in his mind. His skin flushed with heat, and he heard his own voice wail from a distance. "Where is Maggie?"

She caught him as he began to fall, as he finally gave in to the exhaustion and shock he'd held so long at bay. He heard her voice as if from a distance, spoken in a rush as she cradled him on the wet sand. "They are home, darling."

He moaned, believing she spoke of a heavenly rest. Her cool hands lifted his face to look directly into hers—her eyes wide, he knew, at the sight of unchecked tears streaming down his blistered cheeks.

"Listen to me, Gates. The children are safe with Nicolet. They are asleep even now, in their beds, *in our home.*" She released his face and spoke in steely tones. "The fire did not come to Lake View." And under her breath she murmured, "It would not dare."

He struggled to speak. "Yet you are here . . . in this godforsaken place."

"I would not go. Henry—Dear, dear Henry . . . He tried every form of persuasion. But I vowed to remain

50

on this beach until you came or they dragged me to the church to hear the death bells toll."

He relaxed then, safe at last. His office was gone and his livelihood diminished, but the core of his existence—his faith, his marriage, his home—was intact. He thought of the long journey here, his terror of losing what was most dear to him driving him on through indescribable mayhem and ruin. And he considered there was possibly no greater feeling in the world than that of being welcomed into the arms of the one who knows you and loves you most.

They sat on the beach, the rain drenching them and making them shiver, but he could not bring himself to break the embrace. The journey had nearly destroyed them, but they had found each other again—lovers, believers, friends.

CHAPTER 4

It wasn't until Gates squeezed her arm and said, "I know," that Anna realized she'd said aloud what she'd been chanting in her head for the past half mile—*Almost home . . . almost home . . .*

Lake View was a little more than a mile from Lincoln Park, but the going had been agonizingly slow. Fires still burned north of the park's boundaries, and they'd been forced to zigzag through nameless streets, searching for alternate routes through the devastation before they broke free.

And what devastation. In all of her wildest imaginings while she'd stood in the lake and prayed for Gates' safety, she could not have conceived of this. It was truly desolate—once beautiful neighborhoods now reduced to broken columns, crumbled walls, and blackened trees. As they'd trudged through streets lined with smoldering furniture and bundles of broken treasures, she'd found herself wondering what demon had passed through here. What incubus could melt steel and tumble stone? It was as if the war had reignited, the canons bombarding, Sherman marching, landscapes altered, and all so indiscriminately.

She feared the people of Chicago would never recover from it.

Gates seemed unfazed by their surroundings as he'd shuffled along in his mangled boots, exhausted, scorched, and soaked to the bone. Many times, lost in thought, she'd forged ahead, then stopped and waited for him to catch up. And each time she'd been shocked to watch her husband's once erect figure, usually a picture of vim and vigor, now warped and stooped over like an old man.

And all the time little snippets of overheard conversations in the park tumbled through her mind. *We are in ruins . . . all, all are gone . . . I know not what I shall do . . .*

Even when they'd moved beyond the fuming neighborhoods, the gray light of an early rainy morning had simply shifted her mood from shock to grim contemplation. She had only a vague idea of what kind of ruin lay south and west of the park. She had a better understanding of the displaced families. *I know not what I shall do . . .*

When they finally made the turn onto their macadam street and her eyes picked out the brick and stone facade of their house lurking in the gray morning, she was overwhelmed by conflicting emotions—relief that they'd been spared, shame at the elegance and comfort available to them when so many of their fellow Chicagoans suffered. *I know not what I shall do . . .*

Gates was stumbling on the small broken stones, dragging his feet in exhaustion. She fought against every instinct to sprint the last yards and fling open the gates, taking her husband's arm instead, supporting his weight, marching on.

At last they stood in front of their untouched home, she running a practiced eye over the porch and mums and double doors, he contemplating the stone steps with a grimace. She pulled on the iron gate, smiling at its familiar creak when the massive entrance cracked open and Dottie slipped out, closing the door behind her. There was such a look of anxiety on her usually smooth face that Anna halted midstep.

"What is it, Dottie?"

Dottie's mouth worked, but no sound came out.

Anna felt her blood run cold. "Is it the children?"

Dottie shook her head. "No, ma'am. The chil'ren's in they beds, dreamin' o' better times."

Anna nodded encouragement and moved toward

her, but Dottie backed against the door, her hands gripping the brass knob behind her.

Anna frowned and drifted up the steps toward her, cautious as a skater testing the ice. Dottie's eyes never left her mistress, and her hands gripped the knob tighter.

"I din't know what to do, ma'am. You was gone, and the mister." She nodded at Gates, who stood very still on the sidewalk, bracing himself on the iron gate. "They started comin' soon as I lit the lamp. The gaslights is out, and I . . . I . . ." She pursed her lips. "I know'd the first ten or so an' thought as you'd prob'ly be wantin' to help. But then . . ." She looked down miserably as her voice trailed off.

Anna placed her hand on Dottie's shoulder, squeezing. "Why don't we step inside . . ." And she gently worked the maid's hand free of the knob and opened the door.

Dottie mumbled, "I din't know what to do . . ."

Anna stepped through the dark vestibule and opened the door to the hall.

People. Masses of people—whole families with children tucked into their parents' sides—lined the floor of the grand hallway, sleeping the sleep of exhaustion. The massive hall rug was rolled up, the outline of it making a small pathway on the dusty wood floor to the stairs and back door. Piles of luggage and dirty bundles teetered against the pale blue walls. She looked to her left through the doors flung wide open into the parlor. The woven carpet there was gone, and furniture had been pushed against the papered walls to make room for more people. People on the velvet settee and every available surface. People under the grand piano. People she'd never seen before. Her eyes darted toward the dining room, the pocket doors pushed back, the mahogany chairs upside down on the table to make room for people to lie underneath.

And everywhere, permeating every breath of air, was the odor of smoke and burned skin and bodies covered in the sweat of panic and fatigue.

She felt behind her for the doorframe and encountered the solid wall of her husband's chest. She could not draw breath. Her mind raced and froze in intervals. So many people. Where did they come from? Such numbers of children. How could she care for them all? She looked to her husband, who seemed to be at the same loss for intelligent thought.

Then she felt Dottie's work-worn hand take hers and begin to lead her carefully, silently, down the long hallway, past the sleeping masses, past the mounds of blackened trunks and valises toward the only place the woman ever felt comfortable speaking her mind in the magnificent and genteel house—the kitchen.

Spafford rode out against his wife's wishes. She'd begged him to stay and rest. And he'd tried all morning, and failed, and his leave-taking had resulted in one of their rare arguments. He'd left her standing in the door of their bedroom, unable to explain that every time he'd started to lose himself in the bed's softness, he'd jerked awake, running, always running, from fires, from smoke. Looking for her, calling for her, followed ever by the flames.

He'd had a quick bath and found a legitimate mission—to locate more food and water for the horde of people taking refuge in their home. They'd yet to make an accurate count, with guests at various times on three floors, in eight bedrooms, moving through the first-floor rooms to exchange chilling accounts of their flight, going out to determine the fate of friends and family left behind.

They'd eaten breakfast in four shifts, as the coffee and bread became available and the dishes had been washed and rewashed. He estimated the small army of women under Cook's command had fed nearly fifty people by ten o'clock. Tea and supper would be upon them in no time. At this rate their winter stores of flour, meat, and vegetables would be gone in a week.

The opportunity to leave arose when McDaid came to their door, anxious for word of his partner's safety. After a brief moment of joyous hand-shaking and back-slapping, McDaid asked if Spafford felt up to a ride to the artesian wells for water and further west for food. Yes, he most definitely was.

So they wrapped their horses' hooves in leather to ward off injury from streets still hot with burning debris, saddled up, hitched a small wagon to McDaid's horse, and headed out.

They spoke little as they wound their way south, taking in the small groups of people already digging through the rubble of homes, searching through the wet ash for something—anything—to prove that all was not lost. Rumors already abounded of scavengers combing the burned areas, stealing items of value to trade for food and water. But nothing about these people defined them as either victim or scavenger—everyone bore the same look of dejection on their blackened faces, stood with the same defeated slump to their ragged shoulders.

As the neighborhoods became more populated, the path became increasingly difficult with a wagon to maneuver through streets covered with debris from collapsed buildings. Melted, twisted metal that once fenced in grand homes often sprang up through half a foot of ash and lodged into the wheel spokes, and they'd have to halt and dismount and pry it loose. They'd remount and inch forward, Spafford in the lead to survey the path and direct McDaid around piles of brick and stone and over mounds of unknown materials buried in ash.

With street signs missing, the landscape altered so dramatically, and no sun in the overcast sky, they soon lost their bearings. Spafford continued the journey in what he hoped was south and west, past jagged pieces of wall and mountains of rubble, occasionally encountering a person and startled to hear himself asking where a street *used to be*. A point of a finger and a mumbled reply sent them onward.

By one o'clock they were on the corner of North Avenue and what Spafford supposed was Larrabee. The destruction was absolute. Not a wall or tree stood near the gutted area, but the location gave him pause. He had a colleague in this area. He was sure of it.

He signaled to McDaid. "In my recollection the Pickford home would be near here." He turned his horse in a circle and called out, "Dr. Pickford! Dr. James Pickford!"

There was a moment's silence, then a tired male voice intoned, "They are gone."

He searched for the voice. About sixty yards ahead, next to a mound of brick on the west side of the street, a man clutched a sobbing woman to his side. Spafford recognized them immediately and was shocked at the woman's appearance. Although she looked like any one of a thousand people in the park, grimy and disheveled, her hands were bloody and swollen to twice their natural size. He knew in a moment that she'd been digging bare-handed through brick and stone too hot yet to handle, brick and stone that used to be her parents' home.

He urged his horse forward, nodding to McDaid. "It's the Pickfords' children—Maxwell and his young wife."

He gave the horse his head, letting him pick his way delicately through the debris, and observed the couple. He recalled meeting them at this very site, spring of 1870, just months after their St. Louis wedding and relocation for an enviable position at the

Chicago Tribune. Joseph and Carrie Maxwell, the pinnacle of Dr. and Mrs. Pickford's distinguished lives.

He remembered gripping Maxwell's hand in introduction that night, looking him in the eye, and simply knowing the young journalist would be good for their community. But that was a long way from the tall, colorless man now standing immobile in the street, his stricken face empty, his eyes unblinking. And the woman he held so desperately was nothing like the ball of energy that had flitted about her parents' home, filling tea-cups, making introductions, her laughter floating like musical notes across the parlor.

Nothing was as it should be or ever would be again on Larrabee Street.

He reined in his horse and slid to the ground in front of the couple. He had a bad feeling about their situation and struggled to ask the questions. But Maxwell began in the soft, flat voice of one still in shock.

"We came upon a group of scavengers digging for treasure. They found the piano . . ." And he gestured to a cleared area, the iron harp of the beautiful instrument looking otherworldly in the ruins. "I fired my pistol, and they scattered like dogs. But . . . but . . ." He looked down at his wife's hands, and Spafford could see the man was searching for a rational explanation for her senseless reaction to the thieves.

Spafford nodded his understanding and placed a steadying hand on Maxwell's shoulder. "And . . . Dr. and Mrs. Pickford?"

Joseph blinked. "He . . . they . . ." He swallowed hard. "The stairs . . ." And his face went from pale to sickly gray.

Spafford understood. Something truly tragic had happened here, and they could not yet speak of it. They needed time. They needed his wife.

He gripped Maxwell's shoulder. "You must come to my home."

Maxwell's young wife spoke for the first time in a voice mixed with panic and resolve. "I will not leave."

Spafford gambled and took an authoritative tone. "You are reluctant to go, I know. Thieves may yet return. But you need rest. Your hands need treatment, and—" he placed a gloved finger under her chin, forcing her to meet his eyes—"my wife would never forgive me for leaving you here."

He saw a spark of interest ignite in her eyes at the mention of his wife and knew he'd calculated correctly.

He bade them to wait a moment and stepped away to readjust his plans with McDaid. While they turned around the horse and wagon, they agreed that McDaid would take charge of the Maxwells, deliver them to Lake View, then rendezvous with Spafford at the artesian wells in two hours.

They loaded the Maxwells into the wagon, a delicate process with the young woman's injuries, and McDaid settled onto the driver's seat, gazing down at Spafford. He reached into his coat, withdrew an ivory-handled Remington, checked the cartridges, and handed it to Spafford.

"There is mischief about and you travel alone."

Spafford took the weapon, surprised at his partner's foresight in these uneasy times. He nodded his thanks and McDaid tipped his hat.

"Two hours." He slapped the reins, and Spafford stood in the ravaged street, armed, and suddenly sick of adventure, wishing for all the world that he, too, was going home to his wife.

CHAPTER 5

Late October 1871

Anna sat much like she had yesterday and the day before and the day before that—erect at her English desk, pen poised above the linen paper, loathe to write the words that must be written.

She had no way of knowing whether her brother, settled on the Minnesota farm where their father had died, had received news of the Fire. If he had, he would wait patiently for a letter from her, if she had survived, or he would hope for a notice from Gates or any one of their Chicago friends, if she had perished.

She hovered, motionless, over the blank page. She could weave a harrowing tale of their escape to Lincoln Park. She could note that while only three hundred people had died, a hundred thousand were burned out. She could indulge him with the details of running a house crammed with homeless friends and friends of friends. She could exclaim over the price of a pail of fresh water.

But how . . . how to tell him the old Norwegian neighborhood, with their father's carpentry shop and majestic maple trees and rows of tiny pine cottages, was nothing but ashes? How could she describe the look that had crossed Mr. Stensland's face when he'd tried to cheerily report that his grocery of *frukt og grønnsaker* was lost, but he'd been hoping to change careers anyway?

She could anticipate his questions about the Novaks, old Mr. Eriksson, and the Klehm brothers. But what could she, should she, disclose? That they were all burned out, left with nothing, not even a change of clothes? That her house was full of Norwegian mechanics, seamstresses, teachers, and laborers who followed her into the kitchen, into the garden, asking, asking, "What shall I do? Where shall I go?"

Her head and heart ached with the responsibility of it all. Never in her life had her nerves felt so unstrung, and yet . . . And yet . . .

Her head came up and her back straightened to military precision. It was as if her foster mother were standing in the room, so clear were her words uttered to Mrs. Carsen fifteen years ago, words overheard by her dutiful charge returning with the tray for tea: "Our dear Anna was born efficient."

And so she was. Her mother had said it, and she had believed it. Efficiency was nothing more than receiving a task and completing it with ingenuity and alacrity. So. The people in her home were in need. She would use all her connections and skills to help them.

But first she would send this letter. She touched the pen to the paper. *Dear Edward,* she wrote. *All is not lost . . .*

Spafford was all but rubbing his hands together in glee.

The town hall meeting a week earlier had begun as a fierce debate among Chicago's elite on the topic of martial law—a moot point, really, as General Sheridan's "boys" were already in place and maintaining order. But it was D. L. Moody's late entrance onto the stage of the First Congregational Church— now the temporary City Hall—that had transformed a heated exchange into a fervent appeal.

The charismatic preacher had stepped up to the pulpit, looking for all the world as if he'd personally called the meeting, gripped the sides of the lectern's smooth wood, and squinted out at the five hundred men gathered there. And Spafford would never forget how, in the space of one minute, the man had dispensed with bravado and arrogance and won over nearly every heart and mind to a greater cause.

"Men," he'd begun in his booming voice, "the Bible tells us to obey our leaders and submit ourselves. Now, that don't always sit well with me, and it may not sit well with you today.

"But, more importantly, Jesus told us to love our neighbors. Let me ask you men this question: Who is your neighbor? Is he the man to your left or right? Is he the German on the North Side, or the Irishman in Conley's Patch?" Moody had stared out at them with fire in his eyes.

"I leave you today with a challenge: Focus less on questions of authority and more on service to your fellowman. We'll all live better for it."

Spafford had looked around the crowded room at the nodding heads, and his heart had swelled with love for his friend. He'd thought of the devastation he'd witnessed, of the lives forever altered, and asked himself Moody's question: *Who is your neighbor?*

And almost instantly he'd had an answer and a mission: home rebuilding. The people and operation had come into focus like a vista through a photographer's lens.

In his own home he had a collection of highly skilled and hardworking tradesmen in carpentry and masonry, even an architect. These homeless men wanted—needed—work to survive physically and mentally. He had the legal prowess to engineer financing and the experience to negotiate building permits and real estate. Together they would construct homes, relationships, and futures.

He chose the young Maxwells as a test for this mission. With the Pickfords' death, the daughter and son-in-law now owned the land on which the rubble of their home lay. Theirs was a much simpler matter of clearing and rebuilding. Or it might have been, had the intense heat still emanating from the core of stone and brick made immediate clearing possible.

Spafford would not be deterred. While the rubble cooled, he used his business connections and a willing labor force to import and store tools, brick, and other building materials, weaving an intricate web of financial and engineering strategies—a web he prayed would hold up during such uncertain times.

His own finances were under tremendous strain. The recently purchased land might be worthless, but the borrowed money accrued interest, and it had to be paid. He was forced to rely on a small inheritance held in trust in a New York bank. It was intended for the education of his children but would be used for their survival instead.

While he negotiated and coordinated and sent off myriad telegrams, McDaid oversaw the rebuilding of their business. The salvaged documents proved fortuitous. His partner had a hunch that real estate values in the burned district were going to double, even triple, during reconstruction. And he had the documentation to promote their services.

With his business affairs coming to order, Spafford was overwhelmed with a sense of urgency. The weather was worsening, the brutal conditions of winter would soon be upon them, and most rebuilding would come to a standstill. Bricks required the hot summer sun to stay dry. Mortar would freeze and crumble, leaving walls unsteady in the brisk Lake Michigan winds.

But today, ten days after the Fire had swept through their lives, they enjoyed delightful weather—the sun shining, a light breeze blowing. Men and boys wielded picks and shovels on the Maxwells' property, carting reusable materials to one wagon and debris to many others. The refuse wagons made regular trips to and from Lake Michigan, dumping the rubble into the murky depths, collecting the frigid water to pour over stones too hot to handle even with thick leather gloves.

It was while they were combing the debris for undamaged brick that the story of the Pickfords' demise came out. It began with Joseph Maxwell's refusal to go near the center of the wreckage. His quiet but firm, "I cannot . . ." was sufficient for the volunteers, and others began clearing the area, wary of what gruesome evidence they might find.

But in the end there was no evidence. As it became apparent that the Pickfords' bodies had been mercifully cremated by the intense flames, then carried off by the prevailing wind, Joseph edged closer and closer to the heart of the tragedy.

He finally stood in the epicenter and spoke in halting half sentences until all work stopped and every volunteer, respectful of a grieving man's need to tell the tale that had brought such misery, stood stock-still, staring down at their feet or out at nothing. Listening.

Like a thousand others that Monday, the Pickford family had simply waited too long to evacuate. As the fire had marched north, they'd doused the home's brick walls and shingled roof with bucket after bucket of water, hung wet rugs over wooden doors and window casings, and hoped the fire would burn itself out long before reaching their neighborhood.

Mrs. Pickford, crippled from birth, had retired early, exhausted from a long season of excitement and worry and the ongoing debate on evacuation with her husband and children. She voiced the lone opinion that they should stay and fight the fire. For where would they go? And how would she travel? She'd infused her argument with such enthusiasm and adventure, likening it to the burning of Atlanta, that her family had acquiesced, yet again no match for the wife and mother they so adored. Dr. Pickford and his daughter finally retired for the evening, leaving Joseph at the great library windows, standing ready to sound the alarm.

The tale, though spoken with gravity, was filled with the rich detail that only a natural storyteller and writer could manage. Spafford leaned in to the young man's words, reliving the moments with him, anticipating the ending with both fascination and dread.

He hadn't meant to fall asleep, Joseph told them in a voice full of self-reproach and anguish. It could not have been more than an hour. The white heat and smell of the windowpane searing into his resting cheek had woken him. The front of the house was ablaze.

He'd run upstairs, shaken his wife awake, then hurried on to his in-laws' rooms. The doctor was instantly alert, and Joseph hurried back to Carrie. He'd helped her into shoes, yanked a dress over her nightgown, dragged her down the stairs, and burst out the back entrance.

Trapped. The little wooden fence enclosing their property—the very fence that had influenced their purchase, that was so perfect for the safety of small children—was a box of fire. Flames shot five feet into the air, cutting off all escape, igniting trees, closing in.

He'd pulled Carrie back into the house, down the hall, and toward the front entrance. But the front was a wall of flame. He'd looked at her, and she'd mouthed one word: Mama.

He'd raced to the foot of the stairs and shouted the doctor's name. Dr. Pickford had answered, "On our way . . . save yourselves!"

He'd grabbed Carrie's hand, dragged her unwilling form into the smoking parlor, thrown the heavy piano stool through the front windows, and leapt to safety, his wife's body landing heavily on him.

They'd rolled to the concrete sidewalk, blessedly cool and untouched. He'd caught his breath just for a moment, no longer—then dashed toward the shattered window. There was the doctor, descending the stairs, his beloved wife in his arms, surrounded by the fires of hell. Joseph had opened his mouth to shout, waving his arms, when the stairs had collapsed and the surrounding walls with it.

The Pickfords had perished, and he would never forgive himself for it.

When he finished, not a word was spoken, and many a brawny man blinked back tears. Spafford breathed deeply, angry, dispirited, and impotent all over again, wondering *why?* Why did such deplorable things happen to such blameless people? Where was the right hand of God that was sworn to protect them?

The voice spoke deep within him.

Your ways are not my ways.

No, he acknowledged. *They are not.* And he closed his mind to the voice. He could see no purpose in destroying good families, leaving them homeless, penniless on the cusp of winter.

Well. He had his own method of safeguarding these people, and he would see it through, no matter the cost.

Three days later Anna coaxed Carrie down to the work site. It had taken a sincere request for her help in serving the noonday meal and a promise that she would see her husband, a recent rarity with Joseph's obligations to the *Tribune* and his dedication to clearing their plot. Carrie had tried to beg off, claiming her bandaged hands were useless. But Anna had prevailed, encouraging light use to keep the skin flexible while it healed.

They loaded a small carriage with tureens of steaming soup, baskets of crusty bread, a little butter, a surprise of blackberry jam, coffee, mugs, bowls, spoons. They packed it all in as tightly as possible, as the path into the burned district was pockmarked and uneven, and Anna refused to forfeit even an ounce of their dwindling supplies into the hard dirt.

Anna set the horse on a leisurely pace, filling the travel time with tales of her earlier noonday jaunts, observations about the changing landscape—chatter to ease her passenger's troubled mind. As they approached the edge of the burned district, Anna waved to the blue-coated fireguard who saluted back with his bayonet in their daily ritual. She talked about the hundreds of armed sentries patrolling the city blocks, and the scandal of Thomas Grosvenor being shot on the spot for refusing to give the evening's countersign after curfew.

They turned off North onto Larrabee, and Carrie sat rigid while Anna maneuvered their carriage through the crowded street, around wagons and piles of materials, and finally to the edge of the work site.

The district was full of the noise of men hard at work—chiseling, hammering, sawing, shouting orders, calling for supplies. Though the sun shone, a layer of smoke from reconstruction fires hung over them, and clouds of grit and dirt from passing vehicles choked the air.

But the rebuilding begun that morning—the leveling of ground and laying of foundation—was a beautiful and promising sight.

Anna set the carriage brake and looped the reins over it as Joseph ran to the carriage, swept his wife off the seat, then carried her onto the lot like a bride over the threshold. Spafford swung Anna to the ground, then kept her by his side as they watched the young couple. The sad, pale man who could barely speak for his grief days ago now pointed excitedly at rooms and angles outlined with stone and cement. He had Carrie by the arm, cradling her bandaged hand in his, pulling her from side to side, his own enthusiasm inciting a flush on her cheeks.

Anna worked quickly, and within minutes the meal was spread across the back of a wagon and men gathered round, bowing their heads in a quick blessing and again in appreciation for the thick and aromatic soup ladled into their bowls. They stood nearby, balancing their meals on the sides of the wagon, laughing a little, their mood the lightest it had been for two weeks.

As they devoured one helping, then another, the industrious sounds of plot clearing were interrupted by an explosion a block away. The horses whinnied and jerked on their trappings, pawing the ground.

Spafford rushed to calm his gelding. "Easy, Jack."

A man sighed. "There went the McDuff house."

A volunteer swallowed some coffee and said nonchalantly, "I hope McDuff's found more to wear than the nightshirt and pantaloons I saw him wearing the night of the Fire." Silence, then guilty chuckles at this image of a gentleman renowned for dressing to the nines.

"Mrs. Ryerson had on a wrapper and a man's hat

tied down with a handkerchief," another worker added.

More chuckles, then another report. "Tillie D'Wolf wore a calico wrapper with a bed blanket by way of a shawl."

"No!" Gasps sounded all around as the idea of Miss D'Wolf dressed in anything less formal than satin was unheard of.

"Yep. I saw her on the sidewalk, imploring spectators to help her with a pile of cane-bottomed chairs."

"Now, what would a person need with cane-bottomed chairs during a fire?"

They all pondered that as a second explosion shook the ground.

Spafford joined in from his spot near the skittish horse. "Two boys down by Market Street were handing out whiskey, treating anyone requesting a drink."

"And did you?"

He cut his eyes to the women busily packing away the empty cups and bowls in the carriage. "Of course not."

They all grinned.

Joseph spoke into the brief silence. "I saw a man running down Lincoln Avenue with two enormous turnips."

All eyebrows raised at this.

"Turnips?" asked a stonecutter.

"Yes, sir."

"Well, now, how enormous can a turnip get?"

Joseph cocked his head, wheeled around, muscled two large stones from the cutter's pile, and tucked them under his arms. "It looked something like this." And he teetered rather awkwardly around the wagon and into the dusty lane.

It was one of those surreal moments. With the men's heads turned toward Joseph, clouds of dust and sounds of laughter filling the air, no one noticed the driverless horse and wagon careening toward them. There wasn't even a second for a shout of warning or a desperate grab to pull him out of the way.

There was only time for a wail of anguish. For in a flash of screaming steed and flying hooves, Carrie looked up from the buggy and watched, mouth wide in horror, as the frantic horse collided with her laughing husband and ran him down in the street.

CHAPTER 6

Fall 1871

Black bunting graced the Lake View home's facade, Joseph was memorialized and buried, and Carrie Maxwell could not be consoled.

In the space of two weeks that October, she had been orphaned and widowed at the same site under equally extraordinary circumstances. She no longer sobbed, as she had that horrible day when her grief had left her retching and dehydrated and Anna had sent for Coates to sedate her. But she did not speak, either.

73

Carrie dressed each morning in whatever Anna laid out for her from her own closet, completed her toilet, and dutifully ate her meals from the tray sent to the room she now shared with Nicolet. And all the while a steady stream of hot tears ran down her white cheeks.

Days later, during a leisurely Sunday afternoon in the parlor, Maggie finally asked the question that had been plaguing all their minds.

"Papa?" Her voice floated up from the settee where she quietly read. "Why did God take Mr. Maxwell away?"

Every eye was trained on the man of the house, and when he looked up from his own reading, Anna was startled at the steely, almost defiant look stamped on his face. They had not discussed the events of that horrible day, but Anna had sensed in her husband a residual anger toward the injustice of so much senseless tragedy, so much grieving.

"I don't know, Maggie," he said with just enough of an edge to discourage further discussion. "I don't know."

As the household adjusted to this new misfortune, Dr. Coates came regularly to Lake View to minister to the Spaffords' many guests and always finished with a visit to Carrie's room. He unwound the bandages from her hands, approved of the quick healing, and applied more dressing. And each time he would emerge from her room, shaking his head at Anna's questioning look, his eyes reflecting the sadness encompassed there, his step slower and heavier when he departed them.

On one such visit Moody accompanied the doctor to Carrie's room. Anna did not sit with them, as she sometimes did on other visits. Instead, she busied herself with the myriad duties of a crowded household, planning meals, approving the budget, and eventually slipping away into her tiny hothouse for a conversation with the Lord. There, among the fragrant blooms and moist earth, she often clipped and fertilized and talked with God about what was most pressing on her heart. And this day she petitioned Him for Carrie.

She asked for wisdom. She asked for healing. She asked for anointing on Mr. Moody as he ministered to the young widow. And as she worked the soil, sinking her fingers into the rich black dirt, she felt a harmony with the process of planting and nurturing and living. And as she cut a bouquet of late-blooming zinnias, making way for new growth, she felt at peace with the process of death and new beginnings. For hadn't she, in her own youth, suffered the sting of tragedy? And had not her own foster mother—dear, dear Mrs. Ely—proved to her that love can, love *will,* triumph over life's sorrows?

And that was the answer the Lord finally gave her. They would simply have to love Carrie Maxwell. Love her until she triumphed.

Anna stood in the parlor, a broadside clutched in her hands, and translated for the captive Norwegian audience. To The Homeless, the handbill proclaimed in six-inch letters in English. Such notices to direct the destitute to supplies of food, clothing, and temporary shelter were posted throughout the decimated Scandinavian district on the North Side, their publishers either unaware or uncaring that the massive population neither spoke nor read English.

She understood the immigrants' dilemma, as she had lived within the boundaries of their close-knit colony as a child—shopping, exchanging news, worshiping in her native tongue. Her father had built a comfortable two-story flat in a pleasant green suburb in the *Nord Seite,* removed from municipal Chicago, her parents preferring fellowship and compassion from their own people. But like most children, she had adapted to the new language and could function in both societies. Now it was her rusty Norwegian that steadily improved, and she spent a great portion of every day translating newspapers and notices, explaining relief and aid procedures to a population unfamiliar with the outside world.

She left them to discuss the handbill's instructions and crossed to Gates' study, closing the door behind her, leaning back against it, inhaling deeply. The rich smells of leather, books, and polished wood added to her longing for his companionship, for she rarely saw her husband these days.

While she cared for and fed the survivors occupying every corner of the house, her husband worked to secure them permanent lodging. His was the more

heroic of responsibilities. For those wanting immediate accommodation, he negotiated with the shelter
committee for the standard structure—a one-story
house with two rooms and three windows and basic
furnishings. For those willing to lodge the winter at
Lake View, he negotiated building funds and materials for larger, more permanent homes. For this he
was absent for hours before and after the sun crossed
the horizon.

She looked forward to Sundays now with an eagerness akin to her days at the Ferry Institute for Young
Ladies, when she'd been engaged and anxious to see
her intended. She thought about the dormitory room
she'd shared with Mary Morgan, how she had
scratched the initials HGS–AL into the windowpane
with her ring, and how twenty-eight miles seemed so
long a distance between lovers. But on Sundays, glorious Sundays, they would spend the day together,
talking, laughing, dreaming.

Tomorrow was Sunday. The city of Chicago took an
intermission on the Sabbath, and so would they. She
would share her husband with her children and the
congregation of Fullerton Avenue Church. But after
tea he would be hers. All hers.

Anna eased into her bedroom, the baby finally asleep
in her arms, and saw Bessie on her bed, surrounded
by pillows. She smiled, marveling at how innocent
the "little queen" appeared in slumber. It wasn't even
noon, and they'd already had "a day" with the three-

year-old. The waterworks the child could produce when frustrated was beyond exasperating, and she and Nicolet had finally resolved, "When Bessie has a bad day, we *all* have a bad day."

She placed Tanetta in her crib, closed the door with a gentle click, and looked across the hall. The door to Carrie's bedroom stood open. Odd. She entered and was puzzled to find the room empty. Giggles wafted from the girls' room, and she moved toward the door, turning the knob as quietly as possible, hoping to catch them by surprise.

But it was she who was startled.

Maggie stood on a chair in the middle of the room, her arms stretched out to the side, reciting the story "The Little Match-Seller." Her dress, once a stunning creation in blue velvet, hung in pieces from her frame, and a handkerchief covering her head was tied under her chin.

Anna found her voice. "Margaret Lee! What are you doing?" Her dismay was so great at the sight of the beautiful dress in tatters that she did not immediately see the adults in the room.

Maggie grinned. "Mama! I am poor and ragged in Annie's old dress, and no one will buy my matches." Melodrama oozed from her. "But soon I will be a princess!"

Anna's mouth hung open in astonishment, and Annie rushed to her mother's side. "Miss Carrie is remaking my old dress, and we are having a sewing lesson. Do you mind so much, Mama?"

78

It was then that she noticed Nicolet, standing at the bed, sorting through a pile of dresses. And then Carrie's tiny frame peeked out from behind Maggie. Anna took a moment to collect herself while her eldest grasped her hand and whispered, "Miss Carrie is the most wondrous seamstress!"

Anna raised a brow. "It is Mrs. Maxwell, Annie."

"But she asked us to call her 'Miss Carrie.'"

Anna opened her mouth to protest and shut it just as quickly, seeing Carrie's nod. She was so thrilled to find Carrie interacting that she was willing to concede this point of formality. "Then you shall."

"*Ma chérie* . . . ." Nicolet called from the bed and waved Anna over. "Perhaps some of these charming dresses may be a help to *les enfants* staying here?"

Anna was embarrassed that this detail had escaped her and rushed to the governess' side.

While they sorted and exclaimed over forgotten gowns, Carrie pinned and basted the blue velvet on Maggie's slight form, turning her on the chair, murmuring small encouragements until she proclaimed the seven-year-old a true princess and led her over to the large oval mirror.

Anna looked up at Maggie's gasp of delight. In very short order the retired frock had become a shorter and more relaxed model of the latest fashion—squared bouffants, pagoda sleeves, and copious pleats. Anna moved toward the mirror, her hands pressed to her chest.

"Why, Mrs.—" she corrected herself—"Miss

Carrie! You have wrought a complete transformation!" And then she looked at her own dress hanging so dejectedly on Carrie's small frame. She placed her arm around the woman's waist.

"My dear, I long to return the service. We must remake some of my gowns—any of your choosing—to properly fit you."

Carrie met Anna's eyes in the mirror, and the sorrow Anna saw there was heart-wrenching.

"Have you anything in black?"

Anna understood. The young widow was thinking of the mourning attire she would be required to wear for a full year—a weary custom designed to subject women to limitations men did not observe. A woman did not need to wear black to grieve. But she would abide by the rule or give up her place in good society.

"I do, and you shall have it." She pulled Carrie close. "But only for going out. I should like to see you in this season's colors while staying indoors."

Carrie gave her a brief smile of relief, her shoulders a little straighter, her burden a little lighter.

"Now," Anna said, turning Carrie and winking at Maggie, "may we borrow your throne?"

The girls' dress reconstruction project proved so successful that it soon consumed the entire household. Anna and Nicolet went through their respective closets with a practical eye toward usability and alteration and contributed enough fabric to outfit every female in the Lake View house.

After breakfast each morning, the women would gather in the large second-floor hall where a gown of fawn or brown silk or green wool was ripped, pressed, fitted to the recipient, then trimmed per Carrie's instructions in the latest design of covered buttons on the bodice front and pagoda sleeves, shiny silk piping and matching lace on the attached overskirt. By eight o'clock that night, when the last stitch was set, a grateful woman stood arrayed in a modish re-creation that would rival the offering of any city's clothier.

Dottie entered the "sewing circle" one day with a box of waterproof fabric she recalled storing in the attic. A cheer went up and the fabric went down on the floor where it was cut by Carrie's capable and healed hands, then stitched per her instructions into waterproof cloaks with inventive trim for every girl.

And then they started on apparel for boys. Anna selected several retired suits from Gates' closet, and Carrie fashioned them into jackets, trousers, and little knee pants. While the boys squirmed and grimaced through the fittings, the mothers' eyes shone with joy at their sons, properly attired once more.

One morning the ladies entered the sewing hall to find a collection of boys' caps aligned in a row, designed from scraps of felt and wool. "Mama," whispered Annie, "Miss Carrie is one of the Cobbler's Elves." Anna smiled her agreement, but she, and every woman there, knew this was the product of a widow's sleepless night.

The sewing projects had another, greater, effect. Women of varied nationalities and languages and experiences, women who might not otherwise meet, found solace from their own misfortune by gathering together and helping others. Mrs. Novak was clever with a needle and spoke a little French, as her mother had emigrated from Bourg, and Nicolet spoke passable German—a thrill for Mrs. Schmidt, who *never* stretched the fabric and had the utmost patience with a pin. Anna, the hostess and procurer of cloth, often answered Norwegian questions in English, encouraging the ladies to try out new phrases with the ever diligent Miss Carrie. Annie and Maggie joined the circle when Nicolet released them from their studies—Annie to master the art of sewing, Maggie to move around the room, testing foreign phrases on her nimble tongue, mimicking accents and gestures.

As the Lake View ladies ventured into Sunday society, adorned in their "new" gowns, word spread of the *modiste* housed there—a young widow, it was said, who could work miracles with the humblest bit of cloth. Soon strangers knocked on the Spaffords' front door, asking to see Miss Carrie, a second-hand dress donated from ladies in New York or Ohio or Kentucky draped over their arms. Each woman was ushered upstairs and welcomed into the circle where a fitting was taken, refreshment offered, and a time given to retrieve the finished product.

When the woman returned, she was always overwhelmed with the result. For not only had Miss

Carrie and her circle created a costume of highest fashion, they had added to it a slip or a nightgown or a complete suit of underwear—missed items once taken for granted. It was impossible to measure the psychological effect of the new clothing on the weary souls of the giver and receiver.

By mid-November many temporary shelters became available and the Spafford house was home to a more manageable number of twenty-seven—the Spaffords and their servants on the second floor, four families in four rooms on the third. The Schmidts and their three boys would stay until spring, when their home of brick and stone would be ready for habitation. The Novaks and their fraternal twins were uncertain of their future—Chicago had not been the Land of Canaan they'd been promised when they'd left Norway two years ago. The lively Rees family of six would take over the home designed for the Maxwells. In a poignant ceremony no one would forget, Carrie had placed the deed to her land in Mr. Rees' hands and said, "I was happy there. May you also be." Both Gates and Anna hoped the elderly Hundleys would stay with them indefinitely. Mr. Hundley, a renowned architect, had found a new passion in working with Gates to rebuild homes, and Mrs. Hundley was the grandmother their girls had always longed for—patient, attentive, and delightfully witty.

As winter approached, the household settled into a comfortable routine. After breakfast, Nicolet would collect all twelve children in the dining room, cradling the baby and teaching school from materials in the house. She was determined that when the school buildings reopened, *her* children would not have fallen behind. The seven ladies would retire to their sewing hall where a system and pecking order had naturally worked itself out. The five men of the house were not seen during the week, and on the rare occasion one appeared before supper, it had the effect of sending the women into a dither.

Dr. Coates caused just such a stir when he arrived in the ladies' midst one blustery day. The sound of heavy boots on the stair brought a hush to the hall, hands poised over fabric, and all eyes trained on the landing. As the doctor's tall frame came into view, Anna smiled with delight. The man carried himself like an English lord, elegant in his suit coat and tie and fine French bosom shirt. Every lady was atwitter, and Anna could imagine the women flocking to Coates in his youth thirty years ago, drawn by his grace and succor and the shock of thick hair now white and more luxurious for it. He exuded gallantry and valor but without the pretentiousness that often accompanied those traits.

Indeed, it was the doctor's good manners—more in the way he exchanged thoughts, his fairness, his intellectual hospitality—that had drawn first her husband, then herself into regular discussion with him so many years ago.

Coates met Anna's gaze with a small smile and

beckoned to her from the stair. The women entreated him to join them for tea, but he declined, and Anna could see that he struggled to keep his mood light and charming.

She followed him down the stair and into the study where he turned to her with such a regretful expression that she grasped the back of the great leather chair, certain he brought grave news of Gates.

"Is he all right?" She thought of her husband at the work site, how the piles of brick and stone would shift in the wind, how horses driven too fast in the slippery streets would skid and fall, how—

"Gates is well. I come with . . . other news."

She watched him, bracing for what was surely worse.

"I believe your sewing circle recently outfitted a woman—a Mrs. Wilson?" At Anna's confused nod he continued. "The Wilsons have been stricken with smallpox. One of their children first contracted it, then infected the family. I—" He lurched forward as Anna sat down hard on the study floor, her skirt billowing up and out, her face ashen. He squatted beside her and gripped her arm.

"Anna, listen carefully. I am here to vaccinate all in your household who have not been previously vaccinated or infected."

But she was not listening. In a flash she was seven again, running to the drugstore for medicine and brandy while every member of her family—her parents, her three sisters, her baby brother—everyone except her, moaned from their beds. Cholera was sweeping Chicago. The streets were deserted and she ran down the center, her feet slapping against the wet cobblestones, her hands over her ears to block out the groans of the sick and dying.

She had run and run, but her beloved mother had not survived and neither had her brother.

"Anna!" She looked up into Coates' concerned face, feeling her mother die all over again, hurt that her trusted friend could bring her such news. She felt him grip her arm.

"Bessie has not been vaccinated, and Tanetta is too young. They are the most in danger. I will have Dottie bring you some coffee, and then we will devise a plan for your family and guests."

He left her then, and she sat on the floor of her husband's magnificent office, surrounded by the literary offerings of the world's greatest authorities, and felt absolutely powerless, just as she had twenty-two years ago. Where was Gates? She could not do this alone. He would have a plan. He always had the answer.

She heard the footsteps in the hallway and sprang to her feet, smoothing her dress, determined that Dottie would not see her in such distress. Her housekeeper entered ahead of Coates, carrying a tray, and the smell of strong coffee was invigorating.

Dottie settled the tray and stepped to the door, nodding at Coates. He poured the brew into delicate china cups and handed one to Anna.

"We are within the exposure window. It has been four days since Mrs. Wilson was here, yes?"

Anna nodded.

"That is to our advantage. We must vaccinate today. It is effective but not foolproof. The disease can spread with incredible speed."

He added cream to his own coffee. "You know what to look for—fever, tiredness, vomiting, severe back pain. Check for a rash on the face, trunk, arms, and legs." He looked up and found her staring out the great window. "Anna . . .

"When will Gates be home?" Such a long pause ensued that she turned sharply, sloshing coffee onto the expensive rug.

Coates picked up a linen napkin, knelt, and blotted the stain. He cleared his throat. "Gates will not be home. None of the men will. I've placed this house under quarantine."

She stared at the top of his head, unwilling to believe what she had just heard. "Quarantine?"

He stood and nodded, folding the napkin.

"For how long?"

"Up to three weeks."

Her jaw dropped open, and he caught her cup before it crashed to the floor.

"It could be less, depending on infection. We should know within a week."

They were vaccinated and quarantined, and a week passed without incident. Each day a note from Gates was placed outside the front door. "My dearest . . ." he began and told about living in an army tent beside the construction site, about the projects around them, and how he missed having his "ladies" beside him at Sunday services. And then he would write, "Annie and Maggie and Bessie and Tanetta—it is a sweet consolation even to write their names. May the dear Lord keep and sustain and strengthen you . . ." She treasured each of his missives, reading aloud large portions to the ladies and children at afternoon tea, stowing them away with the others in her dressing room.

And then, at the start of the second week, Bessie had "a day." Every woman and child in the house tried to console her, and Anna became truly alarmed when a full hour passed and the tears continued. The child did not want to be picked up or touched in any way. She refused all food. She crawled into her wardrobe, hid behind her dresses, and sobbed.

And then the vomiting began.

Anna held her little body while it heaved and retched and could feel the fever coursing through the child. She sent a message to Coates.

The doctor arrived and made the diagnosis: smallpox. It was moving very fast, he said—shockingly fast. Already the rash had begun to climb up the pudgy legs to her trunk and arms. All she could do now was bathe the child's body with cool water . . . and pray.

Anna carried Bessie around the bedroom that night, singing little songs, both of them drenched in sweat from the raging fever. She refused to imagine her child's beautiful face pocked with scars. She turned off thoughts of lesions or blindness or . . . death.

But as the night wore on and the child's dehydrated body began to shake and heave, Anna could no longer keep up the strength that had sustained her. She held the hot, plump hand of her third child, laid her head on the damp sheets, and cried out to the Lord.

Please, Father God. Please do not take her from me. And the gentlest of voices whispered in response.

She is not yours, Anna.

Anna opened her swollen eyes and looked at Bessie—her plump cheeks stained pink, her lips rose-red with the fever. *She is! She is!*

I am the Lord of creation. I formed her. I knew her in your womb.

Exhausted, despairing, Anna turned her head into the blankets. *Please do not take her . . . Take our house, take our land . . . The world and everything in it already belongs to me.*

Anna shook her head back and forth. *Please . . . please . . .* She felt the lightest of touches—like the downy tip of a sparrow's wing—brush her hand.

Surrender her, Anna.

No! She gripped Bessie's hand tighter.

Trust her to me.

She clutched her child's hand, quoting God's promises, reminding Him of His mercy over and over until sometime before dawn, she gazed upon the rosy face of her little queen and, with a heavy heart, let her go.

CHAPTER 7

The hand in her hair felt so nice, so comforting as it stroked through the long strands, tugging very lightly at the tangled ends. It was just like those times, so long ago, when Anna had rested her head in her mother's lap and closed her eyes as the gentle hand moved through her blond locks, tucking them behind her ear, tracing the shape of her "seashells," as Mama called them.

She didn't want to wake up—the dream was so real. But Mama had been dead more than twenty years now. She opened her eyes and looked into the astonishingly clear blue irises of her child. Bessie smiled and Anna wanted to weep, for the dream had turned unforgivably cruel.

"I love your hair, Mama," said the dream girl in her baby voice. "I want long hair, too. Can you ask Papa again?"

Anna frowned. It was one of Gates' idiosyncrasies to insist his daughters' hair be cut short, and they hated it. He thought it easier to manage and keep clean. The girls wanted to be like all the other children. But why was this part of her dream?

The girl's hands grasped her face, just as Bessie did when she wanted one's full attention. "Mama, can you ask him?"

Anna sat up with a jolt, shook her head, and looked down into her daughter's questioning gaze.

Her mouth opened and she struggled to speak.

"Bessie?"

"Can you, Mama? Can you ask him?"

Anna reached out a hand, unsure of what was dream and what was real, and connected with the smooth, cool skin of her daughter's cheek. A sob broke from deep in her chest, and she pulled the little body into her arms, so overwhelmed with joy and relief that she could hardly breathe.

She rocked Bessie back and forth, telling her in a whisper how much she loved her, how much God loved her. And she praised the Lord over and over again for His mercy.

A knock came and the door opened to Dottie, fear and anguish covering her features. Anna turned her tear-stained face toward the door and smiled, startling the servant. Dottie backed away, but Anna stopped her.

"Dottie! Find the doctor . . . find him now." She could not control the elation in her voice as she turned Bessie in her arms to face the housekeeper.

"She lives!"

Lake View
Early Winter 1871—1872

Thanksgiving could not have been more poignant that year.

Every person in the Lake View home had been through such unimaginable tragedy and was slowly emerging stronger for it.

Bessie's recovery was so instantly complete that Coates pronounced her healing to be divinely given. Carrie's talents were so sought after that she spent three days a week traveling to sewing societies at area churches, demonstrating and encouraging the ladies in fashion redesign. Gates found incredible success in his rebuilding projects, moving families into new cottages every week. Their tenants would be with them into the spring, each family content in the warmth and fellowship and possibilities offered them by the Spaffords.

As the adults and older children sat round the great mahogany table, clasping hands and relating their thanks, hearts were full and light for the first time in almost two months. They sang the "Doxology," let the "Amen" ring, and dove into the food so wonderfully prepared by the women—each lady supplying a dish or two native to her homeland.

Carrie quietly excused herself from Anna's side not fifteen minutes into the sumptuous meal, her cheeks stained red in an otherwise ashen face. Anna watched her friend climb the stairs—a handkerchief pressed to her trembling lips—and blinked back her own hot tears at the reminder of the young widow's loss.

Time. The broken heart needed time.

And then Christmas was upon them with all the anticipation and traditions from previous years. Pine bows, fragrant and sticky, graced the doorframes, elegant poinsettias from Anna's hothouse bloomed at each window, strings of holly berries and brightly dyed popcorn wound up and over the branches of the fresh-cut German Tree.

Chicago homes glowed with the natural resources of the north, but money was tight, and parents spent many an hour counting and recounting nickels, loath to disappoint their children with an empty tree. The good people in New England anticipated the dilemma and sent a train car filled with Christmas surprises. Huge boxes marked "girl" burst with dolls and colored ribbons. Skates and pocketknives and mechanical toys spilled from the "boy" boxes in such quantities that every burned-out Sunday school in Chicago was able to supply a merry Christmas.

At last the day arrived. The children squealed with delight when their stockings revealed their treasures, then moved reluctantly into the dining room for breakfast. Then off the families went to church to rejoice in Jesus' birth, then home again for dinner.

Just before tea a knock came at their door, and Gates' face lit up with hope and surprise. He rushed to the foyer, spoke to someone for several minutes, then returned with a man and a boy of about fourteen. He introduced them as John and Tim Wilson, and the name brought a hush to the room. John held his hat in his hands and told them how honored he was that they would welcome him and his boy into their home. He asked for Miss Carrie, and when she stood, he rushed to her side, thanking her for the beautiful dress she had made for his wife. They'd buried her in that dress, he said. He'd looked upon it for the first and last time at her interment. He'd been in Indiana with his boy when the smallpox struck, he said, the regret still fresh on his face, and only saw his wife and daughter again at their funeral. Then he looked at Anna and told her how glad he was that her daughter had been saved.

Anna stood and reached out her hand, and led him to her place near the fire, and served him tea and a dish of rich lemon custard. And then she did the same with Tim, fussing over him, as she knew his mother had done. She then went to her husband and took his hand, and the tender look that passed between them brought a glisten of tears to every eye in the parlor that day.

Soon it was time for the traditional dinner of roast turkey, boiled ham, and goose pie. They passed dishes of steaming squash and beets and bowls of cranberry sauce until they were ready to burst.

Then they gathered for the Christmas play staged in the parlor with Maggie, naturally, in the lead role, then one more Christmas cake coated with marzipan and sugar that Cook had been hoarding for that very occasion. Then a story, then, mercifully, bedtime.

With the children tucked away and Tim asleep in the study, the adults talked late into the night, cracking walnuts and sipping mulled wine, each one giving thanks for the past, expressing joy for the present, and proclaiming hope for the future. The year's end was near, and although the Fire and its aftermath had ravished their livelihoods and homes, it could not, *would* not, consume their spirits.

• • •

The bitter winter winds that gave Chicago one of her many nicknames whipped through the town and countryside, forcing the citizens into long days and nights indoors.

The schools were open once more, bringing a sigh of relief to more than one mother in Lake View. The ladies still gathered daily in the sewing hall, their talents needed more than ever to turn bolts of donated flannel into blankets, comforters, and bed linens. The Widow Rees was called upon to knit fine wool stockings, and Carrie worked almost exclusively in wool and velvet.

In the middle of one blustery day, heavy boots stomped up the stairs to the second floor and Gates emerged, dragging a heavy crate. The ladies reacted like hens, moving and pecking around the wooden box stamped SINGER MANUFACTURING COMPANY in smudged black letters. Gates grinned, produced a long metal bar, and pried off the lid.

Inside was a shiny black Model 12 treadle with all the newest equipment for custom sewing. The ladies gasped in unison as Gates lifted it out of the straw and settled it onto a nearby table.

"This remarkably heavy machine is for our own Miss Carrie.

The recipient threw her hands over her mouth, her eyes wide.

"It was purchased by Mr. John Farwell in appreciation for her tireless efforts in clothing the women of

Chicago." Having completed his speech, he removed the cabinet pieces, hoisted the crate onto his shoulder, and stomped back down the stairs.

Anna was so excited for Carrie that she didn't bother to get upset about the straw strewn all over her clean floor. The ladies gathered about the gleaming machine much as they would a newborn baby, running their hands over its smooth features, exclaiming over its size and weight, planning for its future. With an ingenuity that would have startled their menfolk, they connected the machine to the cabinet and ironwork stand, tightened the bolts and, within an hour, had it up and humming, the sparkling needle passing in and out of the velvet like a hot knife through butter.

It was the first time since the Fire that Anna had seen such a look of unadulterated joy on the widow's face.

Outside, the business and home construction continued. A little wind and snow was no match for the self-made men of Chicago eager for a return to independence and respectability. Carpenters, in mufflers and mittens, pounded nails, bricklayers sat on scaffolds next to little stoves warming their bricks and trowels, mixing salt with the mortar to ward off cracking in the freezing temperatures.

Chicago was rising like a phoenix.

By spring hundreds of permanent brick-and-stone buildings were underway and nearly completed. Most working-class homeowners rebuilt with wood, but Spafford insisted on fireproof edifices under his control, and he worked hard to keep the prices low.

John and Tim Wilson came often to the Lake View home for Sunday dinner. John was a land surveyor and soon became involved in Spafford's mission, working ahead of the crews on the cold, hard ground, marking the form and boundaries of each piece of land. It seemed a natural progression, then, when two lawyers and a surveyor shook hands that March, and the sign by the new offices at 77 West Madison read SPAFFORD, MCDAID & WILSON.

When the last frost melted away, Anna stood at the edge of her garden, mentally planting the rows of flowers and vegetables. She itched to get started. Peas in by Good Friday, along with radishes, carrots, and onions. She would stagger the sweet corn for early, middle, and late summer harvest, and start the cucumbers, squash, and tomatoes in the hothouse for transplanting. She nearly clapped her hands. Oh, the joy of looking out the kitchen windows and seeing the garden plot green with the upper growths of cabbages and cauliflower, and the bloodred patch of beets, and the stalks of lavender.

She moved about the yard, mentally placing bulbs of tulips, daffodils, and iris. She spotted new growth on the spirea and forsythia bushes and wanted to cheer for the woody rose stems that climbed the trellis.

She loved the rolling lawns and verdant setting of their twelve acres. The yards and garden were sanctuaries to her—simple places where she could hide away from the more difficult moments in life.

But, she wondered, without the difficulties, without the desolation of winter, would she throw open the windows with such abandon to catch the wafting fragrance of the lilac? Would she marvel at each peony and press her face into its lush petals? Maybe not. What an interesting correlation. She would have to think on that.

In May Anna was in her hothouse, coaxing little melon plants to grow large enough for transplant, when the door opened and a familiar voice called her name. She gasped with surprise and delight. It was Emma Moody, wife of the popular preacher.

Anna threw off her gloves and rushed to embrace her dear friend, then immediately held her at arm's length, running her gaze over the petite woman's delicate features, feeling the fine-boned strength beneath her fashionable gown, pronouncing her well. The difficult winter had separated them like never before, and they both talked at once, starting over, interrupting, until they dissolved into laughter. Anna took her friend by the arm and led her through the house to the porch overlooking her garden, calling for Dottie, arranging for tea.

They settled into the striped cushions of the white rocking chairs, and Anna smiled at her friend. "Tell me everything."

Emma launched into one of her hilarious tales of chaos and adventure that accompanied such an enthusiastic man as D. L. Moody. Anna never laughed so much as she did when her friend regaled her with the regular calamities of her life. Emma would pause at a critical moment in the story, prompting Anna to say, "And then what?" And soon she would be holding her aching sides while Emma finished the anecdote, smiling benignly, one eyebrow raised.

Dottie served the tea, and they busied themselves with cream and sugar and lemon until they were settled and the only sound was the creak of the rockers on the wood porch.

Anna looked over at her friend, now serious and contemplative, and tried to help her begin. "And then what?"

Emma smiled. "Mr. M . . ." she said.

Anna hid a grin in her teacup. This new habit her friend had of referring to her husband in the initial seemed rather silly. She could no more call the preacher "Mr. M." than she could refer to her husband as "Mr. H. G. S." She refocused and listened to what her friend was saying.

". . . next month to London for a conference of evangelicals." Emma looked down into her tea. "It is a worthy journey, I am certain."

She remained still for so long, Anna sensed there had to be more to it. She lightly prodded. "And when will he return?"

The answer was so softly spoken, Anna almost missed it.

"September." Emma brought the teacup to her lips, but could not drink and lowered it to her lap. "I know not what I shall do."

There it was again, the phrase that had haunted Anna in the park, that had driven her to aid and comfort the hurting people in her home all those winter months. She covered her friend's hand and squeezed it.

"You shall stay with us—you and young Emma and Willie." Emma was shaking her head no, but Anna pressed her. "Oh, do say yes! It would bring me such joy this summer to know that my dearest friend is only a room away."

Emma's lips curved into a sad attempt at a smile as she looked across the garden. "When I promised ten years ago to cast my lot with his . . ." She trailed off and shook her head. "I never imagined myself so . . . alone." She glanced over at her friend and smiled wistfully. "What does a smitten girl know at seventeen?"

Anna smiled in return. She'd been young and in love and had cast her lot in much the same way. They had all been seventeen.

She thought back over the years, selecting the best memories, and suddenly realized how much she'd missed her husband this winter and spring. A seed of concern lodged in her chest, and she shook it free. She would not imagine herself alone, not for long. The rebuilding of Chicago could not go on indefinitely.

Spafford sat back in his office chair and rubbed his aching eyes with a sigh. The print on the building contracts was too small to read by gaslight. So why did he continue to try?

He hesitated to even glance at the wall clock. He knew it was late—too late to catch the dummy train to Lake View. Again. He tried not to let Anna's certain disappointment add to his weariness. Yes, he'd missed more than an acceptable number of suppers with his family this summer. But it was a sacrifice well justified. Had not the Rees family been overjoyed with their new home? And the Schmidts—were they not comfortable in their little cottage on North Avenue?

He thought of his reasons for entering the real estate field before the Fire and almost laughed aloud. Although he'd loved the law, particularly international law, he'd found it too consuming. Real estate dealings, he'd inferred, would give him more time for charitable and religious work . . . and for family.

But he never could have anticipated the enormity of the Fire or its consequences to the homes and businesses of a third of Chicagoans. And he could not have imagined his passion for construction. Oh, how he loved to walk the streets of Chicago in the early mornings. He would take the horsecar into the city, then walk about the streets already bustling with activity, marveling at the lively work in progress since dawn. He would alter his route to his West

Madison office each morning, maneuvering around the sand heaps and mortar beds beside the new Sherman House on the corner of Clark and Randolph streets, then walk down Clark to Quincy where the Pacific Hotel covered a whole square. He often stood in front of the Palmer House on State Street and watched the swaying derricks hoist their huge stone blocks into the air, holding his breath, like many others, and hoping the massive crane would not drop its cargo or topple this time.

It was exhilarating. Like the Fire itself, the scope of the rebuilding was unimaginable, and he reveled in it.

But it came at a cost to his family. He thought about Anna—laughing in the parlor with Emma. They were always laughing. On the nights he did arrive home for supper, he would enter through the back door and follow the sound of the two young women, usually into the parlor where a competitive game was in progress. He would stand at the doorframe, waiting for the moment when his wife would spy him and rush to his side, her blue eyes bright with merriment and pleasure.

He thought about his children. How long had it been since Maggie had greeted him with "Dr. Livingstone, I presume?" He grinned, thinking how the discovery of the missing explorer last November had intrigued his expressive child. He wondered if all children were natural actors like his. They were forever putting on little shows—Annie announcing, "And now . . . Mary, Queen of Scots," then flinging wide the parlor doors where Maggie would enter, cloaked and crowned, head high, and the two would act out scenes from their history books, complete with executions. His grin widened as he recalled Annie praying one night after one of their productions. "Dear God," she had implored, "don't let Maggie or me ever be queens, but only princesses." He loved to sit in church with Bessie—unbelievably coy at the age of four—while she preened and smoothed her dress and his lapels from the comfort of his lap. He did not know his fourth daughter very well. That troubled him but a little, as Tanetta had just turned one and there was plenty of time to make her acquaintance.

He supposed that every act of benevolence required a man to sacrifice, or it would not be worthwhile. Was it not Edmund Burke who said, "Nobody made a greater mistake than he who did nothing because he could do only a little"?

So he would cede his personal life for a time. There was a greater need for his service here than in Lake View. And Chicago could not rebuild forever.

Anna glanced across the worktable at Emma and fought the urge to sigh. The letter in its customary blue linen envelope had arrived and the news received: Moody would be home in a week.

The children had squealed and clapped their hands and pressed their cheeks to the "kiss" their father had drawn in a little box at the bottom of the page. She would miss the young Emma and her zest for life. And three-year-old Willie had been a wonderful source of amusement for Bessie.

But it was the necessary loss of her friend's constant companionship that brought on her melancholy. As she peeled the prickly husk off the chestnuts and the smell of the first batch roasting filled the kitchen, she let her mind run back over the past months. She could not remember a summer in her life when she'd felt more industrious, given more, laughed more. Together they had remade boxes of clothing, tended a garden, raised children, drunk countless cups of tea, studied the Bible, prayed . . . and missed their absent husbands.

Anna watched her companion efficiently score the chestnuts' leathery shells and pop them into the water to soak. She wondered who or what would fill the void left after Emma's parting. She would not want for activities or conversation—those were always in ready supply in her crowded household. But she dreaded the coming winter months—the short days and long, polite evenings. The romance of the first snow and a crackling fire. The declined holiday invitations. To repeat the days and evenings with the empty fireside chair, with no one to hear her elation or indignation and love her all the more for it.

Emma's husband may have been across an ocean, but hers was tantalizingly near . . . and just as inaccessible. The solitary weeks loomed ahead of her. She looked across the mound of chestnuts to her departing friend and was more than a little alarmed at the words that entered her mind and filled her chest until she wanted to weep.

I know not what I shall do.

PART II

*A friend may well be reckoned
the masterpiece of nature.*
—RALPH WALDO EMERSON

CHAPTER 8

Christmas Day 1872

Thomas Jameson III exited the train and looked around in disgust.

This depot had to be the worst hovel he'd frequented since the war. While the Express No. 3 hissed and cooled on the track outside, the depot's walls collected the engine's grease, and the floor the dirt and tobacco quids of careless travelers. He pushed his way outside and into marginally better conditions.

Chicago was a flat and grimy town, clearly rough and commonplace. Even on this brisk day, just yards from the breezy waterfront, dust particles peppered his eyes, and great clouds of smoke swirled around him. At any moment he expected to hear cries of "Fire!" But the ignorant populace merely went about their business, oblivious to their base surroundings.

He gritted his teeth. A journey of three days, five trains, and seven states had done nothing to relieve his foul mood. He had slept fitfully, had barely eaten, and had cursed his father in so many colorful ways, he'd impressed even himself.

What was he doing here?

The old man had truly lost his mind if he thought he could send his only true son—his namesake—to this place. He was not some pregnant, unmarried chit who had to be packed off to a faraway city to bear her shame in anonymity. He was twenty-eight years old and the wealthy son of a wealthy shipping magnate. And that afforded him impunity, even if his father deemed him rough and unmanageable.

Well. He *was* rough. Four years at the battlefront, watching your friends and neighbors die for a cause you no longer understand will turn an angry boy into a savage man. He'd come home from the war taller and leaner and ready to pick a fight with muscles trained to spring into action on a moment's notice. His hands, enormous on his juvenile frame, were now perfectly proportioned and ideal for cradling a woman's head or snapping an enemy's neck.

But it was his face that made him unmanageable. It was perfectly oval and almost downy to the touch. His beard had never really matured, and when he did stop in for a shave, the barbers always marveled at the silky fluff gathered there. With large blue eyes and darkening blond locks that tended to curl, the effect was deceptively angelic.

He rarely smiled—mostly because he was rarely happy but also because he held in check an implement of last resort: dimples. He'd hated them in his youth because they'd reminded everyone of his dead mother. He now understood their power. Whether his goal was to lure a woman into his bed or an opponent into his trust, he knew that dimples accompanying a deep smile would get him anything he wanted. And that was exactly to his liking. His face was a powerful weapon, and he used it ruthlessly.

Except it had never worked on his father. And that galled him even more. The man was impervious to everything about him and had proved it yet again when he'd stood, sad-eyed, on the train platform in Lynchburg and told him good-bye. He might even have said *bon voyage* in that ridiculous French accent. And then the great capitalist had handed him an envelope full of tickets and addresses and a letter explaining his budget—budget!—and obligations in Chicago.

And he'd decided right then that he hated Chicago. And he could tell already that he hated Chicagoans. The tall man in the dark wool greatcoat was a perfect example. He'd boarded the train in Columbus last night and been an instant celebrity—chatting with the conductor, shaking hands with businessmen, even reading Dickens' *Christmas Carol* by lamplight to a group of wide-eyed children. It was sickening. Now he stood surrounded by bratty schoolgirls shrieking for his attention. What an undisciplined lot. Where was their mother? He spotted a cloaked woman standing near them, slightly removed.

Look at her, he thought. *She behaves just like that wench who married my father—haughty, untouchable.* He knew this type—never content, always looking slightly pained, ready to burst into a screaming tirade or insipid tears, whatever served the purpose. He felt the rage rise within him. He didn't know this woman, but he hated her instantly.

He watched her purse her trembling lips and turn

111

away. He wanted to walk over there and slap the harlot. He wanted to shake her until her neck snapped. His hands clenched and unclenched, and he took a step forward but was cut off by a steward carting a mound of luggage. It was enough to shock him back to the reality of his new situation.

He looked around for a cab. He needed a drink and several hands of high-stakes cards. Then he'd find a way to get out of this hellhole.

Anna stood outside the depot, watching her children greet their father, trying to ignore the gentleman glaring at them so ominously. She did not recognize the man and could only guess that he and Gates had interacted badly on the train ride.

She felt so out of sorts. It had reached the critical point yesterday when the telegram had come and she'd watched the girls' faces fall. "But, Mama," they had cried, "we cannot have Christmas Eve without Papa! *Papa* claps the loudest. *Papa* tells the best stories." And the day, usually so jolly and bright, had been dreadful. Neither Carrie nor Mrs. Hundley could entice them out of their mood. Nicolet and Dottie were visiting family, and Anna was left to bear the brunt of their disappointment alone. Again.

She had hoped that as the day wore on, the excitement of the holiday traditions would rally their spirits. But the strolling carolers and handbell ringers had only saddened them, as Gates had worked out an annual routine in which he would join the ringers and jingle the littlest bell at all the wrong times, sending the girls into fits of laughter. This year Anna had served glasses of punch to the merry musical groups while her children had sat long-faced on the stairs.

At eight o'clock they'd hung their stockings in silence and faded off to bed. She'd tucked them in and retired early, too—all of them haunted by memories of Christmases past.

This morning had been marginally better, as the promise of the three-o'clock train had loomed ahead of them. They'd refused to open their stockings until Papa was home and had prodded her to leave earlier and earlier to meet the train.

Now it was as if *she* were the spoilsport. The girls clung to their father, laughing, teasing, kissing him, and he basked in it. She looked away, breathed deeply, schooled her features, and turned to her husband. He was finally home with them, and they were the happier for it. At least that's what she told herself.

New Year's Day 1873

Tommy Jameson sat at the MacGregors' table at 340 Rush Street amidst the sixteen other boarders, enduring the lengthy blessing, wondering if he would ever eat. The smells of a mouth-watering supper had been wafting up to his second-floor suite since seven o'clock, and he was ravenous.

The clock chimed eight, Mr. MacGregor said the "amen," and they reached for the steaming bowls as a pounding commenced on the front door. They heard the housekeeper answer, and then, "Good evening!" A masculine voice boomed down the hall. "I am Moody. This is Deacon Thane. This is Brother Spafford. Are you well? Are the MacGregors at home?" And the boots stomped toward them before the amused housekeeper could respond.

The dining room door burst open, and Tommy stared in shock as a thickset man in a snow-dusted coat bounded across the room. The man was barrel-chested and short-waisted with ham-hock hands, and he towered over everyone from a rather average height.

In fact, the only thing small about the man was his nose. Combined with his twinkling brown eyes, brows that leapt up and down in animation, and lips that perpetually curved into a grin, the effect was quite boyish.

Many a brow around the room was raised at the sight of this intruder in the rumpled clothes with hair and beard that stuck out wildly as though he'd used a wagon wheel for a comb. These people had doubtless made the same assessment Tommy had made when he'd met Moody years ago: The man cared nothing for his personal appearance. And they were right. But as they would soon find out, Moody was not a man of appearance. He was a man of conviction.

Moody repeated his New Year's greeting to the eighteen diners seated around the massive table. "Good evening! I am Moody. This is Deacon Thane.

This is Brother Spafford. Are you—" And he stopped cold as his eyes fell upon the newest resident.

He cocked his head and addressed him. "Young man, I believe I know you." And he rushed around the table, hand outstretched.

Tommy stood, allowing a small smile.

Moody shook hands with his right, grasping Tommy's shoulder with his left. Moody's eyes roamed over his features, pausing, Tommy knew, on the fading scar across the left cheekbone.

"It was a decade ago, but I'll never forget it. Pittsburgh Landing . . . a sad, sad chapter in our lives. How are you faring?"

"I am well."

Moody nodded, looking him dead in the eye. The two men stood together for a long moment, hands still grasped, until Tommy felt compelled to speak.

"Tommy Jameson. In town from Roanoke. You—" he struggled to speak of it—"helped my friend, Jimmy Wolcott. At the battlefront."

Moody nodded. "That's right. I helped him home to the Lord. I remember it well." He leaned in closer. "And what of you? Will you join young Jimmy in heaven someday?"

Tommy looked around self-consciously, unwilling to discuss such a personal decision in front of such a rapt audience. But Moody was entirely unselfconscious, and when Tommy returned his gaze to the dynamic man, he found the question still lingering between them. Moody patted Tommy's shoulder.

"Well, then, are you employed?"

"Not as yet."

"Come to breakfast, then. We'll speak of your employment and spend the day together."

Moody then addressed the residents. "Do you all come to church and Sunday school? Have you all the coal you need for the winter?"

Heads nodded all around.

"Let us pray." And he and his companions dropped to their knees, the residents left to bow their heads at the table.

"O Lord, thou art gracious and compassionate, and we thank thee for the coming year. May we, thy servants, be faithful. Amen."

Barely had the "amen" been spoken when Moody sprang to his feet and rushed to the doorway, turning abruptly and addressing Tommy.

"Eight o'clock, young man. Be ready." Then he dashed on his hat and darted out the door, his exhausted companions in tow, throwing a hearty "good-bye" over his shoulder.

A moment of silence was followed by a burst of conversation as the tenants peppered the MacGregors with questions about their charismatic visitor.

Tommy took his seat again, returning to the somber mood he'd been nursing all week. He thought of Moody at Pittsburgh Landing, recalling how he'd had a singular effect on each soldier who had dared to meet the preacher's eye. Through the power of personal conviction he'd drawn them in, heart by heart, to a moment of hope. He'd invited them to trust in something more than the politics of war.

Tommy stared down at his empty plate, remembering the preacher's overwhelming personality and the changes he'd wrought in so many lives. And he suddenly found himself afraid of a man, really afraid, for the first time in his life.

CHAPTER 9

The New Year 1873

Tommy Jameson was in a near panic. He cursed as he fumbled with his tie yet again. He glanced at his pocket watch: half past seven. He had to get away from Rush Street before Moody arrived.

Why had he agreed to this absurd meeting? He did not want to relive the war or discuss Jimmy's demise or answer questions about his lack of religious beliefs.

He just wanted to be left alone.

He knotted his tie into a mess, snatched his coat from the bed and hat from the dresser, and tore down the three flights of stairs to the street entrance. He sidestepped the housekeeper, slid across the freshly mopped foyer, and yanked open the heavy front door.

There he stood—D. L. Moody, all smiles and outstretched hand.

"Good morning, young Thomas!" Moody grabbed Tommy's reluctant hand and pumped it like a greased well handle.

"I admire a man who's early." He reached up and, in a thrice, adjusted Tommy's tie into a perfect knot. "Shall we?" And he motioned to the waiting horse and buggy.

Tommy suddenly found himself in an open carriage, tearing across the Clark Street Bridge, gripping the edge of his seat, nearly gasping at the shock of the biting cold air.

Moody drove like a madman. While his long frock coat flapped in the wind, he dodged other carts and waved at acquaintances, regaling his companion all the time with the day's itinerary. Several frantic minutes later, they clattered to a halt in front of a five-story monstrosity on Madison Street. Moody slapped Tommy's knee, and his eyebrows danced up and down.

"Ah . . . the great Brevoort House—kitchen of Jeremiah Whittle and the best eggs Benedict in town." He breathed deeply and leapt off the carriage, tossing the reins to a waiting boy. Tommy had no choice but to follow.

Moody strode through the brass-plated doors, tipping his hat to the bellman, marching to the front-facing restaurant. Only when he was seated did he look around for Tommy, who was even then approaching the table like a wrangler would a wild horse. He was afraid he had crossed paths with a very dangerous man.

Moody smiled and leaned back in his chair, watching him slide into the adjacent seat. The man's intensity was unnerving. "So, Thomas. What brings you to our fair city?"

Tommy took a breath and tried to answer without prevaricating. "I've learned there is a fortune to be made in Chicago." Moody nodded. "That, there is." He smiled and waited. Tommy searched carefully for the right tact. "A man could double his money, it is said, in Chicago real estate alone." Moody acknowledged that statement with a lift of his bushy eyebrows, then waited.

Tommy sipped the coffee that had quietly appeared on the table and tried to settle his thoughts. The intensity of the older man's expression and interest was disconcerting. The silence loomed and he plowed on.

"I have a rather . . . substantial inheritance. I . . . plan to remain in Chicago for one year, at the very least. To that end I will need a small house and its accoutrements." Tommy warmed to his subject, spending his father's earnings with abandon.

"I will need a tailor and boot maker. Also a solicitor and an introduction to the commodity brokers. And, of course, I'll need a fine horse and buggy." He opened his mouth to continue, but Moody interrupted.

"What you need is Christ, my friend."

Tommy was shocked silent. The man's audacity in such matters, in such a public place, was intolerable. Was the preacher so single-minded in his purpose that he neglected social propriety?

Moody leaned forward. "Many a way can be found

119

to relieve the *wants* of men. But only one way can fill the *need*." He held Tommy's gaze for a long moment, then sat back and immediately sprang to his feet, a smile breaking through the beard and mustache.

"Ah, Spafford!" He grabbed the hand of a distinguished gentleman. Tommy hid his surprise. It was the man from the train on Christmas Day. And he had been with Moody on New Year's. Encountering a stranger three times in a city of hundreds of thousands was incredible odds.

Moody made the introductions, and Tommy found himself face-to-face with the answer to his most pressing needs. He listened as Moody related the situation and solicited advice. Breakfast dishes came and went, coffee cups were filled and refilled, and a full hour passed while the men discussed options.

All the while, Tommy studied Spafford—his impeccable manners, his unquestionably learned responses, his ability to assess circumstances and find immediate answers. Here was a man he could use to his own advantage. The fact that Spafford reminded him of his cursed father only made the task more enjoyable.

Yes. He would put up with Moody's evangelism, even though it galled him, and he would endure Spafford's patronizing confidence. For a time. And then he would show these men how it truly pans out to sell oneself to the devil.

In the weeks that followed, Tommy met often with Moody and Spafford—sometimes separately, but generally together. As a trio, they would canvass the regenerating city of Chicago, Moody in the lead, marching into select retail shops on State Street, then stalking down Madison into the ornate business district, then up into the buggy and tearing off to the west side for horseflesh.

Tommy found Moody's breakneck speed irritating but oddly invigorating. The man did nothing in half measure.

And everywhere they went it was the same pattern. "This is Brother Eastley," he would say. "Repented of his sins October last. I shall never forget it." And Eastley would grin in embarrassment while Moody regaled them with the changes in the man's life, always ending with an intense questioning. "Is your family well? Do you have enough coal for the winter? Are you reading your Bible? What, in your opinion, is the most comforting word of Christ?" And off they would dash to the next establishment, Moody bursting through the door, interrupting transactions, loudly proclaiming, "Brother Green is the finest tailor in town! Came to know the Lord as a little fellow. A righteous man, Brother Green." And customers would halt their conversations as Moody extolled Green's virtues, his undying faith, his contributions to the church.

At the end of the day Tommy would resolve to find his own tailor or boot maker or solicitor—someone who was proud to be a "sinner." This kind of businessman he could understand.

And yet he could not deny himself the company of

these two men. They were so well known and optimistic and beloved that Tommy found himself looking forward to each encounter in spite of their oppressive convictions. He would shake off their influence with ribald evenings at the grogshops, swilling liquor, laying odds on cards, propositioning women, and blaspheming the very God he had heard spoken of so tenderly that day. He would not be "transformed," as Moody called it.

One Thursday while dining at the Brevoort, Moody reached into his voluminous frock coat and withdrew a small leather book. He turned it over and over in his hands, and Tommy saw the letters stamped in silver on the black cover—*Holy Bible*. His meal went sour in his stomach. He'd narrowly escaped one of Moody's famous Noon Prayer Meetings last week, and now he feared he was about to be subjected to another of the man's evangelical tirades.

But Moody simply held up the Bible. "This book will keep you from sin, or sin will keep you from this book." He smiled a tender, paternal smile and placed it on the table, next to the gleaming silver and crisp linen napkin. "Your decision."

Tommy looked at that book and silently vowed to a god he did not believe existed that it would be a cold Chicago day in hell before he opened the cover and read a word of it. A cold day, indeed.

Gates found his wife in the dining room, frowning at the elegant place settings for eleven. She looked up at his entrance. "Are we expecting another to our regular party?"

"Tommy Jameson"

She smiled at his jest until she saw that he meant it. And then the blood drained from her face and immediately flushed back into it. She placed a cool palm to her forehead. "You invited that depraved man into our home? To dine with our most esteemed friends?"

"Not I . . . Moody."

She stared at her husband, exasperation on every feature. "As long as I live, I shall not understand D. L. Moody."

Gates smiled. "Nor shall I" He shook his head. "But it is done. Tonight we shall be gracious hosts. Tomorrow we may voice our objections."

Anna pursed her lips, irritated, but unwilling to begin an argument on the cusp of a dinner party.

Gates moved around the table, running his hands along the tops of the mahogany chairs, squinting down at the place settings. "Moody believes Tommy could gain from better influence."

"Truly. His acquaintances are deplorable." Gates raised a questioning brow and she explained. "The MacGregors have sought my counsel on boarding policies. They have never housed a less-desirable tenant."

Gates pondered that. "I confess I don't understand it. Jameson comes from good society."

"But how do we know that? Have we met any of his past associates? Has he gained membership in a church? Does he carry a letter of introduction?"

"Anna, he has the funds, the intellect, the *particulars* of a man in good standing. We may not agree with his . . . activities, come evening, but he is, in every respect, a gentleman."

"Well. He may look like a gentleman, but he has the heart of a serpent." And she turned on her heel and marched into the kitchen.

They lingered over the final course of desserts rich in pastry and cream, enjoying little *tête-à-têtes* around the table, until the excitement from one conversation drew everyone's attention.

Moody spoke animatedly of an Order of Deaconesses in the Church of England—women schooled and ordained to the ministry for home missions. He was so impressed by the English pioneer program, he told his audience, that he was working to persuade Miss Emeline Dryer to launch a similar school in Chicago. Miss Dryer, seated on Moody's left, blushed with the compliments and smiled indulgently.

Anna was so pleased for her friend. Her dedication to Christian service was matched only by another at their table—Emma Moody. Miss Dryer was an excellent teacher and first-rate administrator—the perfect test subject for such an ambitious project.

Moody raised his water glass. "I am all taken up with this, and I daresay you will be, too, when you learn of the opportunities for missions and evangelism." All smiled and bobbed their heads. All except Tommy.

"I am *taken up* with none of this." Tommy looked directly across to Miss Dryer. "Because the only proper place for women outside of the home is in domestic service."

Everyone—even Moody—was speechless with this declaration, for every woman at that table had held prestigious positions in Chicago's burgeoning community. Moody's water glass hung suspended before his lips, and Gates was uncharacteristically without comment.

Miss Dryer, radiating confidence and intelligence, met Tommy's look with a cool gaze of her own. "You find the idea of female leadership in the church . . . offensive?"

Tommy shrugged. "It is not so much offensive as unrealistic."

Miss Dryer held the same unruffled tone and look. "How so?"

"Women have delicate brains that should not be damaged by studying the same subjects as men."

Miss Dryer's mouth turned down slightly, and a heated blush crept up her lace-covered neck. Anna fumed as the debate volleyed back and forth between the two adversaries. Her husband and dinner guests watched in rapt fascination.

Miss Dryer sat a bit taller. "And what of Miss Susan Anthony?"

"Ah . . . the lawbreaker."

"The suffragist."

"Yes, the voice of reason . . . from a prison cell."

Miss Dryer smiled patiently, unwilling to give ground with this man. "But even if you cannot support her fight for the female vote, certainly you can admire her logic."

"I might . . . if I believed she understood that which she purported to change"

"And she must not understand the issue, owing to her . . . 'delicate brain.'" She waited while Tommy folded his napkin into precise triangles and placed it next to his plate.

"Tell me, Miss Dryer, do you support Miss Anthony's views on temperance?"

"Certainly. I am an active member of the Women's Christian Temperance Union."

"Ah. And you fully comprehend the Union's mission?"

"Indeed. It is a moral charge supported by reason and evidence."

Tommy smirked and raised his water glass to his lips.

Miss Dryer pushed forward. "Do you wish to join me in this cause?"

Tommy laughed. "Indeed not."

"Because you cannot imagine such a lifestyle?"

Emma drew a sharp breath, and Tommy leaned forward, his voice striking out like a cobra. "Because, Miss Dryer, while you support a movement for *temperance,* you preach and practice total abstinence. Your incomprehension of the word alone is astonishing."

Anna hated him in that moment—hated him for being right, for echoing what her husband had said to her at supper not three nights ago. But mostly, she hated him for causing the stain of humiliation on Miss Dryer's cheeks, for putting the entire room in a state of unease, for neglecting the responsibility of a gentleman.

She stood, and the rustle of her gown seemed unnaturally loud in the uncomfortable silence. She smiled brilliantly at no one in particular and said the only thing a hostess could at such moments.

"Shall we adjourn to the parlor for coffee?"

Spafford leaned against the doorframe of the YMCA's great room, a smile teasing the corners of his mouth, and watched Moody wield a heavy broom with great vigor, his coat and vest off, his shirt-sleeves rolled up. He whistled while he worked, his breath puffing out into the cold air.

Of the many characteristics Spafford admired about his friend, it was Moody's belief that no task was beneath him, no duty so disagreeable it should be left undone that drew his regard. Certainly one of the tenants was responsible for this task, but Spafford knew Moody had entered the room, discovered it undone, and received great joy in quickly accomplishing it.

He also knew that Moody would not brag of it, that he would, in fact, revel in the puzzlement it would cause the man assigned the task. It was part of his playful nature, the same nature that made him so popular with children, that found him romping wildly in a crowd of boys and girls, beating them at their own sports and games, laughing with them until tears ran down his face.

The man was not without flaws—he could be dictatorial, insisting on his own way. He was impulsive, blunt, and sometimes lacked perception. And it was this latter flaw that brought Spafford early to the YMCA.

Anna was furious. The late addition of Tommy Jameson to their supper table may have been forgivably spontaneous, possibly even inspiring, if all had gone well. But the evening had ended on such a sour and tense note with feelings hurt and indignation high that the mood still lingered in his home. Because her nature was one of restraint, Anna had not voiced her anger. In fact, she had said very little since the previous evening. And that troubled him.

And so he had come to sort out the happenings of last evening and propose that it not occur again. He had come to the source of the dilemma.

Moody finished at that moment, gathered his clothing and turned, his face breaking into the wide smile Spafford had come to rely upon. As Moody hurried toward him, he became so enveloped by the man's expressive, unashamed love and acceptance that Emily Dickinson's words in a letter to a friend overwhelmed him—"I felt it shelter to speak to you," she had written. She felt it protected . . . she felt it safe. So. The topic of this conversation would be hard, but he felt their relationship was secure.

Moody barreled up, his hand outstretched. "Spafford! Come into the office where the fires are lit and the coffee is hot."

Spafford followed him into the cluttered room and settled onto a hard, rickety seat. Moody sat with a sigh, gripped the arms of the chair, and looked around.

"How I love this place. When I was young and homeless and had nary a penny to my name, the building gave me shelter. And the men here gave me a chance when no one else had any use for me."

They smiled at each other for a long moment, then Moody surprised him. "I expect you are here about young Thomas." Spafford nodded and Moody took a deep breath, letting it out slowly. "He thinks himself a man when he is really just a boy. A lost boy." He said it without malice or condescension, and a pained expression flitted across his eyes.

"He strikes out in that vicious way of his—I suspect because he is ashamed of attachment, although he would never own up to it. He shuns belonging. He has no father or relation here . . . no close friends." Moody leaned his head back, contemplating the low ceiling.

"He's a love-starved boy, my friend. And I know a little something about that." He trailed off and when his voice returned, it was husky with emotion. "At times I put my hand on his shoulder in the same place, in the same manner as a kind man once put his hand on mine, and the boy recoils as if I've branded him." He blinked, and Spafford watched a trickle of tears flow into his beard.

"He avoids discussions about his family, about his friend who died in the war, about anyone dear to him. And I want to tell him, even our Lord felt despised and rejected and unloved. Who among us has not felt that pain? If there is such a person, I have never found him."

Moody shook his head, retrieved a handkerchief, and blew his nose.

"But none of that excuses his conduct last evening. I know he caused your wife pain, and I will speak to him." He leaned forward. "And I will ask for your forgiveness, my friend."

Spafford let go all of the arguments he'd prepared for this encounter. They mattered little now. He nodded, shook the conciliatory hand stretched out to him, and realized that Moody would endure a thousand uncomfortable evenings with Tommy Jameson if it meant the young man could love and be loved.

So he sat on his hard seat and took the coffee offered him and thanked God for D. L. Moody—lover of the unlovable.

Tommy pushed open the door so violently, the housekeeper crashed against the opposite wall and stayed there, mute. He glared at her. "Where is he!"

Her mouth worked, but no sound came.

He moved within inches of her, his face red, spittle

gathering at the corners of his mouth, and smiled darkly when she whimpered.

"Moody!" His menacing voice echoed through the hall and up the stairwell, and the housekeeper slid down the wall in a dead faint.

"Moody!" He sprang across the foyer, throwing open doors until he came to the dining room and found him there.

Tommy stood in the doorway, breathing hard from haste and rage, and shook a sheet of cream stationery. "I have heard from the devil himself—the sorry wretch that is my father."

Moody nodded at Emma, and she slid from her chair and through the connecting door, clearing no dishes, saying not a word. He watched her go, wiped his mouth carefully, and contemplated his uninvited guest.

Tommy paced beside the table. "He's uprooted his household and moved to England. England! More than three weeks prior! What kind of man quits his country, crosses an ocean, and writes his son after the fact?"

"Well, now, I'm certain he meant—"

"It must have been that . . . *woman*—the plague who ate away my youth and blinded my father, the spineless man"

Moody pulled out a chair. "Sit with me, Thomas, and we shall puzzle this out together."

Tommy ignored the offer and continued to pace. "I knew it was a mistake to leave. I knew her influence was too strong."

Moody tilted his head, acknowledging the point. "The influence of a woman can be right powerful."

Tommy squinted at him, contempt oozing out of every pore. "Is it possible an opportunity came along quite sudden-like?"

Tommy snorted with derision.

"Is it possible his business required a change of this nature?"

Tommy dismissed the suggestion with a flick of his wrist. "He is a shipping magnate. Nothing is required of him."

"Is it possible this is but a dreadful misunderstanding?"

Tommy looked at his new friend, saw his earnestness, his willingness to understand, and decided to let fall the facts, or at least some of them.

"My father bought me a one-way ticket to Chicago because he couldn't stand me. Did I ever tell you that? He couldn't stand me because I couldn't stand the trollop he married."

Moody's expression never wavered.

"And he never wanted me when my mother died. Did I tell you that? He didn't want me then—" he tossed the letter onto the table—"and he doesn't want me now."

He brushed away the hot tears that sprang from his eyes and made him even angrier. He glared at the letter, then his confidant, and finally slumped into the offered chair.

"And now I have no one. No one."

They sat in silence for a long moment, Moody rubbing his chin, Tommy staring straight ahead, exhausted from the outburst.

"I had a brother," Moody began in a hushed voice so different from his usual exuberance. "Isaiah. He was the firstborn and oh, how my mother loved that boy. But he up and left home one day. Never told a soul he was leaving. Just—" he waved a hand— "walked away"

Tommy listened, wondering what this brother, this Isaiah, had to do with him and his present troubles.

Moody continued. "I well remember the long winter nights when we all sat round the fire, how Mother would go on telling us about Father and his goodness—she was never tired of talking about him.

"But if any of us mentioned Isaiah . . . Well, all would be hushed in a moment. She never could speak of him without tears. She said it would have eased her heart even to know he was dead." Moody was speaking now as if to himself, his hand absentmindedly rubbing, rubbing the stubble on his chin.

"On one particular day of the year there was a family gathering to thank God for the harvest, and on this occasion, Mother always put out a chair for Isaiah. But the chair was always empty."

His voice was so quiet now, Tommy had to lean closer to hear it.

"A parent never stops hoping for the good he sees in his child, Thomas." He gestured to the letter. "Your father has written you. He has put out a chair,

Thomas—an empty chair—waiting for you. Hoping. Pray it is not in vain." And with that, he stood like an old man and shuffled toward the kitchen.

Tommy watched him go, then called out just as the door began to close, "Moody!"

Moody slowly turned and studied him.

Tommy struggled with the question, overwhelmed with the wanting and fearing warring within him. "Your brother . . . did he ever return to your mother?"

Moody's eyes softened and a slow smile spread across his face. "Why, yes. Yes he did."

The door did close then, and Tommy was left alone at the table with his thoughts. His thoughts and an empty chair.

CHAPTER 10

Winter and Spring 1873

Tommy strode down the sidewalk to Moody's house, his black boots crunching on the fresh snow, his mood much as it had been since his father's letter had arrived—sad, angry, contemplative. When the mood consumed him, as it did today, he sought out his friend—usually at tea, for he knew the man loved his wife's tea cakes.

Moody was the closest thing to a father that Tommy could imagine—attentive, loving, respectfully challenging. He often walked the public square with the preacher, hoping onlookers would think him the long-lost son of D. L. Moody. It was a wonderful fantasy, and he entertained it often.

A child's hearty laugh floated toward him, and Tommy watched as a schoolgirl of about eight expertly pitched a snowball at her much-younger brother. Though they were clad in layers of clothing, he recognized them as Moody's children, Emma and Willie. The woman with them handed the little boy a ready-made ball. As he clumsily flung it, she pitched another at the same time, congratulating him when it connected with his sister's back, correctly guessing that he would never know it had come from her hand.

Tommy walked past them to the front door and banged the heavy knocker. A moment later the children's governess approached him on the front step. She was covered head-to-toe in navy winter wool, a plaid scarf wrapped around her face and neck, leaving only eyes and nose visible.

"May I help you?"

Tommy gazed into chocolate-colored eyes, sparkling with mischief, and felt his mood instantly lighten. "I've come to see Moody." A snowball whizzed between them and exploded on the door. She did not flinch, but her freckle-covered nose wrinkled, and he distinctly heard her giggle.

"I'm afraid you've just missed him. Might I tell him you've called?"

A snowball connected with her shoulder, showering both of them with fine white powder. Her eyes widened, and she held out her hand. "I do beg your pardon." She turned and glared at the older of the two children, but her little snort of laughter ruined the effect.

"I believe—" Tommy stepped away from her just in time to avoid another snowy missile. "I daresay—" and he reached out a gloved hand to stop another one from connecting with her head.

He was bending over to gather his own snow arsenal and show the little devils a thing or two when a carriage pulled up to the little cottage. He recognized it as Moody's and made to step toward it when Anna Spafford emerged. He smothered a curse. Abruptly he changed course, tipped his hat to the governess, and strode off in the opposite direction, leaving two women to stare after him—one, he knew, in extreme distaste. A sentiment he entirely returned.

A week later Tommy walked through Lincoln Park with Moody, telling him of his plans to enter the real estate market, gingerly seeking his counsel. "Spafford's your man for that project," Moody told him, somewhat dismissively, Tommy thought. But he didn't want Spafford's advice, didn't want to be beholden to him or anyone in his employ. The man was too much like his father.

He kept up with the shorter man's rapid pace, forming his next thought, until they came to a sudden halt on a little wooden bridge overlooking a frozen pond. Skaters zipped back and forth underneath, gliding, leaping, spinning on the ice.

A familiar voice floated up to them, and Tommy recognized the blue cloak and plaid scarf from the snowball fight. There she was, racing across the pond, chasing Moody's children, her laughter a bright little melody. He was intrigued by a woman who played and laughed with such abandon. She seemed completely unspoiled by social constraints. He would press Moody for an introduction.

"Your governess seems to enjoy herself with your children."

Moody looked at him in surprise. "Governess?" He looked out toward the ice, then back at Tommy. "I wish it were so, as Mrs. Moody surely could use the help." He sighed. "But she will not allow it."

They continued watching, Moody clapping his hands when Emma made a stylish turn. Tommy, unwilling to leave the woman's identity a mystery, cleared his throat and tried again. "She is a . . . relative, then?"

Moody frowned, then his eyebrows leapt up with comprehension. "Ah . . . . you speak of Mrs. Maxwell."

Married, Tommy thought, disappointed. *The most interesting women are always married.* Not that a woman's marital status had ever stopped his pursuit. It just complicated things.

"She's boarded with the Spaffords since her husband's death," Moody continued, surprising him. "A lovely and talented woman, Mrs. Maxwell."

Indeed, he thought, admiring her trim form.

Widows always appealed to him, for they knew how to please a man and quite often longed for the opportunity to do so again. He would have to arrange an introduction and discover just how talented this widow was.

Anna smiled as she ran her hand along the polished stair rail. Planning Carrie's birthday had been just the thing to shake away the winter blues that had plagued her these long months. Not even the afternoon's leaden skies and gusting wind could dampen her mood as she'd sat with Carrie by the fire and presented a birthday gift of perfumed soaps and sachets.

Carrie had the distinction of being born on February 29, a leap year. Last year they had "leaped," but Carrie had been in the early stage of mourning, compelling her birthday into a quiet home affair.

This year, as there was no February 29, Maggie was determined to celebrate both days surrounding it. Friday, after school and before tea, Carrie had been crowned and declared a princess—but not a queen, as that always left open the possibility of a beheading. She had been treated to High Tea and several private performances by her royal court, and her every wish throughout the evening had been granted. At nine o'clock the princess had wished for bedtime, and—true to their word—her ladies-in-waiting retired to their rooms without a breath of complaint.

This morning Carrie had been greeted with a sunrise birthday cake and her first gift: new ice skates.

She had gasped in pleasure, then clapped her hands and commanded that her royal court—and their mother—accompany her to Lincoln Park for a trial run. They'd returned for dinner, rosy-cheeked and famished, to find the table filled with all of Carrie's favorite dishes: baked apples, goose pie, creamed corn, and coconut pudding.

Now the Spafford home was filled with upwards of fifty happy guests, and as she rounded the final bend and looked out over the crowd, Anna found a further reason to rejoice. Standing inside the foyer, shaking the sleet off her scarf and cloak was Emma Moody. Anna nearly raced down the busy hallway, so great was her pleasure in seeing her dear friend. The two women grasped hands, both talking at once, dissolving into laughter. Anna handed the heavy cloak to Dottie, pulled her friend's arm through hers, and steered her toward the parlor.

"Thank you for coming!" They wound through the jovial crowd. "Now that you are here, I shall truly enjoy myself."

Emma pursed her lips and leaned closer. "You may not think so when you discover that Mr. M. has—"

"Mrs. Spafford!" Moody's voice was like a trumpet blast in the crowded room. "A wonderful gathering on a wretched night! Are you well? Of course you are, or you would not be hosting such an event! Quite a number of people you have here. Now, where is your husband?"

Anna looked toward the punch bowl where Gates

was supposed to be stationed and met the direct and insolent gaze of Tommy Jameson. Anna's smile faded away, and a throbbing began at the base of her skull. And then a slow anger spread through her veins as she wondered at the preacher's audacity in bringing that man back into her home. Tommy raised an eyebrow, and Anna refused to react or even look away.

Moody harrumphed. "Well, never mind, never mind. I am off to make an introduction. Mr. Jameson would like to become acquainted with Mrs. Maxwell."

She turned her head in time to see Moody grin and wink devilishly at his wife.

Anna found her voice. "I wish that you would not."

Moody raised a questioning brow, and Anna placed her hand on his arm. "Please. No good can come of it."

"My dear . . ." Moody patted her hand. "It is simply an introduction. What harm can come of that?"

Anna could think of plenty of injury Tommy Jameson could do to the young widow. But before she could put her thoughts into words, Moody was gone, pushing his way through the room.

Emma turned toward her friend. "I am so, so sorry, Anna. I know Mr. Jameson grieves you and is not welcome here. Mr. M. knows that as well. But I could not reason with him. He was determined . . ."

Anna heard her friend's remorseful voice as from a distance while she watched the scene unfold across the room.

140

There was Moody, his hand on Tommy's large and well-garbed shoulder. And there was Carrie, beautifully flushed from the evening's excitement, the mahogany velvet gown she'd finished just that afternoon setting off her fair skin and dark eyes. As Moody talked and gestured, Tommy took the young widow's hand, a smile spreading across his handsome face until dimples appeared in each cheek. The effect was devastating.

Anna felt a tremendous anger roil inside her chest as she watched the young people interact. A woman could be a fool for a man as striking as Tommy Jameson, and Carrie was looking more foolish by the moment—laughing gaily, her free hand fluttering near her smooth neck, drawing his interested eye there. She was twenty-one years old and no match for a seasoned rogue.

But Anna was. Mr. Jameson had come to the wrong house in pursuit of the wrong woman. If he wanted a contest for the young widow, he would have it. And he would lose.

She watched them throughout the evening. She noted how Tommy was careful not to monopolize Carrie's time but always managed to be within her line of sight. He brought her fresh glasses of punch and sweet tidbits from the table, and the dimpled smile on these occasions was enough to stop her in midsentence.

As the clock struck eleven and guests began to leave, Anna stood with Gates and Carrie near the foyer, helping them on with winter cloaks, saying their good-byes. During a brief lull, while Gates was out assisting with a wagon, Carrie turned to Anna, her eyes alight with pleasure.

"Is not Mr. Jameson the perfect gentleman? I'm quite impressed with him. He's been in Chicago but two months and still feels rather a stranger, so I've invited him to come to church with us tomorrow night!"

Anna made her features as smooth and taciturn as a bridled pony while Carrie gushed.

"He should be comfortable there." She put a hand to her mouth and whispered like a schoolgirl. "He looks like an angel."

A fallen angel, Anna thought but kept her lips tightly sealed.

"I wonder that you have not introduced us before now. He is a friend of your husband's, yes? And Brother Moody's?"

Anna looked past her young friend to Mr. Jameson—lounging in an armchair, one leg crossed casually over the other, one eyebrow raised sardonically at her. Oh, he was smug in his conquest.

"Oh, Anna. What a happy meeting this was!"

Anna squared her shoulders and looked Carrie dead in the eye. "Guard your heart, Mrs. Maxwell."

Carrie's smile dimmed at her hostess' harsh tone, and Anna was not sorry for it. "Guard your heart."

The silence between them that spring brought both relief and strain.

The ladies laid out the garden plot from opposite ends—each measuring eighteen inches from the last row, planting the wooden stake, pulling the twine taut over ground that was finally dry and broken up and ready for planting. Anna's garden grew in proportion each year to the number of people eating at their table, and this year's would be her largest yet.

Carrie was a hundred feet away, yet Anna could clearly see her furrowed brow and lips drawn into a tight line. Their relationship had diminished to polite conversation over mealtime and household tasks since the introduction of Tommy Jameson into the widow's life.

Within a week of the party, the man's name had spilled from Carrie's mouth so often that Anna could no longer stifle the sigh she generally regarded as theatrical in her own children. A fortnight passed and Carrie was plaguing her hostess with ideas for enticing the man into more church activities, finally appealing to Gates when Anna proved noncommittal. After a month of placidly denying Mr. Jameson an invitation to supper, Anna had been forced to sit with her young friend and lay out for her, in the clearest terms possible, without the benefit of witnesses or documentation or even gossip, why the man was not welcome in her home.

With an early April storm blowing against the parlor windows, Anna had told Carrie of her own negative experiences with Mr. Jameson, her impression of his character, how he resorted to sarcasm and belligerence in order to win even the smallest point. She'd acknowledged that Gates had spent a fair amount of time with the young man—usually at Moody's request—and found him troubled, removed. She'd brought into question Tommy's heritage—for he had spoken little of it—his lack of acquaintance or recommendation, his disinterest in their faith.

But it had fallen on deaf, smitten ears. Mr. Jameson's behavior with *her* had been everything that is amiable and pleasing, Carrie had argued. He had taken no liberties, neither had he been removed. He had sat with her in church each Sunday evening since they'd met, intent on Brother Moody's message, discussing the particulars quite agreeably with her as they'd taken a turn about the courthouse square. While it was true that he did not readily discuss his family, she'd sensed the topic brought him pain and would not press him.

In the end, Carrie had labeled Anna's distrust of the man as unfounded suspicion based on a bad first impression and general distrust of bachelors. Although it grieved her to disagree, she'd said, she would not sever her new association with Mr. Jameson, as his company brought her great pleasure.

And so, Anna was relieved to hear no more of Tommy Jameson and his dubious qualities. But at the same time she mourned the loss of Carrie's happy chatter. And she abhorred the rigid silence that stretched between them now like the prickly twine connecting each garden stake.

She felt a heaviness settle on her heart as she bent and retrieved the next marker. Robins chirped in the fresh spring air, and the sun warmed her back through the cotton day dress. And somewhere, deep within, she remembered another time—before the Fire—when life was full of beginnings and uncomplicated relationships and a happy rhythm interrupted by even happier events. And she knew with a sudden awful clarity that she could never, would never, return to it.

CHAPTER 11

Spring 1873

S pafford stared across the crowded horsecar, fairly sure he'd made the right decision. He was loathe to involve himself in women's issues. But the occasional suppers he'd attended in his own home were overwhelmingly polite, and he sensed a strain between Carrie and his wife. An overheard conversation on this very train had seemed to provide an opportunity, and he'd presented it.

Now Carrie was on her way to interview with the proprietor of Higgins Dress Shop on the north edge of the city. The shop needed a talented *modiste,* and Carrie, he reasoned, needed a measure of independence. A solution was at hand.

He worried a little about his wife. The long winter was always a bit hard on her, but she usually leapt into spring with great spirit—testing the soil, coaxing it to dry enough to let the field hand break up the clods with a little more manure before she began the planting. But this year the field hand had come to *him*, asking if they'd be needing his services, as he hadn't heard from the missus. He'd mentioned it to his wife that very Sunday, and she'd looked up from her dinner, rather distractedly, and nodded—Yes, yes, he could come at any time. But her eyes had been filled with such a weariness that he'd left messages with all the staff the next morning to be sure not to burden their mistress with tasks they could complete themselves.

He wondered if keeping the third floor filled with boarders was taking its toll on her. He wondered, because she never complained. Anna was the most resourceful, disciplined woman he knew—a first-rate problem solver. When she came to him with a dilemma, he knew it was only because she had exercised every option within her command without resolution.

If she was wrestling with something—something beyond her control—she would seek his counsel in due time. So he would put aside his worries until then. He snapped open the newspaper and read, rocking with the rhythm of the car, confident, satisfied.

Anna knelt in the rich black dirt of her garden, staring down at the shallow trench, trying to remember what seeds she had just scattered. Her head ached, and she wished for a cool drink of water. Was it carrot? No . . .

146

yes. Carrot with a little radish mixed in to help distinguish the new sprouts from the early weeds. She reached for the watering can and sprinkled the seeds and felt the prickling at the backs of her eyes again. She fought back the tears and won.

It was ridiculous, this melancholy that made her shoulders droop so that she consciously squared them, the heaviness that made her feet drag, the memories that distracted her. She shook her head, covered the seeds with the fine soil, and reached for the next batch to scatter.

Are we weak and heavy-laden . . . cumbered with a load of care? Her hand halted in midair, so startled was she at the clarity of the poem read to her months ago. *Precious Savior, still our refuge—take it to the Lord in prayer.* The memory was vivid . . . Coates sitting with her by the crackling fire, reading from the little book of hymns and other verses while the snow fell in large, wet profusion beyond the pulled drapes. The tray sat between them, and she slowly stirred the sugar into her tea as he read. *What a friend we have in Jesus, all our sins and griefs to bear.* They had talked at some length on that poem and the power of prayer. They had spoken of the biblical Hannah, the once-barren mother of Samuel, who had cried out to the Lord, "Remember me." *Oh, what peace we often forfeit, Oh, what needless pain we bear . . .* The poem wrapped itself around her, holding her tight in its solace and truth. *All because we do not carry everything to God in prayer.*

She sat very still in the garden, thinking . . . waiting . . . until the tender voice of the Lord floated on a gentle breeze and whispered to her.

Come to me, Anna.

The tears flowed then in slow, hot rivers down her cheeks. *Abide with me.*

She looked across the neatly planted rows and tried to put into words what she found hard to explain, even to herself. How to describe her weariness when she had servants' and boarders' hands to help with every task. How to account for her loneliness when she was surrounded daily by loving children and friends. How to detail the sorrow she felt from her husband's increasing absence—a necessity, she understood, for attending to people with greater needs than her own.

In the end there were words, but no complete thoughts, and no easy answers from the Great Counselor. But just as the poem said, she found a solace in the garden as she carried every need, every want, every hope—everything—to God in prayer.

The knocking on her bedroom door was so soft, she almost didn't hear it. She remained still, hoping her visitor would go away. But after a moment the door latch released. She opened her eyes to the soft reds and yellows and greens pouring through the second-floor landing's stained-glass window. She opened her eyes to Emma Moody.

"My dear," Emma moved to Anna's bedside. "Are you ill?"

Anna watched her friend take in the dressing gown and compresses and dark, airless room at midday. She raised herself to a sitting position and smiled a little.

"Just a headache."

Emma pursed her lips and moved toward the window. "May I?" At Anna's nod, Emma drew back the heavy curtains, throwing the room into natural light, and pushed the glass open. A fresh breeze stirred the fine hairs around her face as she looked out toward the garden, then turned with a small smile.

"Anna . . ." She hesitated, then sought out a chair in the corner, bringing it bedside and perching on the edge. "I have . . . news.

Anna waited, oddly detached.

"Mr. M. has been invited to Great Britain for a revival tour. Mr. Sankey and his wife also go."

There was such a pleading look in her friend's eyes that Anna immediately understood her dilemma. And her spirits were instantly lighter as she envisioned another summer of companionship and afternoon teas and laughter. It would be just the thing to shake her from the melancholy that daily held her in a terrible grip. She rushed to make the invitation.

"You will stay again with us? Oh, do say yes!"

Emma opened her mouth, then closed it. She leaned forward, placing her hand over her friend's, speaking with the utmost gentleness.

"Dearest . . . I go with them"

Anna's spirits, so high just moments ago, plummeted to a new low. *No. No, Emma,* her heart cried out. *Please do not leave me.* She struggled to clear the agony from her throat.

"For how long?" She almost held her breath as her cherished friend looked into her face.

"Two years."

Years . . . years . . .

"He has a goal to win ten thousand souls."

Anna's own soul bled out any hope she had for an enjoyable summer. The days stretched endlessly before her, and her breath caught on a sob.

Emma grasped her hand tighter. "Anna . . . Can you tell me what is wrong?"

"Nothing." She looked down at their hands, then back up, letting her feelings roam free on her features. "Everything." The tears broke free and she brushed them away with an impatient hand.

Emma studied her, letting her regain control, offering her a dainty pink handkerchief that matched the trim on her cotton day dress.

Anna wiped her face, over and over, but the tears still came, and her throat hurt from holding back the sobs.

Emma held her hand in companionable silence, her own eyes sad and wet from unshed tears. "You are lonely?"

Anna nodded, wiping her face.

"Perhaps no one understands that better than the wife of an evangelist." Emma smiled a little and sighed. "Men—" She corrected herself. "Busy men cannot grasp the solitariness of the domestic life.

They do not see us waiting in the parlor, watching the timepiece, listening for the carriage wheels to stop at the front gate." She shook her head. "So we must tell them."

Anna appreciated her friend's advice but could not envision herself at the dinner table, facing her husband, saying, *I am lonely, Gates.* It just seemed selfish. Who was she to compel her husband to her side for quiet evenings on the porch or by the fire when needy Chicagoans cried out for his expertise?

She looked out the window at the brilliant green of the maple tree's new leaves. Two sparrows leapt from limb to limb. How she envied their carefree, innocent existence.

"Anna?"

She focused again on Emma, her sorrow lying like heavy stone on her chest.

"Talk to him . . . tell him. You have nothing to lose and everything to gain."

But Anna had learned long ago that when petitioning others, high expectations—or any expectations at all—only brought disappointment. So she was lonely. She would find more activities, interact with more people. This was her problem to solve, alone.

CHAPTER 12

Summer 1873

Anna stood at the edge of the crowd, smiling in spite of her sorrow. They were gathered in the great hall of the Chicago Avenue Church, celebrating friendship and faith, honoring D. L. Moody's witness, and sending him off to the British Isles in grand style.

But Moody was never one for pageantry. So as soon as the formalities had become too much, he'd slipped away and joined the children in their games, teasing and romping with them until they pounced and pinned him to the floor. And he laughed and laughed until the tears ran down his face.

Anna watched as her own girls vied for the man's attention. They loved him like an uncle and had entrusted their souls into his care. Just that spring, Annie and Maggie had sought out the preacher because they'd wished to join the church. They had told their mother about it late one night—how Moody had questioned them separately and quite thoroughly about their salvation and discussed their responsibilities as Christians. "God says, 'Trust me,'" he had told them. "And God will bring us through all our difficulties, if we will only trust Him." So they had. And they'd rejoiced in their faith ever after.

She let her gaze roam across the room. There was Ira Sankey—the portly musician with the interesting beard and muttonchops that made him so easy to identify. And John Farwell—the dry goods merchant and Moody's benefactor—who looked on the party with the same sadness she felt, for he had a premonition, he'd told Gates, that the Moodys would never return to Chicago for more than a visit. In the corner were Gates, B. E Jacobs, Major Whittle, and other board members of the YMCA. J. H. Cole, who would take the pulpit in Moody's absence, Dr. Coates, and Miss Dryer stood in a circle of women, undoubtedly discussing the ministry and home missions training she would start immediately.

And then her eyes lit upon Carrie Maxwell and Tommy Jameson. They sat on a bench with their heads close together, talking fervently. Anna could not deny they made a handsome couple—he with his blond angelic facade, she with her fresh youthful innocence. For weeks after her frank discussion with Carrie, Anna had searched her heart for some ulterior motive in disliking, mistrusting, the man—some reason other than the ongoing reports of his disreputable behavior. But in the end she'd been forced to conclude that Carrie and Moody simply saw something in Tommy Jameson that she could not.

She looked about the room and concluded that, in a way, an era was ending. Barriers between rich and poor, men and women, mission and ministry had been burned away with the Fire, and much of the success centered on the man who was leaving them. No doubt Moody was so focused on his new mission in Europe

153

that he was oblivious to the hearts breaking in this very room—hearts that had come to depend on his and Emma's steady love and compassion. Hearts like hers.

Tommy Jameson slouched at the table, fumbling with his napkin, avoiding his friend's gaze. Another sleepless night had taken its toll. He knew his face was puffy, that dark circles framed bloodshot eyes. He remembered another morning, months ago, when he'd sat in this same restaurant, ate the same breakfast, hoping to put off the man who was now leaving him.

Moody broke the silence. "Well, my friend, we have come full circle."

Tommy looked up then, straight into the loving gaze of the only man he'd ever trusted.

"I shall miss this place," Moody sighed. "And I shall miss you, Thomas."

Tommy was speechless. Never in his life—not one time—had anyone missed him. He choked down the emotion that had constantly threatened to erupt since Moody's announced departure.

"Just five months past, we sat in yonder seat—" Moody pointed with his chin to a table by the window—"you and Spafford and myself." His voice was very soft and tender. "I took you into my heart that day, and you have been there ever since."

Tommy looked across the table, his pulse beating wildly, his mind screaming, *Please don't go! Don't leave me!* It was excruciating having words of such desperation in his heart, words he could never utter. He swallowed hard.

Moody leaned forward. "I want to tell you a story—a tale of a father and a lost son." He waited until Tommy nodded, then leaned back and began.

"There was a young man, arrogant, with no regard for his father's authority. One day this son demanded his inheritance, left home, and lived a wild life. He was called a prodigal—wasteful. By and by he squandered everything and found himself feeding pigs to survive. Now it took a while, but the poor fellow finally came to his senses. He thought of his father's hired men, how they always had plenty to eat, and determined he would go home, beg his father's forgiveness, and live as a servant . . . if his father would let him."

Tommy had crossed his arms in defiance as the story unfolded. He was no fool. He knew what Moody was driving at, and it offended him. But Moody pushed on.

"What this boy didn't know was that his father had been watching and waiting for him, even from the day he'd left. And when the father saw his son approach the gate, he ran to him and welcomed him home. He told everyone, 'My son was lost and is found!' And they celebrated with a feast and music and dancing."

Moody concluded the tale with his characteristic spirit—eyebrows jumping, hands gesturing—and sat back, waiting for his young friend's response.

"You think I should beg my father's forgiveness." Tommy laughed—a short, humorless sound from a tight, aching throat. "Trust me when I tell you that I would not be welcomed by him or anyone near him."

Moody shook his head. "My friend, this is not the story of you and your father in England. The father of the prodigal is the picture of God. And as the father of the prodigal is waiting for his son, so God is waiting for you"

Tommy was angry now, but his anger was mixed with such a sense of longing that he found himself confused, and he lashed out where he thought it would do the most damage.

"Then your God is a fool."

The blasphemy struck home, but not as Tommy might have predicted. Moody's shoulders slumped and his mouth drooped, and when he spoke, it was with a heaviness Tommy had not experienced in the charismatic man. "Oh, but the devil has a hold upon you."

Tommy raised a brow. "If that were true, why would someone like Mrs. Maxwell have such an interest in me?"

"Because she happens to think, as do I, that there is something worthy in you . . . something aching and tender that needs to fight its way out"

Tommy shook his head and stood. "I like my own way"

Moody stood with him. "As do I. It was a long

while before that truth went home to my sinful heart." He put his hand on Tommy's shoulder and locked pleading eyes with weary ones. "The world will deceive you but never satisfy you." He squeezed the shoulder until Tommy almost winced. "What evil is left for you to do? Must you do it until even the world rejects you?"

Tommy's heart constricted and his lips parted, but the words were frozen in his throat.

Moody leaned closer. "Call upon God. Ask for mercy. That's what you want. Ask Him to have mercy upon you."

Tommy wrenched himself free and fled to the restaurant door. He burst through it and stood on the sidewalk, looking this way and that, seeing nothing, a battle raging in his soul.

Moody emerged behind him, whistled for the buggy, and led him to it like a nurse with a blind man. Tommy climbed into the seat, and they drove off. And not another word passed between them.

Within minutes they were on Rush Street approaching Tommy's boardinghouse. The panic was building in his chest—Moody was going away! He would never see him again! His whole body started to shake, and the emotion threatened to strangle him. In his head he was crying out, *Please don't go! Don't leave me!*

Moody reined in the horse and jumped down from the seat. Tommy climbed down after him, unsteady. Moody held out a hand, and Tommy gripped it, and

Moody covered it with his left. And then a hot tear splashed onto their hands. And then another. Tommy watched the falling tears with fascination. He could not remember the last time he had cried. Yes, he could—at the battlefront, the night Jimmy had died.

Moody inhaled deeply and let the breath out on a whisper. Then Tommy felt Moody's strong hand on the back of his neck, very gently pulling his head down, down onto the preacher's shoulder until his forehead rested against the soft and worn frock coat. He felt Moody's arm against his back, holding him in a powerful embrace. Then he felt the rumble in the man's chest as he began to pray. Ever softly, he prayed for God's mercy on his lost boy. He prayed for guidance, for protection against the powers of hell. Tommy's body continued to shake, and his tears soaked the preacher's coat, and Moody held on tighter. Finally, he asked for God's blessing and for His perfect will to be done. The two men embraced on Rush Street, man-to-man, father-to-son, until Tommy stepped away, wiping his eyes.

Moody stood still on the sidewalk, nodding his head, his brow furrowed, his cheeks wet. He gazed up into the clear June sky, drew a shaky breath, then looked for the last time on Tommy Jameson.

"I would take you on my shoulders and carry you into the kingdom of God if I could. But I cannot. I can only tell you of one who can." He gripped Tommy's shoulder once more, pulled himself into the buggy, and drove away.

Tommy watched him go, the tears still coursing down his cheeks, and thought he'd never met a stronger, more tender, more considerate man than D. L. Moody. He realized with sudden clarity that he loved the preacher, revered him. And he knew in the same moment that he'd just lost the best friend he'd ever had.

Spafford kept his promise to Moody that summer. He found a reason twice a week to seek out Tommy Jameson for lunch or coffee or expeditions to a new building site. And each time, Tommy's mood was a little darker, a little meaner. Mrs. Maxwell was a regular topic of conversation, for her success at the dress shop kept her working long hours, and Tommy found that inconvenient. Occasionally Spafford would mention his wife and her increasing work in the community. But that topic was always met with silence and a look of such disregard that Spafford soon gave up mentioning her at all.

In early August Anna and the three eldest girls walked home from the Marine Hospital nearby in Lake View. The girls swung their baskets that had carried fruit and flowers to the sailors, discussing their experience, choosing hymns they might sing on their next visit.

They skipped through the iron gate and up the steps and dashed through the great double doors, leaving Anna to trail behind. She was lost in thought and passed along the hallway, nearly missing the flash of color moving through the parlor.

She turned and saw the stricken face of Carrie Maxwell. Anna was so surprised to see the widow in the midafternoon that no greeting came to her lips. She recovered in moments and hurried into the parlor where she encouraged Carrie to join her on the settee and share her troubles.

It came out in a rush—how Mr. Jameson had refused to attend church services once Moody had gone, how he'd begun to question her faith, then mocked it. Then today, how a young woman had come into the dress shop, garish and loud, demanding to see Miss Carrie and their most expensive fabric for which she would pay handsomely—well, not *she,* but Mr. Jameson of Rush Street, her benefactor.

Carrie was deeply ashamed of her naïveté. With tears streaming down her face, she knelt at Anna's feet and begged her forgiveness, for her pride and coldness, but mostly for the way she had discredited Anna's intuition. She laid her cheek against Anna's knees and admitted, "You saw in him an unworthiness that I could not."

Anna placed her hands on Carrie's head and tried to form an appropriate response. She could not fault the widow, for her behavior in the courtship had been in every way appropriate. She felt no pleasure for being right about Tommy Jameson's character. She felt no joy at the dissolution of their romance.

She felt relieved and a little hopeful that the strain of the past months would subside and that they could, again, be friends. So she spoke the words, and they embraced, and Anna convinced her restored friend to wash her face and stay for tea and regale her with the latest news from town.

Anna opened the door to her hothouse, not a little leery of what she'd find. She had not been inside the little room in weeks, as she had thrown herself into community work and had found neither the time nor the heart to come here.

She walked down the tiny center aisle, looking left and right, surprised at the tidiness and growth sprouting from moist pots. She looked around in confusion. Zinnias were blooming—zinnias she had not planted. Pink tea roses climbed a makeshift trellis, their fragrance wafting out and over her. The greens of hearty paper whites pushed out of their bulbs.

Someone had been here, tending the inside garden while she had ignored it. She wondered who—Carrie? No, the widow's services were too much in demand this summer to tend flowers. Dottie? Nicolet? Doubtful. Neither of them viewed the garden as more than a necessity to stock the larder. Anna turned full circle and noticed a stool tucked under the long shelf. Where had that come from? Who would . . . Her mind played over the rooms in the house. Had she seen flowers in the foyer this morning?

She walked out of the hothouse and through the kitchen, glancing about her for the first time in months, and emerged into the grand hallway. There on the hall table, inexpertly arranged but lovely nonetheless, was a slender vase of early mums and zinnias. She stared at the vase, and the answer came to her—Annie. Her eldest daughter had been invited into the hothouse for special projects since the age of four. Now, seven years later, she had taken it over when it became clear that her mother had abandoned it.

She reached up and touched the watch pinned to her breast and thought of her own mother, how she had died one summer, leaving them with bluebells and lily of the valley pushing against the walls of their little cottage in glorious bloom. She remembered how she had lain down at the edge of those flowers, inhaling their sweet fragrance, thinking that if she could just keep the plants blooming, her mother might return and clap her hands in her merry way and say, "Well done."

And now she realized that her own daughter had quietly tended the flowers, growing them, cutting them, arranging them in little vases all over the house, hoping . . . hoping for the same reaction.

Anna turned and slowly climbed the stair, each step calling out her failure—as a mother and wife and friend. The ever-present dull ache spread across her shoulders and up the back of her head, pressing them down in shame and unworthiness. She walked through her bedroom door, closed it with a gentle click, pulled the drapes, and climbed into bed. She could not face the day and the disappointments it revealed. The darkness and oblivion called to her, and she closed her eyes and answered.

CHAPTER 13

October 1873

Anna thrust her hands into the warm, doughy mixture—blending, turning, kneading. It was the one skill her Norwegian mother had instilled in her before she'd died, and Anna sought solace in it now. *"Snakk med deigen . . . fortell den om dine problemer,"* her *mor* would say. *Speak to the dough . . . tell it your troubles.* And Anna would squeeze the eggs through the flour in adolescent frustration, physically working out her misery until she pounded the bloated mass in final satisfaction, shaped it, and settled it in the heavy pan to bake.

But now she worked the dough in steady abject silence, her fingers moving mechanically. What could she say? That the unchanging routine of her life was unbearable? That her marriage was a farce? That was the real crux—her marriage.

Outwardly nothing had changed. They still lived harmoniously in the same house, attended the same church, dined with the same friends. They had four lovely and obedient girls. In all, they made a pretty, well-crafted portrait in their family pew on Sundays.

But it was just that—a portrait. If one picked away

at the paint and got to the canvas of their particular portrait, she feared it would be entirely, frightfully, blank. Gone would be the basic reliable coating of the vows they so eagerly pledged to each other that bright September day. She mentally reviewed them—"to have and to hold." She saw the wisdom now of linking those two together. If one did not "have" her husband, if work and boards and committees and church duties had him, then the holding would fall by the wayside, relegated to a less-busy time and place. "In joy and in sorrow." She recalled the joy she used to find in pleasing her husband—entertaining him at the piano, trying new recipes, enticing him into the bedroom. She could not remember the last time she'd applied fragrance to her wrists and neck as a subtle signal of her desire. And sorrow . . . well, neither of them was particularly good at expressing or detecting that emotion. It was that hearty European ancestry, that tendency to lift one's chin and buck up under the weight of sadness. "To love and to cherish." This one disturbed her the most. Gates was extremely loyal and, no doubt, felt he loved her. But she . . . she could not honestly say she loved her husband. She worked at the emotion, probing it, turning it over in her mind, searching for something, anything to reignite that essential of all emotions. Why, if he came through that door right now, she would—

The door swung open, and Carrie burst into the kitchen, hands waving, loose strands of hair flying around her flushed face.

"I had to come right away! I've had a telegram—a *telegram*—from New York! It says—" and she searched frantically through the pockets of her sewing apron for the black-edged paper. "I must have laid it aside. Oh! How could I have forgotten it?" She gave her head a furious shake. "Oh, never mind . . . never mind."

She gripped the edge of the worktable with both hands. "I have heard from E. Butterick & Company on Broadway in New York City! Their chief designer—a Mrs. Chapman—is thrilled with my designs and summons me to their workshop posthaste. A letter is to follow with the details." She clapped her hands together and looked skyward.

"Oh, Anna, is it not the most wondrous and exciting news? Isn't God simply wonderful and gracious to arrange this for me? A new life in New York!" Her eyes shone with exhilaration and unshed tears. She looked around the kitchen as if seeing it anew.

"I must return to the dress shop. I told Mrs. Higgins I'd be away for just a tick, and—" She squinted at Anna's watch. "Good heavens! It's been closer to thirty. I must dash!"

And with that, she spun on her heel and hurried down the hall, calling over her shoulder, "We shall celebrate the news tonight!" The front door slammed with just enough force to punctuate her excitement.

Anna waited, her hands deep in the dough, for some kind of feeling to wash over her—elation at Carrie's good fortune, joy at an answer to prayer, envy for her good friend's adventure, worry for her safety in such a big city, jealousy, sadness, curiosity . . . anything.

She waited, and there was nothing.

She searched her heart and felt only the regular dull thumping of the muscle in its rhythmic cycle. No racing exhilaration, no sinking dread, no crushing panic, no jolting surprise. Nothing.

And she wondered at what point it had come to this. She looked back and remembered a spectacular summer Saturday, July twelfth, the day Betsy Roberts married James Hutcheson in the bower of St. Michael's, the day she stopped asking God to mend her broken spirit, the day she finally, irretrievably, went completely dead inside.

She looked at her doughy, work-worn hands—so much like her mother's and grandmother's—and finally dared to ask herself the crucial questions: Could she wake up tomorrow and face her staff, her tenants, her children? She could not imagine it. Then would it not be better to simply end this daily cycle of despair?

Yes, she decided. An end always brings about a different beginning.

So she meticulously washed the dough from her hands, dried each finger, and folded the damp towel. She untied her apron, shrugged it off her shoulders, and hung it on its regular hook on the back of the pantry door.

She walked out of the kitchen, down the hallway, and through the foyer, ignoring the wall of family

166

portraits, the unopened mail on the table, and calls for her attention. She reached the massive double doors, opened them, and walked out of her life.

Perhaps, she thought, *forever.*

The ragamuffin scurried along Market Street, head down, hands shoved deep into his pockets. When he came to the end of the tall wooden fence, he slowed, looked both ways, then ducked behind it.

Except he didn't go behind it—he went *between* it and the older fence built two feet behind it. And he was really a *she.*

She collapsed onto the soft earth between the fences and yanked off the cap. Why in the world did boys wear these things? They made her ears itch.

She rubbed her scalp and marveled again at how light her head felt now that the heavy tresses were gone. She harbored no regret for hacking them off with the rusty knife. It served two purposes—it completed her disguise, and it ensured that no man would ever want to touch her again because of her hair.

She'd nearly gathered it all up, tied a satin bow around it, and sent it off to her uncle. But though he was vile, though it would please her to enrage him, she was worldly enough for her fifteen years to know that he must never find a reason to come after her. Never.

She donned the cap again, settled into her hideaway, ignored the rumbling of her empty stomach, and engaged in her favorite activity of late: people watching. Yesterday she'd wrestled with the new fence until she'd loosened a board and created a peephole just large enough to see through but not be seen.

Market Street provided plenty of activity as a crossroads between the genteel neighborhoods and the less-savory business district. Thus, ladies and gentlemen of distinction would occasionally cross paths with laborers and opportunists. The interaction between these groups fascinated her, and she'd watched more than a few pockets being picked.

She relaxed against the fence and must have dozed, because when she opened her eyes, a lady seemed to appear out of nowhere. She seemed to glide along the wooden sidewalk, looking neither left nor right, in no particular hurry, on no pressing mission. She carried no reticule and wore no hat or gloves. She was unaccompanied by servant or spouse—odd in this part of town.

As the lady drew closer, the girl was overcome by her mysterious presence. She was lovely and without expression, moving effortlessly, gracefully, nearer.

The girl reached out her hand, and the name came unbidden to her lips—the name she had not spoken in two years, had vowed to speak nevermore.

"Mama?"

And with that one word, that single utterance, something broke loose in her and filled her with such a longing and a rage that she was propelled to her feet.

In her mind's eye it was not a sunny morning, but the dead of night. And the freshness of fall was replaced by a heavy foglike smoke that stung her eyes and clogged her throat. And this time when she crossed the street, no strong arms held her back, telling her it was too late, telling her to run—run for her life.

She felt her legs moving, free from the confines of a nightgown, but still she could not breathe. Her chest was in a vise, and her heart thudded mechanically, but the air would not fill her lungs. Her ears rang, but not with the screams for loved ones or shouts for help.

She reached the sidewalk and stood resolutely in the middle of it. The woman continued toward her, looking absently forward, noticing nothing. Indeed, they would have collided had not the girl held up her hand, palm out. The woman focused on the hand and simply stopped.

The girl looked her over. Everything about this woman was so familiar to her—the hair knotted at the neck, the tasteful day dress, pressed and pinned with a watch, the dainty handkerchief tucked into the sleeve. The slight scent of lavender wafted between them, and the girl fought the urge to weep. She knew the erect carriage, the air of authority, even the hollowness in the woman's eyes.

She stood there, remembering her former life, and briefly she was in a room that no longer existed. She was at the piano, pressing the keys with an ease that always surprised her, finding comfort in the solitude of a solo instrument. Her mother passed the doorway but did not come in. She rarely came in, for she appreciated her daughter's unwillingness to interact with others. Children were such a bother. The girl tried to shake the sudden memory and the ache that began to consume her, not for the loneliness of her young life, but for the solace of always knowing what to expect.

But the ache took on a life of its own and began to build in her until she combined it with anger over her loss, shock over her uncle's depravity, and worry over her daily survival. She let the mixture simmer, then boil, then directed every drop of it toward the woman who would not be her mother.

"I'll take your watch." The woman looked at her with her hollow eyes and made no move to hand it over. Instead, she spoke in a voice almost bereft of emotion.

"I cannot help you."

They faced off on the dirty sidewalk, the girl afraid of nothing, the woman feeling nothing. The girl arched a brow and leaned a little further into the waves of lavender.

"Well, I did not ask for your help. I asked for your watch."

The woman surprised her and made no move to cover the timepiece or to flee. Instead, she appeared to focus on her adversary, taking in the chopped hair, the creamy skin, and the ill-fitting clothes. The woman cocked her head a little to the side and said with interest, "Who are you?"

"I am the boy who wants your watch."

The woman actually smiled, not in pity, but in understanding. "You are no boy. But I think with time and a little more dirt, you could pass for one . . . at a distance." She made to continue on, but the girl blocked her path.

"I'll have your watch. Then you may go."

The woman looked at the timepiece then for a long moment. When she looked up, the hollowness had returned, as well as resolve.

"This was my mother's watch. It is all I have, and I will not part with it."

Perhaps it was the woman's determination, or the mention of her mother, or the idea of a keepsake. Whatever it was, in one instant the girl determined she would do anything to have that watch. She reached out for it and was met with a surprising strength in the woman's grasp over her wrist. She wrenched her arm free and struck out with the other, knocking the woman back. But the woman did not flee. Instead, she stepped forward to pass.

The girl again blocked her path and, this time, knocked the woman to the ground. The woman sprang immediately to her feet and began to hurry toward a shop a hundred yards away. The girl calculated the distance, grabbed a broken tree limb from the ground, and gave chase.

The first blow caught the woman on the shoulder blade, and she stumbled but did not fall. The second blow caught her in the ribs and sent her to her knees.

She struggled to rise, but the girl grasped her shoulder and flipped her onto her back.

The girl stood over her, tree limb poised for another blow, and looked in rage at the spot on the woman's breast where the watch had been. Gone. She raised the limb higher.

"Give it to me."

The woman shook her head "no."

The girl swung hard and met the woman's upraised wrist. She swung again and connected with the woman's head. As the woman fell back, the girl reached down and pried open the clenched hand.

The watch . . . gold, delicate, ticking softly with assurance. She snatched it up and stood for a moment, following the second hand's movement, transported by its familiarity. *Tick . . . tick . . . tick . . .*

Mama, she cried in her heart. *Why didn't you wake up? Why didn't you come out?*

Two years had passed, yet she still relived that horrible scene, daily, nightly . . . on particularly bad days, hourly. She saw herself standing in the street, waiting for her parents and brothers to come out of the burning house. But they never came. She had bolted through the door at the first sign of danger and left them, asleep in their beds, to perish.

She looked over at the lifeless form of the stranger and fingered the watch. Mama was dead. And God would never forgive her for that.

PART III

He who has never hoped
can never despair.
—GEORGE BERNARD SHAW

CHAPTER 14

Anna had been awake for some time now. She hadn't moved, hadn't let even an eyelash flutter. She recognized the lavender smell of her bed sheets, amazed that the little sachets had perfume to give after a year of hard use. She knew the texture of the worn cotton cuff on her favorite nightgown—pale pink, lace at the hem, ribbon at the neck. She knew she was safe.

It wasn't pain that kept her motionless, although her head ached where the tree limb had connected, her left wrist felt heavy and stiff, and drawing a deep breath proved difficult with tightly wrapped ribs.

She was still because while remaining so, nothing was required of her. She simply breathed in and breathed out, listening to the hushed conversations outside her door.

She was pleased to learn that her attacker had not been found. Poor girl. *Protect her, Lord,* she prayed. *Forgive her.*

Dr. Coates remained close-by, murmuring assurances to frightened tenants and staff. Dear, dear Coates. He'd done so much for them, for their city. Her children knew nothing of her experience. Good. Their tender hearts were already full of the suffering around them. She'd counted four men who came and went with negative reports on locating Gates.

Gates. She found herself straining for the sound of

his boots on the stair. The very timbre of connection between the leather of the sole and the wood of the step would indicate his mood. If the footsteps were soft and unhurried, he'd had time to review the details, make a conclusion, and devise a plan. If they were sharp and rapid, he'd just been located and would call for information. If they were heavy and measured . . . Ah, this would signal battle. His ascent on the stair would indicate nothing about his disposition to the masses, for he kept that firmly controlled and hidden. But she would know.

She'd been formulating her statement in the quiet of the room—what she would reveal, how she would reveal it. She would let him speak first, listen without interruption, acknowledge his concern. And then she would tell him about the struggle inside her—the daily compulsion to leave always fighting the conviction to stay.

He would have a solution to her dilemma, something logical, something moral, something that required three steps, from A to C, and then, sensibly, a resolution. And then she would tell him again. And again. Until he understood that this was not a problem solved through logic.

Oh, Lord, she prayed, *help me to speak in truth and grace.*

She heard the doctor call his name, then felt him stand, as all men were wont to do when her husband approached. She listened. Heavy, measured steps. Her spirit sighed. It was to be battle, then.

Spafford climbed the stair, engrossed in thought. He could not recall a time when he'd been so angry with his wife. Why had she ventured into that part of town without an escort or a weapon? She was neither a flighty nor frivolous woman. She must have had some purpose, although she'd told no one of it.

How many times had they discussed the danger of a society under such economic and moral reform? Chicago was healing substantially, but it remained a haven for corrupt men who would do evil for personal gain. She knew the rules of venturing out during this dangerous period.

He paused at the bedroom door just long enough for a report on her condition. Head injury, cracked ribs, swollen wrist—probably sprained. Bruising, no blood, no fever, small possibility of internal injury. Had not regained consciousness.

His heart stopped for a moment at that last statement, and he swung open the door a little too hard. The room was peaceful, aglow with late-afternoon sun, fresh roses bedside. He eased the door closed and approached his unconscious wife, slowly, uncertainly.

Midway to the bed, his step slowed. He could tell by her composure that she was alert and had been for some time. He closed the distance and stood over her, arms crossed. What kind of act was she performing, feigning unconsciousness, frightening them?

"Anna." She opened her eyes.

His look was stern, and he began to address her. But, uncharacteristically, he stopped, surprised by something in her expression.

They looked at each other for a long moment, calculating. She seemed to be waiting for him to speak. When he did, his inflection was low and deliberate.

"Coates is just beyond this door. Why do you worry him so with your stillness? Have you no voice to call out?"

She waited. He regarded her silence with irritation.

"You must tell me who did this to you so that we can bring him to justice. The assault on the good people of this city must stop."

She used her sound wrist and one knee to work her way into more of an upright position. He watched her struggle, caught up in his own need for control.

She sighed. "Do sit, Gates. You are not a teacher, and I am not a reckless schoolgirl."

He raised a brow at her impertinence. "Schoolgirl, certainly not." He considered her again, then placed his hand on the mattress and sat, rigid with displeasure. When her continued silence proved unnerving, he resumed questioning.

"Do you have pain?"

"A little." She regarded him steadily but did not elaborate. He worked to remain cool. "Well then. As soon as you are able, the police will take your statement."

She seemed to be choosing her next words with care, attempting an even tone. "I have nothing to report."

"You did not see your attacker?"

"I do not wish to make a report."

His brow shot up, emphasizing the mockery of the situation in his slow, even words. "You wish this man to remain free so that he may attack others?"

She looked toward the window, her smooth features revealing nothing to him. His patience was thinning.

"Anna."

She dragged her gaze back to him.

"You had a family to visit near Market Street? Someone in need?" Again, her silence indicated nothing. "Your mission was . . . unknown. To *anyone*."

That, in itself, was curious in their system of checks and balances. Their household did not tolerate secrecy or any type of clandestine activity that could lead to distrust within the community.

She met his gaze, and he saw that she would delay this conversation no longer. He watched her draw a breath as deep as her damaged ribs allowed and begin.

"I was leaving. I had to leave."

He studied her, intent on her expression—utter calm, not a hint of emotion.

"Where were you going?"

"I don't know."

"For how long?"

"Long enough."

It took just a moment for the full weight of her implication to land on his heart with a sickening thud.

The color drained from his face. He nearly choked when he voiced what she would not.

"You were leaving . . . me."

She placed her bandaged hand over his. "I am so weary, Gates. Weary of the hurting people at our door and in our home. Weary of caring, constantly caring. The lack of privacy is exhausting. There is not a moment of personal or spiritual rest. The duties of this household and our mission leave no room for individual renewal, and there is guilt for even wanting it."

He took it all in—her words, her poise. His vocation had trained him to recognize that this was not evidence gathered in haste. Her weariness had evolved over time. How much time, he wondered.

"You've never told me this."

"You're never here."

She spoke without malice, and the mere lack of emotion in her statement—that it was presented as cold fact jarred him.

"Your duties in this city, your contributions, are inestimable. And yet . . . it took four men and several frantic hours to find you today." She paused, and the pain in her eyes cut him to his core.

"Where do you live, Gates? Do you draw comfort from your employees and find peace at the newest construction site?" When he gave no immediate response, she pressed him. "Where is your home?"

He felt compelled to present even a little defense. "I am home every night."

"You are. And there is comfort in that. But tell me, what is Maggie's favorite color? When did you last hold Tanetta on your lap?"

He looked away. She knew he could not answer that. But he'd venture that few men in his position could. He stared out the window and directed the conversation back to her state of mind.

"How long have you been so . . . weary?"

He felt her hesitation and wondered if she calculated the time or simply was loathe to tell him.

"This past year, the work, the children . . . I'm terribly busy. But . . ." She leaned toward him. "I could bear it all if I were not so constantly . . . alone."

A year. His wife had contemplated leaving for a year. How many times had she considered flight before today? And what had stopped her? He suddenly found himself wanting to find her attacker, simply to thank him for halting his wife's retreat.

They sat together, her words ringing in the air. For long minutes he looked everywhere but at his wife, struggling with it all, then turned and asked the question to which he prayed she had the answer. For he did not.

"What is the solution?"

Her face fell. He saw that she grasped his uncertainty, that he considered this a problem outside his expertise and, therefore, one of delegation.

She shook her head. "I don't know. It is a problem within, not easily fixed with tasks or committees." She fixed him with a stare of hopelessness. "You must look within."

He withdrew his hand and stood. His mind was numb from his wife's stark revelations. His pride was wounded to find that amidst two years of rebuilding a city strife with chaos, his own family was crumbling. His soul ached with despair.

And so he chose the same path his wife had chosen just hours before. He opened the door and fled.

The doctor stood in the shadows of the dark foyer rubbing the silky petals of the fresh-cut mums between his fingers, waiting. He'd delivered every child in this household, and he was about to deliver a man—and a marriage—from ruin. Even if it cost him a valuable friendship.

He heard Spafford before he saw him. The sound of the man barreling down the stairs was so out of character for one usually so restrained that he froze in place, mesmerized.

Spafford skipped the last stair and nearly ran to the door, his head lowered like a charging bull, his hand lunging for the knob.

"Spafford." The doctor's deep voice had the effect of a slap to the man's body and brain. Coates watched him pivot, blink, and stand at attention, scanning the foyer. When Spafford spied him near the hall table, he attempted every tactic of control available to a man—deep breaths, shoulders back, chin up.

But, the doctor observed, Spafford's face admitted everything his body denied. He approached, step by cautious step.

"She is awake, then."

Spafford inclined his head, maintaining eye contact, swallowing hard.

"Completely alert?"

"Completely."

"Excellent. Excellent."

Spafford inched toward the door. "If you will excuse me—" The doctor interrupted with a gesture toward the closed study. "Might I have a word?"

Coates watched Spafford eye the distance between the two doors, the heavy oak of the entrance urging him to go, propriety compelling him to oblige his guest.

The doctor smiled and stepped closer. "Shall we?" And propriety as always, won out.

Spafford grimaced and led the way into his private domain. He stopped in the middle of the room and looked about, then sprang into action, pulling back heavy draperies, opening every window to the crisp autumn breezes.

The doctor closed the door and watched Spafford air the room at a frantic pace. He stood for a moment, then without invitation, folded his elegant frame into a club chair, the rich leather creaking with satisfaction. He spoke immediately.

"I have yet to meet a woman as determined as Anna." Uttering her name aloud had the effect he'd hoped for, as Spafford came to a standstill. "I have every belief that she'll simply will her injuries to heal, and they'll rush to accommodate her."

Spafford stood with his back to the west window, the afternoon sun framing him in silhouette, hiding his expression.

"However," the doctor continued, "I have noticed an ... agitation in her these past months. It is nearly imperceptible in a character such as hers—nothing like women given to theatrics or histrionics. I'm afraid she's taken the hurting people of this city to heart, locked their pain away, and finds in it all a hopelessness."

Spafford bristled. "She's told you as much?"

"I am her doctor. And her friend."

Spafford nodded and turned toward the window. When he spoke, his voice was filled with an equal measure of question and accusation.

"What happened here today? What made her depart so abruptly?"

"Nothing more than any other day." The doctor watched his friend closely. "She's simply reached her limit."

Spafford moved away from the window and paused at his massive desk, frowning. He pulled out the chair, then pushed it back, moving on to the bookcase.

"She sets her own limits. Not I."

"True," the doctor acknowledged. "And yet she would model her efforts after yours. And therein lies the problem. Your labors seem to know no limits."

Spafford scanned the neat rows of books, up and across, until he reached out and chose a thin volume of Browning's most recent poetry. He gripped the book and took the offensive.

"I believe the apostle James tells us that faith without works is dead."

The doctor nodded. "Yet I would supply that works, to the detriment of mind and spirit, are futile."

A stunned silence filled the air between the two powerful men. They'd matched wits on the plight of mankind in this very room on many occasions. But never was the subject so personal, so revealing.

Spafford gripped the book of poems and fixed the doctor with his gaze. "What would you have me do?"

The doctor understood this was not a rhetorical question for a spirited debate. For possibly the first time in his life, the man before him—the man who led committees, directed business deals, wielded authority in every situation—knew not what to do.

He gestured to the book in Spafford's hands. "If I may quote from the great poet in the Psalms—'Oh, that I had wings like a dove! for then would I fly away, and be at rest.' "

Spafford shook his head, irritation on his features. "Speak plainly, Coates."

"You must take her away from here."

Spafford's eyes widened, and he laughed derisively. "Impossible. I have obligations to the community, clients, the church. I cannot afford the consequences of time away."

"Can you afford the consequences of remaining here?"

Spafford stood stock-still, staring at the doctor. The scent of autumn wafted through the open windows

185

and filled the quiet room. Afternoon sun danced across the desk, enriching the colors of paper and wood. Across the street a pianist played Schumann's "Traumerei."

The doctor came to his feet. "You must fly away, dear friend." He crossed the room and paused, his hand on the doorknob. "Here you will find no rest."

And he left, closing the door softly, leaving his dearest friend standing in the center of the room, alone. Completely and utterly alone.

CHAPTER 15

Spafford watched the sun come up from the east window of the parlor. He watched the stars fade, the sky lighten, and the brick of his neighbor's house glow like the pumpkins in his mother's garden.

This was the last room he'd wandered into during the night, and where he'd stayed to watch the day break. He needed to see the sun pass the horizon because he was a man who believed in symbolism— the budding tree, the empty cross, the dawn of a new day.

He looked down at the open notebook in his lap and slowly turned the. pages. Lists. Lists of activities, people, and readings to help his wife. Lists of Scriptures and poetry, words of wisdom and encouragement from respected thinkers.

And then, paragraphs. Written questions and answers about his work first. Then his faith. Then his marriage. And as he'd recorded each of these thoughts, he'd come to a conclusion that rocked him to his core: He had become his father.

There, on crisp paper, written in ink, were lines and lines about the responsibilities of his profession—challenging cases and business deals, the politics of rebuilding a fire-ravaged city. The paragraphs about his faith were just as detailed with Bible verses and ancient creeds. The text showed a confident and persuasive man.

He turned the page to the moment of epiphany. One sheet, a list of names: Anna, Annie, Maggie, Bessie, Tanetta. And beside the names, birth dates, ages, and inches of white space. How long had he sat with pen poised over paper searching for some prescient detail? What made Annie laugh? What *was* Maggie's favorite color? There was a limited choice of hues for a child of nine. Which of his four children were musically inclined? Did Anna still play the piano? And how could a wife love a husband who could not list even one of her childhood dreams?

Like his father, he had a worthy profession and a picture-perfect family. He was a good provider. And just like that great respected man, he had become disconnected from his family's lives. And they had let him.

He closed the book and stood. The house was waking; people were stirring. It was a new day, and he had a life to change. His own.

The sounds of morning drifted into her dreams, and the familiar dread started to spread through her body. Another day—the same day, over and over again. Her head pounded. *I must get up,* she thought and breathed deeply to sigh but stopped short at the pain in her ribs.

And then she remembered.

Her skin flushed at the knowledge of the trouble she'd caused. Yet she was relieved, in a way, that she'd finally done it, that she'd found the courage to walk away from it all, even for an afternoon.

Anna stretched her hand across the sheet, turned her head on the pillow, and saw that Gates had not slept here last night. And felt . . . nothing. There was a time, months ago, when she'd wake and find him gone and long for the days when they'd lain there in the still of the morning, holding hands, praying for their children, for each other.

But that emotion, like all the others, had passed, and she'd come to accept that the grander purpose of their lives overruled her own silent wishes and dreams.

The door opened. She kept her face turned away and hoped Dottie would simply leave the tea on the stand and not inquire about her mistress' well-being and patter on about the household and the children.

She tensed, listening. There was no rattling of tea things, and no one approached her bed. Instead, she heard water flowing into the basin and the unmistakable sounds of washing up.

Gates? Why was he here at this hour? Her head ached even more, and she felt nauseous. She willed him to go away.

She listened as he carefully laid out his shaving utensils, following his movements in her mind. He wiped the wet towel over his face, softening the whiskers. He stirred the compound, swished the brush four times, and applied the cream to his face. He picked up the razor, carefully examined the sharp edge for nicks, and began.

She used to love to watch him in this wholly masculine routine. She'd sit by the vanity and lift her chin when he did, puff out her cheeks, purse her lips. She loved to run her fingertips over his suddenly smooth face. But now the sound of the blade scraping over his skin made her want to scream.

And the shaving seemed to go on and on. She turned her head on the pillow and met his eyes in the mirror. He smiled. She fought the urge to sigh.

"Good morning, Anna. Did you sleep well?"

She did not want to do this—have this polite morning conversation that seemed so fascinating when they'd first married. Her wrist started to throb from the tension, and she had no gracious response, so she remained silent.

He turned to her, wiping a towel over his smooth face. "I've spoken to Cook and Dottie, and I've sent messages to your volunteer posts. I will speak to the children after breakfast." He sat on the edge of the bed. "You may rest as long as you need."

She supposed she should be grateful for his thoughtfulness. She should smile and say, "Thank you." But she struggled to rouse any emotion toward him whatsoever.

He looked at her for a long moment, and she saw the tired lines around his mouth and the puffiness under his eyes. He had not slept.

He stood and moved to the armoire, selecting a fresh shirt. He shrugged into it and fastened each button, as if doing it for the first time. He tucked it in, adjusted the sleeves, and moved toward the door. He stopped there, and when he finally turned to her, she could see that he struggled with something deeper than the issue of her well-being.

"Anna . . ." He fought to keep a smile on his face, and lost. "Things can change. I can change." He did smile then and left.

She stared at the closed door. That might have meant something to her a year ago. She might have latched on to that bold statement, and the hope in it might have sustained her for another week, or month, or year.

She was thirty-one years old and trapped in the mechanics of her own life. She would get out of bed. But not yet. Not yet.

Spafford stood in the doorway, arms crossed, watching his eldest child fuss with her sister's hair. She attached a wig of some strange material tied with blue and yellow rags. She soothed and plaited, tugged and whispered, and with a delicate tweak of the ear, finally declared—in French, no less—the masterpiece *fini.*

And it was a masterpiece. Her small hands had managed to take a wild mop of fabric and transform it into a curly crown, showcasing her sister's natural spirit. He felt an urge to applaud her efforts, to shout, "Well done, Annie!" But that would appear silly in these sober times. So he lingered at her door, watching, waiting for them to notice him.

Moments later Annie twirled into the middle of the room like a *danseuse,* her proud chin thrust forward, her eyes scanning the crowd. She spied him and came to an abrupt stop, her skirt twisting and settling around her. "Papa," she said, and gave him a half smile and a little curtsy that produced an odd feeling in his chest.

Bessie had the surprised look of a thief caught pocketing jewels and without a word scampered through the doorway connecting this room to hers, curls bouncing in delight.

He looked after her, amused, then settled his smile on Annie. "May I?" He gestured toward the vanity bench so hastily vacated. She nodded and he stepped carefully into her domain.

It was a lovely and feminine room, lavender walls awash in midmorning sunshine, white linens glowing in contrast. Every item was artfully arranged to draw attention, yet appeared to be part of an entire scene. It struck him that this was one of the loveliest rooms in his house, and he couldn't remember the last time he'd seen it in daylight.

He settled his tall frame on her delicate bench and regarded his eldest. She returned his gaze directly and quite seriously with a look that said Papa in her room at this hour could only spell trouble. And she was ready for it.

He smiled again and began. "Your mother is ill." She nodded, hands folded primly in front of her. He marveled at her composure. She didn't look alarmed, merely curious.

"She will be abed for several days, perhaps a week" He leaned forward and rested his arms on his knees. "I would like to try an experiment. I would like for you to manage some of your mother's duties while she recovers." He took a breath before listing the duties and was interrupted by her quiet voice.

"I know what to do."

"Do you?" He raised a brow.

"Yes. I know the things to do when Mama goes to bed."

He was puzzled by her choice of words and must have looked it because she continued.

"When Mama shuts the drapes and pulls the covers up to her chin, and we must be very, very quiet, I know what to do."

His entire body went absolutely still. As her meaning washed over him and the words echoed it his brain, he searched for something comforting to say to this child. But it was *he* who needed comfort.

"You have . . . helped your mother in this way . . . many times?" She nodded, and he was breathless. "Just . . . lately?"

Her face screwed up as she thought hard on that question, then shook her head. "I get to be Mama twice a week now. Before summer I was Mama just . . . sometimes." She rushed to assure him. "Dottie says I am very good."

He regarded this child who was so much like her namesake and wanted to weep for her role in this crisis. "Yes, I am certain you are"

She smiled slightly at his praise and raised her chin. "Now, if you will excuse me, Papa, I must check on the children." He nodded and watched her glide away—a child checking on her children.

The door closed and he hung his head in the lavender room. So many thoughts, none of them good, raced through his mind. But there was one lurid thought above all the others: He had not loved his wife. Not really. He had not listened, had not cared, had not recognized her melancholy for what it truly was.

But Coates knew. Dottie, the staff—they had made a game of it to shield his children from the truth. And now he had the same information and longed for the former bliss of his own ignorance.

Or did he?

Was it not better to know the whole ugly truth at once? To hear the doctor's worst prognosis? To see the accountant's bottom line?

Yes.

He was a man of action. He solved problems. His wife was unhappy—no, it was more than that. She despaired.

So he would find a way to ease open the drapes and draw back the covers. Because if he did not, if winter came and the trees were bare and his marriage was as cold and dead as the sod, he feared he would never believe in anything ever again.

CHAPTER 16

It was guilt that finally drove Anna from her bed. Guilt that someone else—Nicolet, and probably Dottie—was caring for her children. Guilt that her convalescence had driven Gates from their room.

He'd come and gone for several days, selecting clothing, always smiling and polite, always closing the door with a gentle click. But he hadn't slept here. She was a little surprised that she cared about that fact, cared in a way that was *wifely.* For even when they'd shared barely a word or thought for days at a time, they'd always shared the intimacy of a bed.

It had amazed her at first how two heads on a pillow, arms and legs entangled, breaths deep and rhythmic, could ease away any misunderstandings and tensions of the day. Without any real discussion, they'd taken St. Paul's decree to heart and had never let the sun go down on their wrath. Then again, wrath was uncommon between them. She struggled to recall the last time they'd argued over anything, anything at all. No, the sun would set and rise, and she was more apt to lie awake next to disappointment and disillusion, never confessing it, never troubling her bedmate with the ache in her soul.

He'd left their bed so as not to disturb her injuries, he would say. He'd left to give her time to heal. But she knew the underlying reason and was surprised that it troubled her.

And now she stood with her hand on the knob, unable to make herself turn it. Guilt had gotten her up, but futility kept her within the room. She no longer felt the urge to run, yet she found no peace in remaining.

Enough.

She took a breath as deep as her bound ribs allowed and opened the door.

Spafford tried not to grimace as an unladylike squeal pierced the air, followed by a chorus of giggles. It had seemed like a wonderful idea, inspiring even, to have tea with his little ladies. But how quickly he'd lost control.

Just now, two-year-old Tanetta, powdered and dressed like a china doll, had climbed onto his lap and begun, quite solemnly, to feed him cake. Her lack of coordination resulted in more frosting on his cheeks than in his mouth, much to the delight of her sisters.

He wiggled his eyebrows up and down and marveled again at the restorative power of children's laughter. How his soul had needed this moment.

Tanetta reached across him for another sweet and nearly lurched out of his arms.

"Mama!" she squealed and clapped her enthusiasm, bits of caking flying.

Spafford looked up and spied his wife on the stair, captivating in an afternoon gown of caramel and ivory, the sleeves full and covering her bound wrist. He watched her smile and noted that it never quite reached her eyes and felt a pang of guilt that he was responsible for a good measure of that.

He saw her take in the scene, never meeting his gaze, never leaving the stair, and understood her reluctance. She may have rejoined the household, but she was not yet prepared to interact full-scale. He took command of the situation.

"Ladies, I have thoroughly enjoyed your company this afternoon." They all beamed at him, the laughter still in their eyes.

"Perhaps you could greet your mother, then hurry up to your rooms for a game of—what did you call it, Maggie?"

"The 14-15, Papa." She sighed dramatically at his forgetfulness, then leaned in to whisper, "If we solve the puzzle, we could win a *thousand* dollars!"

He was fighting the urge to smile at his wonderfully theatric daughter when Dottie appeared out of nowhere. He never ceased to marvel that his house-keeper seemed to know just when and where she was needed before he ever opened his mouth to call out.

She moved from child to child, washing hands, straightening dresses, all the while offering advice on proper behavior. Within moments all four of the girls stood at the foot of the stairs, eldest to youngest, silent, awaiting their mother's signal.

Anna held out her right hand, and Annie stepped up, gently grasping her mother's fingers, smiling all the way to her dimples, proffering wishes for good health and recovery. Anna nodded and murmured her appreciation for such a responsible daughter. Maggie was next, restrained only by force of will, kissing her mother's hand and speaking *sotto voce* of certain information she would pass along at another time. Anna nodded a conspirator's nod. Bessie stepped forward, hesitant, at a loss for words. Anna dropped to her level, whispering little nothings while Bessie bobbed her head in agreement. A quick kiss and she was on her way.

Dottie then placed Tanetta on Anna's lap, and Spafford's heart contracted as he watched mother and child meld together. Anna laid her cheek against the downy head pressed onto her shoulder, closed her eyes, and rocked a little as her youngest smiled dreamily, content in the bosom of life and love. They stayed that way for long, tender minutes until by silent mutual agreement, they parted with a kiss.

And then, within a thrice, he and Anna found themselves alone, she on the stair, he in the parlor, neither of them moving or speaking, both of them lost in the moment.

He finally stood, cleared the crumbs from his clothing, and walked to the foot of the stairs. He held out his hand, and she looked up, uncertainty written on every feature. He gave her what he hoped was an encouraging smile.

"Shall we go for a walk?" Her expression did not change, but she continued to hold his gaze. He tried again.

" 'Twould be a shame to miss Chicago in the fall." And he meant it. But the greater shame would be allowing their relationship to disintegrate even further by failing to face the truth. He waited, palm up, steady, determined to begin the restoration, determined to reconnect with his wife. Today.

She hesitated, then placed her hand in his, and he helped her down the stairs. He held out her cloak, and she stepped into it, tying it awkwardly, the same uncertain look on her face.

He opened the door and they stepped into the afternoon glow of the harvest season. And he found his heart crying out, even as Ruth once cried to Naomi—*intreat me not to leave thee . . . intreat me not to leave thee . . .*

Anna let her husband lead her down the wide front steps, through the iron gate, and onto the macadam street. He'd tucked her reluctant fingers into the crook of his left arm and trapped them there, covering them with his free right hand. And they strolled along the street, looking every bit the comfortable couple out for an afternoon constitutional.

She was thinking about how the children had looked—clean and untroubled and well loved. She was recalling how Gates had seemed to enjoy amusing the girls and Dottie had effortlessly directed a quick and proper greeting. She was reviewing all that and wondering at the ease with which the household had seemed to march on without her.

But what had she been expecting? Chaos in her absence? Or hysteria upon her return?

She did not view herself as particularly dramatic, although her abrupt departure and street encounter appeared otherwise. She was not one to wish turmoil on others because they failed her . . . was she? She was resourceful, reliable, stable. Wasn't she?

She mentally shook her head. She had trouble concluding anything concrete about herself and her purpose anymore. Except this: She could not—would not—assume the same role, the same life she'd left. So where did that leave her?

She walked the exact path she'd taken days ago, in a similar frame of mind, blind to the brilliant colors and dusky smells of autumn. Everything about her moved on reflex until Gates' voice startled her out of her introspection.

"How was your day?"

"My . . . day?"

"Your activities."

"I have no activities. I am resting." And her voice sounded dead, even to her own ears.

They walked on in silence until she felt him regard her. "You are looking much improved."

"Thank you."

The familiar knot started to form in her stomach. It was the same awkward dance they'd danced when courting, except the burning curiosity and passion were gone. Those fervent emotions were replaced with apathy and barely controlled tolerance. And yet this was what she'd wanted most from her husband—his time, his attention, his . . . affection. And now that she had it, she only wanted to escape from it.

He drew her closer, and the bile rose in her throat. "Remember the picnic, when I first held your hand?"

Her ears started to ring. Her skin grew clammy. She was suffocating from his nearness and looked about in a panic. She watched a pile of restless leaves shuffle across the crushed stones, and she broke free to chase after an offering of brilliant yellow maple.

Bending and plucking it from the ground made her breathless with pain, but she kept walking, determined to stay clear of her husband. She rubbed the waxy leaf between her fingers, planning her next move should he come too close, vaguely aware that her behavior was ridiculous, bordering on manic.

She came to the end of their street and halted, every nerve screaming, contemplating a path left or right. But Gates' voice stopped her, and he moved to block her flight.

"Anna." His voice was husky with emotion. She stared at his boots, unable to meet his gaze.

"You may hate me. You may despise me. You may hurl things at me." And his voice took on a slight tremor. "But do not treat me with indifference. That, I cannot abide."

She followed the movement of an oak leaf as it tumbled into the ditch, wondering how they'd arrived at having such an intimate conversation on a public street in Lake View. Wondering if there was any hope for two people so far removed from each other. Wondering, wondering . . .

"You must forgive me, Anna. Even if the Lord had not commanded it, you must."

He was right, of course. She'd spoken those very words to her children on countless occasions. What she'd never considered until this very moment, though, was that she'd demanded of them an impossibility. When one is truly, deeply, hurt, one could not be commanded to forgive and simply do it. It was infinitely more complicated than that. One needed to learn to trust again. One needed . . .

"Time." She spoke without meaning to, and the forcefulness of her voice shocked them both. She turned to face him and spoke with as much sensitivity as she could muster. "I need . . . time."

She searched his face, knowing what he wanted to ask: How much time? He wanted a goal to work toward—a day and an hour. He wanted an end to this unpleasant interval in their marriage. But he surprised her, smiled a little, and nodded. No demands. No expectations. Intriguing.

He gestured to the left, and they took a turn toward the setting sun. She noticed that although he remained close to her side, he made no move to touch her. She knew that flew against his code of chivalry and appreciated his sacrifice for her needs all the more.

They walked on in silence, and she felt as if they'd come to a quiet shaking of hands. He had agreed to allow her a measure of time and distance, while she had agreed to let him try to repair the damage done from a year's neglect. It would be taxing, frustrating. But perhaps—she could not quite dare to hope it— perhaps they could salvage the friendship they had begun so many years ago. She could not promise more.

Gates matched his pace to hers, accommodating in every way. She marveled at his ability to keep his demands in check. She knew her husband. When he wanted results, he got them, on his own terms, in very short order. She stole a glance at him and noted how his brow furrowed, how he gnawed on his lower lip— little-known signs of her husband's deep struggle within.

She gambled and opened herself up just a little, hoping she would not regret it. "What is it?"

He looked across the way, hands behind his back as they strolled. He opened and closed his mouth several times before he asked, "Will you tell me what happened on Market Street?"

She hesitated, determined not to lie about the experience but reticent to put the girl in more danger. She looked straight ahead and gave the only answer she could.

"Someday . . . someday."

A week passed and every time Anna had reached for her mother's watch, she'd thought about the girl. She'd been filthy and dressed as a boy, but there was something familiar about her. And then it had struck her late one night—that hair. She doubted any amount of filth could cover the striking platinum blond thickness poking out from under the wool cap.

She remembered sitting in a parlor several years ago, listening to a child prodigy play through Liszt's preludes, marveling at the melancholic interpretation of one so young but absolutely spellbound by the way the pianist's head glowed in the lamplight. She'd never seen hair so blond it was white, so full it looked impossible to brush, so alive that she wanted to touch it.

She could not register whose home she'd visited, or even whose child had played. But she could never forget that hair.

And then, while sitting at the piano yesterday, thinking of the watch and the haunted look in the girl's eyes, she suddenly had a name: Elizabeth Duncan, the unhappy wife of a prominent banker.

She saw it all in a flash—the parlor, the piano, the street where the house once stood.

The revelation about her attacker's identity was followed with worry. Such a talented and cared-for child could be on the streets for only one reason: The Fire. An idea formed, and she felt the first exciting tremors of a worthy mission. But only one person could be trusted with this information, and she knew what she must do.

Coates arrived midmorning and found his patient resting in her bedroom. While Anna remained in her dressing gown and propped up in bed, he noted that the windows were open and uncovered, that light and fresh air filled the room. He made no comment but was thrilled at the subtle change.

She smiled as he filled the doorway and invited him in with a slight gesture. "Good morning, dear Coates."

He returned the smile and the greeting they'd exchanged for more than a decade. "Good morning, dear friend." He settled himself into the bedside chair, his doctor's bag at his feet, and waited, as he always did for the patient to share her request or grievance in her own time, her own way.

A moment of silence passed in the comfort of old friends until she reached for a slim volume on her bedside table. He let her stretch for the book, gauging how much pain it cost her, watching for a grimace, a wince. There was nothing but ease in her movement, and he knew that implied her ribs were healing nicely.

She opened the book to where a blue satin ribbon marked the page and, never glancing at the text, quoted: " 'Oh, the comfort, the inexpressible comfort of feeling safe with a person; having neither to weigh thoughts nor measure words, but to pour them all out, just as they are, chaff and grain together, knowing that a faithful hand will take and sift them, keep what is worth keeping, and then, with a breath of kindness, blow the rest away.' "

He nodded at her. "The timeless words of George Eliot."

"Yes."

She removed the ribbon and closed the book. "I understand you have begun to replenish your library."

"That is so"

She offered the book to him. "It would give me great pleasure if you would take this book, this marvelous outpouring of thought and spirit, and know that I value our friendship for the very reasons Eliot names."

He accepted the book, running his fingers along the spine, glad that his patient, his friend, was returning to them—changed, no doubt. Changed and, perhaps, stronger.

"Thank you, Anna." He laid the treasured book in his lap and regarded her with a physician's eye. "Now tell me about your activities."

She sighed. "Dottie brings me breakfast, Annie shows me never-ending lists of activities before she leaves for school, and I am relegated to my room until midmorning."

He knew she was frustrated, but he was happy for

the decline in her overrun schedule.

"I engage in light activities with the household and my hot-house until tea, when Nicolet brings the girls to join me. They are so well behaved, I am convinced someone—" she shot him an inquisitive look— "*someone* has threatened or bribed them into submission."

He gave a shrug and a look that said, "Not I."

"At five o'clock Gates returns home, and we take a lengthy promenade through Lake View."

He was so surprised at this his jaw went slack. Horatio Gates Spafford? Home at five o'clock? He didn't think it possible.

"The evening is filled with children's games, dinner, and spirited conversations with the boarders. I am afraid I now have Annie's bedtime, but I hope to extend it soon."

The recitation over, she relaxed against the pillows and awaited his clinical response.

"Well," he began, still astonished by the news of Gates' much-shortened workday. "Your schedule explains the healthy glow, and the daily walks are an excellent idea. Yours?" She shook her head no, and his surprise developed into a stirring of hope for this marriage. For he knew real healing could only come from Gates' willingness to make dramatic changes in their lives.

He thought it might be wise, at this point, to leave the status of her marriage undiscussed, to have her sort it out for herself while he focused on her physical recovery. And so he let the moment pass and touched her bandaged wrist. "May I?"

She nodded and placed her wrist in his outstretched hand. He was less ginger in his handling, watching for signs of pain or stress. Those he did not notice, but as she looked away, he saw her brow knit and her mouth turn down. Clearly she struggled with the real issue that brought him to her side today. He removed the bandage's clasp and began to unwind the dressing. She took a deep breath, let it out, then began.

"On Market Street, near where I was found, there is a child—a girl, nearly a woman."

She paused, and he continued to unbind her wrist, appearing mildly interested, though he knew this was the first time she'd spoken of the events on Market Street.

"She is disguised as a young boy . . . a ragamuffin. She is very strong and can wield a tree branch like a club. See if you can coax her off the street and into your clinic."

He cradled the bruised wrist in the palm of his hand, examining it closely, bending and testing it.

"And how will I know her?"

"She has the most striking hair—white, white blond, now chopped as a boy's and dirty. But there is no disguising it. You will notice it immediately."

He lowered the wrist to the bed and looked into his dear friend's eyes. He would never understand this woman's capacity to give and forgive. How different the world would be if hearts were as gentle as hers.

He stood and placed the wrapping into his bag. "And how will I do this? How will I coax a young girl dressed as a boy to follow me downtown to a clinic?"

"Tell her . . ." She looked at him, her friend and confidante, and he saw the seriousness of her mission. "Tell her you knew her mother"

CHAPTER 17

Anna walked beside her husband, reflecting, wondering. Just before tea today she'd reached inside her apron pocket and felt the edge of fine linen paper. And without looking, she knew what it was, and a shiver of anticipation went through her.

In the early years of their marriage, she would often awaken to find resting on the pillow, or folded on the tea tray, or tucked between two pots in her hothouse, a note from her beloved. Most times the notes were short reflections of her, of nature's comparable beauty, of God's enduring grace. Some were as brief as two lines. Some were poems of one or two stanzas, and these were her favorite.

Today she'd slipped off to her hothouse and slowly drawn the linen paper from her apron, her pulse racing. She'd read and reread the lines, her heart full of their unadorned meaning. She recited them in her head even now.

Dusk

When the day comes to a close
Suddenly there is time to ponder
What fills my day?
What haunts my way?
I know it is you . . .
It is you I lost
Before the day came to a close

And suddenly there is time to wonder
You fill my day
You haunt my way
I know it was you . . .
It was you I lost
Before the day came to a close.

Gates was working his way back to her. That was what the poem spoke to her heart. But it brought her a second message—that she would have to work her way back to him.

She was no poet, but she knew what inspired her husband. So she slipped her hand through his arm, returned his sudden smile, and began.

"I would like to tell you a story."

He raised a curious brow, and she told him about Coates' mission to find the girl—the orphaned daughter of the banker, Ira Duncan, who had perished with his wife and family in the Fire. She spoke of her

interest in bringing the child into their home—perhaps adopting her, if he was agreeable and the legali-
ties could be unraveled. She watched him closely as
she spoke, searching his face for displeasure, feeling
his arm for tension.

But he simply listened to her story, then asked questions about the Duncans. What did she remember of
the parents? She spoke honestly of her impressions,
for that was all she had from such a brief encounter.
Where had the child lived these two years? She did
not know, had only just learned the girl was living on
the street. How would their own children react to this
idea? She thought they would be intrigued, as she
was.

They talked as they had in years past, exploring the
positives and negatives of such a change in their
household. And when they had exhausted the topic
and come to a conclusion to welcome the child, Gates
surprised her with a story of his own.

Moody had written. His letter had been full of the
evangelist's activities—the towns visited, the souls
saved. Emma had sent her love, and Anna's heart
contracted with longing for her dear friend. Moody
had closed with a sincere invitation to the Spaffords
to join the crusade, for as little or as long as they
desired. Anna came to a dead stop in the street.

"Are you considering his invitation?" She knew her
voice came out breathless, and she wasn't certain if
she was thrilled or dismayed with the notion of overseas travel.

Gates smiled. "I am. But only if you are agreeable to it." He looked deep into her eyes. "Perhaps it is time to get away from Chicago. Perhaps it is time to rest."

She was flabbergasted. Gates? Resting? She knew few men as driven as her husband. She could not imagine him leaving his business, his projects, his responsibilities—even to join Moody.

Gates gently drew her back along the path, his hand over hers in the crook of his arm. He spoke of the benefits of the invitation—the chance to tour Europe, the pleasure of seeing their dear friends, the possibility of visiting her childhood town. As he talked, Anna's excitement grew.

And they walked the streets of Lake View, working their way toward each other as the dusk of the poem settled, and the day came to a close.

It had been one of the greatest challenges of his career, but he had found her.

Coates sat in the Spaffords' parlor, watching the young girl move about the room, marveling at the transformation a hot bath and clean clothes could work. When she had emerged from behind the fence two days ago, he'd glanced at her, then looked a little closer, then watched her pass the bench in front of the shop on Market Street. He'd waited only an hour before she'd returned, hurrying along in her baggy and ragged clothes. She'd carried a stout stick and clutched a paper bag to her chest.

He'd been coming to the bench for three days and staying for several hours—first in the early morning, then at lunchtime when the traffic was much heavier, then at dusk. He'd had a thought that a girl who was willing to go to such lengths to disguise herself might prefer to move about under the cover of darkness. He'd been right.

He'd gone to the clinic that night, pondering the best way to retrieve a child from the streets, praying for guidance, wishing for Moody, when the Lord had performed a miracle. Just before eight o'clock he'd heard a tapping at the back door and opened it to find the girl. She'd stood in the wash of the gaslight, stooped over with pain, panting and shaking. He'd led her inside and diagnosed botulism—food poisoning—probably from the contents of the paper bag. He'd given her a concoction of mustard, salt, ginger, and pepper in hot water to induce vomiting, plied her with cup after cup of strong green tea to kill the lingering bacteria, then drawn her a hot bath. She'd soaked for an hour and emerged wrapped in a blanket, all pink and sleepy, and he'd tucked her into a cot in one of the exam rooms and closed the door.

He'd slept in a chair outside her room that night, sure that if he retired to his own rooms, he would wake to find her gone and fail his mission. He'd found her some clothes from the clinic's donation box, and she'd appeared in them late this morning, hungry, wary, and curious. She'd watched him as he'd steeped more green tea and cut thick slices of bread. They'd spoken very little—More tea? Yes, thank you. Jam for your bread? Please.

And all the while, he'd been transfixed by the child's hair. It was hacked off at different lengths above her shoulders but was glorious nonetheless. Not even Anna's description could do it justice. White gold and thick, it flowed straight from her scalp like an icy waterfall. She'd caught him studying her and looked down, frowning. He'd realized he'd have to work quickly or risk losing his opportunity.

As it was a Sunday, the clinic was closed, and Coates could devote his full attention to his mission. He'd recommended a drive past Lincoln Park, telling her that the fresh autumn air would only improve her condition. She'd taken her time before agreeing, weighing her temporary comfort, he knew, against the motivations of a strange man—kindly doctor or no. She'd finally nodded her agreement and spoken one word: "Lizzie." He'd smiled, bowed, and formally completed the introduction.

They'd clip-clopped along the edge of the park, taking in the glorious reds and oranges of a spectacular fall, the burlap bag of Lizzie's sole possessions tucked behind her legs. When he'd continued north into Lake View, she'd shown no alarm. And when he'd stopped in front of the Spaffords' home and told her he had a patient within, she'd let him help her down from the carriage and lead her inside.

Now he watched Lizzie run the tips of her fingers over the rosewood surface of the seven-foot square grand, and he could see, even from his perch on the corner settee, the pain and longing on the girl's features. Back and forth went her fingers, up and down the hidden keyboard until they rested in perfect symmetry on the closed lid.

A flash of yellow drew his gaze to the hall doorway. Anna stood just inside the room, watching the child. He followed her gaze and saw what she saw—a sad girl caught up in a reverie, unaware yet of her determined hostess with the steady gaze and the tender smile. So deep was the child's concentration that she raised her head to Anna's voice like a drunkard.

"Will you play for us?"

Lizzie jerked her hands away and hurried to the other side, putting the piano between them, her back pressed against the muted gold wallpaper. Her eyes darted around the room, resting accusingly on the doctor. "What is this?" her voice hissed, and her eyes narrowed.

Coates dared not speak, so tenuous was this moment. He watched, fascinated, as Anna inched toward the piano and very gently folded back the lid and raised it until the hinges caught. She rested her hand on the instrument's rounded corner and smiled at the girl.

Lizzie stared down at the ivory keys, then back up at Anna. "What do you want?"

Anna continued to smile and gestured toward the instrument. "I wonder if you might play for us."

"I do not play."

"That is a pity. You were so gifted."

Lizzie's eyes widened, and Coates knew she caught the light reference to her past. She opened her mouth to speak, but closed it tight. As Anna continued to smile at her, she looked around the parlor—at the elegant chairs and Boston ferns and enormous fringed rug. Coates thought it was a practiced look, as if she were assessing the quality and value of its contents.

"Elizabeth . . ."

Lizzie's head snapped back to Anna, and she cut off her hostess before she could continue. "Who are you?"

"I am Mrs. Spafford."

"How do you know my name?"

"I came to a party at your parents' home on Ontario Street . . . years ago. You played an enchanting piece on a piano much like this one."

Lizzie stared at her, unblinking. "You knew . . . my mother?"

Anna shook her head. "I did not know your mother." Lizzie looked away, and she continued. "But I remember a little bit about her."

She edged around the piano until she was within an arm's reach of the girl. "She was quite petite and proper. And she loved to give parties." Lizzie was nodding her head almost imperceptibly. "And she gave her only daughter her name—Elizabeth."

Coates watched Lizzie, thinking he'd never seen such bravura on a girl so young. He wondered if the street life had developed it or if the bravura had led her to the street. He watched her shrug and school her features into a smooth blankness.

"My mother is dead." The cold declaration hung in the air, out of place in such a warm and cozy room. She looked toward the hassock placed invitingly before the fireplace and jutted out her chin. "I do not have what you are looking for."

These words, so softly and forcefully spoken, puzzled Coates. But Anna showed no surprise. She simply reached out a hand and brushed Lizzie's arm, making no reaction when the girl jerked away.

"My dear, I was only looking for you."

Lizzie sat between the doctor and the eldest daughter—Annie, was it? She passed the rolls, still hot and buttery from the oven, left to right, just as her mother had taught her. When every savory dish came her way, she inhaled its warm fragrance, assailed by memories of suppers long ago. She was famished and leery of worsening her condition at the same time, glancing at the doctor for approval. He nodded or shook his head no, always smiling, never drawing undue attention. No one berated her manners or told her she must try a little bit of everything. No one plagued her with questions.

It was maddening.

She was dining at the table of a woman she had brutally attacked and left for dead just a fortnight ago. She kept expecting a knock at the door and the police admitted to arrest her. The past twenty-four hours seemed like an elaborate ruse—the doctor had probably placed the spoiled food where he knew she would find it, then waited for her to come to his clinic so he could bring her here where she could be confronted and . . .

She spread some strawberry jam on a roll and tried to still her shaking hands. She needed to behave normally, but she could hardly remember what normal was.

The girl—Annie—said something to her, and she looked up for a moment, startled. The butter dish was hovering before her, and she passed it to the girl. That was all Annie had wanted from her. Butter. Why were they all treating her so nicely? Why did no one ask her about the watch? She nearly jumped when the man—Mr. Spafford—stood and suggested they retire to the parlor for dessert.

She filed into the adjoining room with the rest of them, suddenly self-conscious in her too-small dress and chopped hair. She'd been completely surprised to see that all the girls had short hair—and they weren't trying to pass themselves off as boys. She sat on the hassock, her hands folded in her lap, her feet crossed at the ankles, her mind whirling with confusion.

The Spaffords had stayed home from church this evening and someone suggested they sing some hymns. Lizzie watched as Mrs. Spafford sat down at the piano and began a song in the key of G. It was a haunting tune, and halfway through, the left hand began to echo the right-hand melody. And then Mrs. Spafford began to sing.

"Softly and tenderly Jesus is calling, calling for you and for me. See, on the portals He's waiting and watching, watching for you and for me."

Lizzie thought the woman's piano skills were fairly good and her voice quite lovely.

"Come home," she sang, and every voice in the room echoed in harmony, "come home . . ." And she sang it again. "Come home, ye who are weary, come home."

Lizzie looked around the room and felt the familiar heaviness descend on her. For two years she had wanted nothing more than to "come home" to a place like this, a place that existed only in her dreams. She sat with her back to the crackling fire and thought that perhaps, just this one evening, she would live in the dream.

And when she woke up tomorrow between the two fences, cold and hungry, she would hand this memory over to Morpheus, where it would remain . . . just like all the rest.

Lizzie stayed with the Spaffords that night and woke in the morning to soft linens and a house smelling of apples. She opened her eyes and took in the glow of the lavender room. She sat up and spied a lovely fawn dress draped over the foot of the bed, along with clean underwear and stockings. And shoes . . . girls' shoes.

She dressed and eased open the door, listening. Voices carried up the stairs, and she descended, step by cautious step, to the grand hallway. She followed the sounds into the kitchen, finding a group of women deep into the process of making applesauce.

She watched as two women plucked the bright orbs from a bucket of water, coring and chopping them in rapid movements. Another woman stood at the massive black stove, stirring a pot filled with bobbing red skins while Anna mashed a steaming mixture of boiled fruit through a cone-shaped sieve. The room was filled with the heady smells of warm apples and cinnamon and the dry fall foliage as it wafted through the open windows.

Anna looked up and smiled at her young guest, making no fuss, simply motioning her over to the large worktable. There, Anna spooned steaming applesauce onto a thick slice of bread, then went to the icebox to retrieve a cup of cool milk. Lizzie consumed both with barely restrained eagerness. After another serving, introductions were made, and Lizzie was recruited into the process, carefully spooning the hot applesauce into sparkling glass jars.

The day passed in industrious, fragrant camaraderie, interrupted only by the girls' return from school. They sampled the newest batch, pronounced it good, and joined Lizzie at the table, filling jars and chatting about their day.

At five o'clock Gates stepped into their domain, tasted the sauce, and begged to borrow his wife for an afternoon stroll. At their departure Annie declared herself "Mama," monitoring each step of the canning process under the amused smiles of the working women. Then she formally extended Lizzie an invitation to spend another night and requested a glance at the supper menu.

Lizzie observed it all in curious silence.

Three days passed with similar scenes of domestic productivity. Lizzie entered the kitchen each morning to find the women engaged in preserving yet another autumn crop—carrots, beets, and pumpkin, all making their way into waiting jars. She blended into the process, following directions, working diligently, nodding each afternoon when Anna would extend the invitation to stay another night. The evenings were spent in comfortable quiet with Miss Carrie as she altered dresses to fit the budding form of a girl not quite a woman. Lizzie watched in the mirror, studying the way loose fabrics became fashionable gowns under Miss Carrie's efficient hands.

Before supper on Friday Anna drew Lizzie into the hallway and asked if she would like to spend every night with them. Lizzie's mouth hung open in astonishment.

"You want me to live here?"

Anna nodded.

"For how long?"

"As long as you wish." She pressed her case as Lizzie frowned and backed away. "You could share a room with Annie and Maggie and go to school with them and—" She broke off as Lizzie began shaking her head violently.

"I will not go to school." The statement was bold and passionate and took them both by surprise. Lizzie looked down at her dress, then toward the large doors leading into the foyer, a blend of fear and sadness on her usually bland face. Anna reached out and grasped Lizzie's cool hand. And for once the girl did not jerk away.

"No decision must be made at this time, my dear. We shall enjoy your company as long as it is given us."

Lizzie nodded and drew away until she reached the stairs, then climbed them with a steady, weary march—like a prisoner to the gallows.

Late that night, long after the household had retired, Anna came awake with a start. She lay there, listening. Drifting up from the first floor and under her bedroom door were the unmistakable tones of the piano.

She slipped from the bed, donned a robe, and crept to the foot of the stairs. Every first-floor room had been closed off from the hallway. But from under the parlor's large double doors floated the sorrowful notes of Beethoven's "Moonlight Sonata."

Anna sat on the stairs, closed her eyes, and listened to the music played with such melancholy by such a young girl. Though the song was hushed, she played with intensity—giving every phrase its own meaning, building crescendos and decrescendos into the piece until the final notes sounded and lingered in the quiet house.

And then there were long minutes of silence.

Anna sat very still on the stair until the parlor door opened and a girl dressed as a boy emerged. She carried a burlap sack over her shoulder and stood in the hallway, looking neither left nor right. Anna waited until she reached for the foyer door, then called out.

"Please don't go."

Lizzie froze in place. Anna stood and moved cautiously along the hallway until she stopped beside the ragamuffin. Lizzie stared down at the floor, her face hidden by the bill of the wool cap. Her voice came out low and flat.

"My uncle . . . is a bad man." She waited, but the only reply was the ticking of the hall's grandfather clock. "If I go to school . . ." She shook her head.

Anna spoke just as softly. "Mr. Spafford is a lawyer, a very good lawyer. He can help you, Lizzie, but not if you run away."

Lizzie looked up then, fear making her eyes wide. "If you can find me, so can my uncle."

Anna smiled a little. "Let us speak to Mr. Spafford on the morrow. Perhaps you find, as I do, that solutions are always clearer in the morning."

Anna waited until Lizzie nodded, then walked her to the stairs and watched her ascend. She waited with her hand on the rail until she heard the soft click of Annie's bedroom door, then turned and considered the door standing ajar to the parlor. She walked toward it, then entered and stood at the piano.

There, placed perfectly in the center of the closed

lid, its surface smooth and delicate, was the emblem that had forced the change in both of their lives several weeks ago, the emblem that represented to them a brighter, more innocent time: her mother's watch.

CHAPTER 18

Spafford found his wife asleep on the parlor's settee early the next morning. He'd awakened alone in their room and knew from the sheets' coolness that she had not spent the night in their bed.

His heart had lurched with panic for a moment, afraid she'd left him again. But then he'd come more fully awake and reason had returned, and he'd set out to find her.

He smiled as he watched her doze. She looked so young and carefree as she slept. She looked like Annie. He loved the way her cheeks flushed and her lips parted and how her spiky eyelashes brushed against her pale skin. He would have to write a poem about that.

He moved to where her head rested on the firm cushion, gently raised it, sat, and settled it onto his lap. She opened her eyes a little, smiled, and reached for his hand. They rested together for a quarter of an hour as the sun rose and began to light the room, and then she began to tell him about Lizzie. But this time she started at the beginning . . . on Market Street.

He listened with surprise and not a little awe that his wife could be so concerned with the welfare of her attacker. He remembered how she'd refused to give a report to the police. He'd thought her merely stubborn then. He thought her courageous now.

Anna finished with last night's encounter and her all-night vigil, and they lapsed into silence, both lost in their own thoughts. They looked up in surprise when a soft knock sounded on the parlor door. Carrie peeked in and Anna sat up, beckoning to her.

Carrie retrieved a chair and perched across from them in her robe, surprisingly unselfconscious, Spafford thought. Clearly something was troubling her.

"Last night," she began, then shook her head. "No, I believe it has been several nights now." She smiled. "Lizzie has been sleeping in my bed. At first I took no notice, because one or more of the girls often visit me at night." Spafford and Anna looked at each other in surprise.

"Lizzie has terrible nightmares. I awoke two nights past to hear her calling for her mama to 'come out.' She was truly panicked, and I managed to console her. Last night, though, she was white-faced and sweaty and telling an uncle to 'get away.' When I tried to wake her, she struck me."

She looked imploringly at the Spaffords. "I think some truly horrible crime has been committed against that child."

Spafford nodded. He'd been considering that very thing, and the thought of it sickened and infuriated him. They sat together in silence until an idea began to form in his mind. He looked at his wife.

"You say she is a musical prodigy?" Anna nodded. "You think her talent might be recognized by a professional? Perhaps in a music conservatory?"

The women exchanged a look, and Carrie spoke. "Perhaps in New York?" He nodded and she smiled brilliantly, clapping her hands. "Oh, that would be wonderful—for both of us!"

They spoke in an excited hush about the possibilities in the short time before they set sail for Europe. Spafford had sworn the women to secrecy about their trip until the details could be worked out. But there was a greater urgency now, and he would be forced to break the news and call in some favors.

He left the women to their planning and crossed over to his office, already setting the day's agenda. He would call on John Farwell and convince him to finance Lizzie's education. He would cable an acquaintance in New York about music schools. He would summon a man from the police force and ask him to investigate the whereabouts of Lizzie's uncle. And then he would make certain that odious predator never worked in this town again.

The impulse to do it was so strong that she snatched her hands away and sat on them. Her fingers—once so limber and delicate—would not perform the intricate arpeggios and scales up and down the keyboard, and Lizzie was overwhelmed by the urge to slam her hands down on the keys, slam them until they obeyed.

A wave of renewed terror washed over her. What if she couldn't recover the skills? What if she failed the audition? There was not enough time. Miss Carrie would be gone in the morning, and the Spaffords would be leaving ten days hence, and . . . The familiar harsh voices reverberated in her head. *You're not good enough. Everybody knows that.* She wanted to clap her hands over her ears to shut them out.

Oh, *why* did Mrs. Spafford have to find her? Why couldn't the woman have just left her on the street where there's no hope, no future, not even a tomorrow? She was going to disappoint everyone. And then they would leave, and her uncle would find her, and—

"You are a delight to Him."

Lizzie looked up, startled, and stared at the little girl standing a few feet away. "What?"

Maggie moved closer. "When I'm mad at myself, or a mean girl like Mary Jo Whitman pulls my hair and makes me cry, I just say out loud what Mr. Moody told me, what God thinks of me. 'You are a delight to Him.' That's what Mr. Moody told me."

Lizzie was silent with disbelief.

"Try it, Lizzie. God said it." She leaned in to whisper, "It's in the Bible." And then she smiled and skipped away.

Lizzie gaped after her. A delight . . . The only time she remembered being a delight to anyone was when her mother would sit her at the piano in a roomful of people and they would stare at her as she played a collection of difficult pieces carefully selected by her parents to impress their guests. And then she would make a mistake—she always made a mistake—and she was sure her parents were sneering, and their pleasure would turn to disgust, and she would never, never look up to confirm it.

But maybe . . . maybe . . . God was different. She brought her hands out in front of her and considered them. Her fingers were long and graceful—much like her mother's had been. She tried to picture God as her audience . . . tried to picture Him there on the settee, nodding and smiling. And then she tried the words, tentatively at first, then with conviction.

"You are a delight to Him."

She sat at the beautiful piano, the afternoon sun making the rosewood glow, placed her hands on the smooth keys, and said it over and over again. And finally, finally she started to believe it.

Tommy refused to believe it. When the word had spread that Mrs. Maxwell was considering a move to New York, he'd simply thought it a ruse to regain his attention. And it had worked.

He'd showered the widow with notes and bouquets of flowers, and they had all been graciously received, then ignored. He'd plied Spafford with questions about her plans, and the man had been forthright, if not effusive. And now, here he was at the Lake View home, welcomed by hardly anyone, pretending to wish her well with the other guests.

He longed for Moody. Moody would intervene on his behalf. Moody would look into his soul with that penetrating gaze and see his sincerity toward the widow. Moody would make his intentions clear when he could not.

He leaned against the parlor doorframe with barely controlled anxiety, scanning the joyous crowd for her face, alarmed when he could not find her. This, he knew, would be his reaction every time, at every party, if she were to leave on that train tomorrow. And he hated that.

Out of the corner of his eye, he spotted the skirt of her dress—corded silk of palest green—as it rustled up the stairs off the grand hallway. He pushed himself away from the doorframe and gave pursuit, dashing to the foot of the stairway and calling out, "Mrs. Maxwell!"

Carrie halted on the stairs, and he saw that he'd startled her by the panic he heard in his own voice. He gazed up at her, wordless, and cursed the complexity of an emotion that could rob hint of clear speech and thought.

"What is it, Mr. Jameson?"

"It . . . it gives me great pain to think of you gone from here."

"So you have communicated. On a number of occasions."

Fool! He berated himself. He must be sincere, yet fervent. He felt sick, so great was his desire to hold on to this woman. Oh, how he wished he had Spafford's gift for quoting the great poets.

She sighed at his silence and continued up the stairs.

"Carrie!" He watched her react to his discourtesy. He saw her grip the rail, square her shoulders, and turn, summoning a coldness into her eyes and voice that brooked no argument.

"Sir. We are not of an acquaintance that you may address me with such familiarity."

He sprang up the stairs until he was at a level with her, "Then let us change that! Let us shake hands and begin a courtship right here, tonight, in Chicago."

"I leave for New York on the morrow."

"Must you go?"

"Yes."

"You would not stay?"

"No."

"Not even for love?"

It was a bold question, more of a challenge, really, and he observed a lovely blush spread up her neck and across her freckled cheeks. She stared down, unblinking, and it was a half minute before she spoke.

"I cannot love you, Thomas Jameson."

He shook his head, disbelieving. "Cannot? Or will not?"

She looked up then. "It is all the same in the end. I cannot, I *will not,* love a man who so clearly does not love himself."

He met her steady gaze and accepted the truth in her statement and let the old veneer of bravado fall away until all that remained on the stairs was the lonely and terrified boy from Virginia. He took her hand and thrilled when she did not immediately withdraw from his grasp.

"Then show me—show me how to love."

She searched his desperate face, and he wanted to weep for the longing and compassion her own features revealed.

"Oh, Thomas . . ." And he heard the anguish in her whisper. "Only God can show you that."

She took his hand between both of hers for the briefest of moments, her grip firm and sure, then released him and turned away.

"Good-bye, Mr. Jameson."

And when the great tower chimed ten o'clock the next morning, the first of November, Tommy leaned against the window of his boardinghouse room, heard the ringing of the engine bell, and knew with a raging certainty in his heart that she was gone.

PART IV

Forgiveness is the fragrance of the violet which still clings fast to the heel that crushed it.
—RUSSIAN PROVERB

CHAPTER 19

November 1873

A schoolteacher. The repulsive man was a school-teacher. Lizzie had sat across from Spafford in his study several days ago, her face parchment white, her breathing rapid and shallow, her voice a monotone like a child who'd just witnessed a horrific accident, who'd learned her mother was never coming home.

Spafford had soothed and coaxed until he'd finally convinced Lizzie that she was safe, that she could be frank with him, and she'd reluctantly mentioned a school—a prestigious school—where her uncle could be found. He had pictured the man in custodial service, cleaning or repairing or keeping the grounds. But he never could have imagined that the man who had taken such advantage of a child in her grief was daily influencing young hearts and minds.

He understood her fear now. The Spaffords had no legal claim to her welfare, and she had no rights as a child. If she reentered Chicago society, the law would land on the side of the uncle, and she would be returned to him regardless of her protests. In two years she would be eighteen and win emancipation from the man forever. But that could be a very long two years.

Spafford paced the floor of his Madison Street

office, the words of Asaph, the great musician in the Psalms, drumming through his head. *Defend the poor and fatherless . . . do justice to the afflicted and needy.* Do justice . . . do justice . . .

McDaid and Wilson, partners and fathers, sat behind their desks voicing options. Taking Lizzie on the overseas trip was the best way to ensure distance. But like most of Chicago's children, she had no birth certificate—all birth records were destroyed when the courthouse burned—and could not sail without proof of citizenship. Applying for a duplicate could alert the uncle, and their cause would be lost. And there was no time.

The lack of certificate could also be a problem in New York. The school applications were lengthy and required multiple personal references and documentation. Telegrams were flying back and forth between John Farwell and Miss Carrie as they filed petitions and scheduled auditions. And there was no time.

The McDaids were willing to keep Lizzie in their home until the details could be worked out. But Spafford felt an enormous sense of urgency in removing her from Chicago. And he had less than a week to accomplish it.

Dear Lord, he silently prayed as he paced, *bend down and hear our petition for this child.* And then his blood ran hot and thick as he thought of the reason for Lizzie's crisis. *And take your vengeance on this evil man . . . or I will.*

● ● ●

Later that day Spafford heard the soft knock at his office door and absently called for his visitor to enter. The door opened and closed, and at the ensuing silence Spafford looked up and into the drawn face of Tommy Jameson.

The change in the man was astonishing. Gone was the confident swagger, the aggressive stance, the arrogant tilt of his chin. In their place was a bewilderment that made the man fidget, looking about the room at everything and nothing.

Spafford put down his pen and watched him for a moment, eventually breaking the silence. "I've had a letter from Moody." At this Tommy focused. "He is well?"

Spafford nodded and reached into a drawer. "He included a note for you."

He handed over the envelope and watched Tommy slide it back and forth between his thumb and finger, then trace the words inscribed on the front. Long moments passed as Tommy stared down at his name and frowned, then ever so softly spoke.

"I am . . ." He hesitated and shook his head.

Spafford prompted him. "You are. . . ?"

Tommy never looked up. "I don't know who I am."

Spafford was elated. Moody had been reluctant to leave his "lost boy" when he felt a transformation was within reach. He'd garnered Spafford's promise that he would look after Tommy, and Spafford had kept his word, making contact at least twice a week.

And now it had come to this. He responded casually.

"No man, for any considerable period, can wear one face to himself and another to the multitude without finally getting bewildered as to which may be true."

Tommy stared at him, his eyes wide and bottomless. "That is . . . brilliant. You should record it . . . somewhere."

"Yes, well . . ." Spafford reached behind him and pulled *The Scarlet Letter* from the wall-to-wall shelves. "Nathaniel Hawthorne said it first." He placed the book on the edge of his desk and pushed it toward his guest.

Tommy looked at it, then back at the envelope.

Spafford suddenly felt a burden for this man that he'd never felt before. He knew this was a delicate and defining moment and he should act on it before it passed them by. But he was a poet. He did not possess Moody's candor, found it impossible, in fact, to be so blunt on such personal matters with anyone outside his close circle of family and friends. How would he begin? He mentally selected and discarded quotes from the great poets . . . too indirect, too complex, too—

Is there anything too hard for me?

The voice of God stilled his anxious thoughts. This was not about his own prowess. H. G. Spafford was not directing this moment. He waited, listening.

You love me because I first loved you.

Of course. He came out from behind his desk and motioned Tommy to the club chairs in front of the

236

fire. They sat in contemplative silence until a log hissed and fell and Spafford found his opening.

"In all my life I have never encountered another man like D. L. Moody." Tommy looked at him with such longing and misery that Spafford felt his heart contract with compassion for the man. "He loves the most unlovely people—the corrupt, the degraded, those who would steal from him, those who would destroy him. Unruly children. Me. You." He took a deep breath and let it out on a sigh.

"It is an uncommon trait for man." He watched Tommy closely. "It is not of this world."

Tommy turned Moody's envelope around and around in his hands, staring into the fire but listening. Spafford was amazed at his own calm and pushed forward with the Gospel.

"It is an astounding truth, but God loves you, Thomas . . . just as you are." Tommy shook his head and Spafford leaned forward. "*Just as you are*—noble and wicked together." He pressed the point home.

"Go to Him. He heals the brokenhearted and binds up their wounds—one of His many promises in the Psalms."

Tommy looked down at Moody's letter, carefully tucked it into his inside coat pocket, and stood. Spafford stood with him. After a pause Tommy held out his hand, and Spafford took it, then pulled him into an embrace and held him for as long as Tommy would let him.

And then Tommy was through the door, and Spafford looked to heaven and made his third petition to the Lord that day: *Follow him.*

Tommy wandered the crowded Chicago streets and had never felt more alone in his life. One by one the people who had come to matter to him in this dusty town were leaving for other cities, other adventures.

He never should have started to care. That was it. When he had been ruthlessly selfish, when he had used people for his own pleasure, he'd never given them another thought when they'd passed out of his life. In fact, he'd helped some of them on their way with a swift kick and a "good riddance" and enjoyed their disappointment.

He was a fool for changing anything about his survival.

He turned the corner off LaSalle and came to a halt before the Chicago Avenue Church, staring at the motto inscribed over the main entrance: "Welcome to this House of God are strangers and the poor." He considered how he'd been a stranger once and was received here. It had been months since he'd stepped through these doors, and he put out a hand and opened them and walked inside.

The room glowed with afternoon sun as it spilled through the stained-glass windows, catching dust particles as they spun by. It was as silent and peaceful as a mausoleum. He stood near the back row, pulled the blue linen envelope from his pocket and broke the seal. Inside was a single sheet of matching paper and Moody's familiar hurried scrawl.

Dear Thomas,
Though an ocean divides us, I still weep for your soul. I pray you would surrender your heart at once, for it would be a pity to spend one more day rejecting the love of Christ.
Moody

He sat in a wooden pew on the last row, staring down at the words on the linen paper. No one had ever wept for him—no mother, no father, no friend, no wife. He'd rarely even wept for himself. Yet here was a preacher, an ocean away, remembering a sinner in Chicago. And grieving.

It was more than his rebellious spirit could take.

He reached into his inside pocket and withdrew the Bible Moody had given him almost a year ago. He'd been carrying it with him since the day his friend had boarded the train and left for Europe. He traced the words on the cover and turned the book over and over in his hands, as Moody had. Oh, how he missed that man.

He drew a shaky breath, opened the cover, and saw written there, in Moody's hand, a note: *Matthew 6:33.* He turned to the index, found the page number for Matthew, and kept turning until he saw the heading for chapter six. Across the page, next to number thirty-three, was a sentence underlined in pencil. *Seek ye first the kingdom of God. . . .* Beside it was another reference: *John 1:12.* He found it and read, *But as many as received him, to them gave he power to become the sons of God . . .* Sons of God . . . it was underlined twice.

Moody had planned ahead for this day—the day Tommy would actually crack open the book—and set out a quest. Tommy remembered the preacher once saying to a group of men, *"When you study the Bible, be sure you hunt for something."* So he had filled the little book with clues.

Tommy followed the path Moody had laid out John 5:24, Psalm 139, Jeremiah 29:11-13. He turned the fragile pages, and his breath caught on Hebrews 13:5-6. *I will never leave thee, nor forsake thee . . .* He read about sin in Romans, sheep astray in Isaiah and remained in that section, ending with the promise in chapter 49, *Yet will I not forget thee! Behold, I have graven thee upon the palms of my hands . . .*

The church had become cold and dark in the winter afternoon. Tommy could no longer see the text, but his mind spun from the words he'd read. No one could keep all those promises. No one! He threw down the book and leapt to his feet. He stomped back to the entrance and pulled on the door. It wouldn't budge. He tried again, but it was as if the doors had been welded shut. He wheeled around in disgust and marched toward the side doors to the connecting rooms. Locked. He pounded on them with both fists, then listened for a response. Nothing.

He stood at the front of the church, sweating from frustration, the Bible verses ringing in his head. *For all have sinned . . . Christ died for us . . . If any man will come after me . . . I am thy God . . . I have summoned you by name—you are mine . . .*

He closed his eyes and saw Moody weeping. He opened them and saw the pulpit where the man had challenged him each week. He walked down the center aisle and remembered the people who had gone forward each Sunday—foolish people, he'd thought. He heard the singing. He heard the praying. He felt the familiar pull toward the altar and moved far away from it. His will warred against his heart.

And the battle, this time, was fierce.

Tommy collapsed in the last pew beside the Bible, his head in his hands, remembering the preacher, remembering . . . Jimmy. He rarely allowed himself to think about that night ten years ago—how his childhood friend had lain there, mortally wounded from Confederate cannons, struggling to fill his bleeding lungs. At midnight the chaplain had been summoned to help Jimmy die, and into the tent had walked D. L. Moody. Tommy had given up his campstool and stood in the shadows listening to the story of how Christ had left heaven and come into this world to seek and save all who were lost. It was the first time he'd heard that story, and he'd believed every word of it as he'd listened to Jimmy rasp and fight the pain and, finally, breathe his last breath on that promise.

And then Tommy had spent the next decade fighting the memory . . . and the truth. It was as Moody had said—he had sought out every evil in the world. And it had never satisfied him.

His throat was clogged with the dueling urge to cry out for mercy and curse the Savior. He wanted to tear the room apart and hold it close. His hands shook and his heart raced, and hour after hour he wrestled with the Lord on the last pew of Moody's church.

And somewhere in the night, Thomas Jameson III, motherless boy, prodigal son, laid his sorry life before the Cross and accepted the glorious mantle of what he had been all along—child of God.

CHAPTER 20

November 11, 1873

It was a moment of pure emotion, and Anna struggled to contain it. The express train that would carry them to Pittsburgh hissed and steamed on the track, its vibrating energy increasing the excitement coursing through her. Two years in Europe! She could not, dared not, have dreamed of such an adventure a month ago.

She watched her husband guide a young porter to their trunks and thought of the long evenings when she and Gates had lain in bed, holding hands, planning. After two days in New York, they would board a ship for France and visit their many friends there—

Bertha, her schoolmate who had married a doctor and moved to Paris, Nicolet's extended family, the Moodys. Then off they would go to Switzerland to settle Annie and Maggie in school and Nicolet nearby with Bessie and Tanetta. And then a private trip, a second honeymoon across Europe.

She had in her reticule the note she'd found resting on Gates' pillow the morning after one such night of planning.

> *Here between the was and the will be,*
> *I cannot help but recall the early days . . .*
> *I am overwhelmed with longing and love*
> *for family and for God.*

She echoed his sentiment and marveled at his ability, once again, to convey his feelings so succinctly, so perfectly.

In the rush and preparation for this journey, through the myriad details of farewells and instructions and packing and promoting Lizzie, she had left little room for personal reflection. Now, while she waited on the platform, she was feeling what the children suffered no qualms in expressing—complete joy. She felt the pull of adventure, like their passenger coach connected to the steam engine, and thought there was nothing that could ruin this moment.

And then she saw him.

On the platform, not ten yards away, was Tommy Jameson. And his luggage. Her happiness dimmed.

What was he doing here? And why was Gates shaking his hand so cheerfully? Perhaps it was coincidence. Perhaps he had business in Pittsburgh. And now Maggie had joined them, babbling and flushed, and that horrible man was smiling down at her with his blue eyes and dimples.

Anna looked away. She would not allow Mr. Jameson to spoil this adventure with his mere presence. In twenty-four hours they would change trains and be rid of him for two whole years. She looked at her mother's watch, smiled, and marked the time.

It was worse than even Anna could have anticipated. Not only was Mr. Jameson traveling by the same trains to New York, he had also booked passage on the same France-bound ship. He was crossing to find Moody.

She had gaped at Gates when he'd told her the news, believing it some sort of tactless jest. Yet, there Mr. Jameson had been as they'd switched to the Pullman car the next morning. He'd marveled at the famous Horseshoe Curve outside Altoona at dusk with Bessie standing on his lap, squealing and pointing as the caboose revealed itself on the massive loop. He'd choked down the station restaurant's meat pies without complaint. He'd carried Maggie onto the next car as they'd made their final exchange in the dead of night. And he'd looked irritatingly fresh as they'd disembarked in the Jersey City terminal.

He had greeted her with the utmost politeness at

each encounter and entertained the children thoroughly, and she quite possibly disliked him more for it. She did not understand his motive. Did he believe she would influence Carrie toward him because he was momentarily a gentleman? Did he hope to gain Gates' trust and, therefore, endorsement in Europe?

Gates had begged her patience and tolerance with the man, and she had obliged. But his presence had tainted every new experience: the ferry crossing of the Hudson River to Manhattan, the elevated car ride down Broadway, even their excursion to Pier No. 50 where their ship—the great SS *Ville du Havre* was docked, its enormous black bow towering over them.

Anna had breathed a sigh of relief when Mr. Jameson declined to accompany them to Normal College, Lizzie's new school. She was surprised at his refusal, as it was abundantly clear they would be meeting Carrie at her new apartment and taking her to supper.

But as they stood in front of the gothic facade of the new facility for gifted girls, all ill-tempered thoughts of Mr. Jameson left Anna's mind. She gazed up at the banks of arched windows and knew with the maternal certainty innate in women that Lizzie would be happy here. School was in session, and their little group walked from room to room, marveling at the beauty of the facility, listening intently as the administrator explained the curriculum and procedures—not to the Spaffords, but to Lizzie.

Then off they flew to Carrie's rooms, where the

widow had worked a little creative magic. The common space was compact and elegant with muted tones and cozy furnishings. But it was Lizzie's bedroom that drew a collective gasp. For Carrie had recreated the lavender room from the Lake View house, right down to the white trim and crisp linens. Lizzie moved from bed to window to dresser, eyes wide, caressing each item until she turned and threw herself into the widow's arms. Safe, at last.

Lizzie stood outside the tall white building on Union Square the next day and silently repeated her mantra—*You are a delight to Him . . . You are a delight to Him . . .*

She was about to audition for the teachers at Steinway Hall—teachers who would be able to determine after one keystroke, she was certain, whether she was worthy of their instruction. If not for Mrs. Spafford's arm across her back and the tight hold, she might have fled by now. In fact, she had almost made up her mind to break free when Mr. Spafford knocked for the third time and the door flew open to reveal a rather eccentric-looking man.

He was no more than five feet tall with hair that was all but gone, making his bald pate shine and emphasize the few strands that danced about in the brisk New York wind. He stared at them with piercing blue eyes over the top of tiny glasses, raised an incredibly bushy eyebrow, and spoke in a baritone worthy of the opera.

"You are late." And then he turned on his heel, and they had no choice but to follow.

Across the marbled lobby and up the winding grand staircase they went, nearly running to keep up with the little man. Lizzie no more than glanced at the arched galleries and rows of gas-lights as they wound up, up, up to the fourth floor, where the man disappeared behind a massive pair of doors.

Mr. Spafford stood with his hand on the knob, slightly out of breath, an amused expression on his face, and whispered to her, "Ready?" She nodded, and he opened the door.

She stepped into a shrine to the piano. Along the inside walls were a variety of Steinway's instruments—the square grand, the upright, the art case with its lavishly carved box and legs, the tiny "boudoir" model like the one just delivered to Miss Carrie's rooms. And showcased in front of the floor-to-ceiling windows stood two concert grands, intertwined, lids up, glowing in the brilliance of the midday sun. The little man perched on an overstuffed chair in the center of it all, arms folded, legs crossed at the ankles, and watched her take in the room.

The studio was both peaceful and oppressive, for no sound entered from the street. The hush was absolute, and Lizzie actually jumped when the man spoke.

"Pick one"

Mrs. Spafford helped her remove her coat, then without hesitation Lizzie walked to the concert grand.

She sat on the tufted stool, stared down at the ivory keys, and marveled at the detailed nameplate. And then, the audition began.

The little man barked out orders in his rich voice—"Scales! B-flat major! E minor! Unison! Opposing! Chords! A-flat! Invert! Invert!"

Lizzie called upon every ounce of instruction and control in her short life, and answered the commands by instinct. In the middle of one such instruction, he appeared at her side and spoke softly, the word coming out like a song. "Play."

She began with Chopin's "Prelude in B Minor"—a moderate, fluid piece—and the man backed away, and she was alone with the music. She poured her heart into the melancholy song, letting the instrument's rich bass tones showcase the running left hand, her skin tingling as the music floated up and out and enveloped the room. When the last note rang out, she looked up and spied the man looking out the banks of windows, hands folded behind his back. She released the sustain pedal, and he spoke again.

"Another."

She launched into a Bach Invention, marveling at how the brilliant purity in the treble mingled with the mellowness of the middle register. She felt she could play a piano of such magnificence all day.

He asked for another, and Lizzie thought at once of Chopin's "Nocturne in E-flat Major"—how the grand would respond to the waltz quality in the bass, how the rapidly running notes in the right hand would sing out and over with little difficulty. It was an extremely difficult piece, but it had never seemed easier on such a worthy instrument.

Without turning, he requested Beethoven's "Hymn to Joy." She thought it an odd request but played it nonetheless, letting the powerful chords ring out, applying the pedal sparingly. And when she reached the end of the short hymn, she did something she'd never before done in public. She improvised.

She kept the melody in the right hand and created a running left hand, worthy of Liszt, as accompaniment. And then she modulated to a minor key and played as Schumann might. And then she returned to the original piece and finished with a resounding series of chords.

And then she wondered if she'd just ruined her audition.

But the little man turned from the window, tears streaming down his face, and rushed to her side. "Delightful . . . delightful!" He dashed past her to the Spaffords, who had never moved from the doorway and stared in not a little bit of awe at their young charge. The man skidded to a stop before them.

"She is . . . magnificent." He dashed to the center of the room, flung wide his arms, and laughed, the tears still streaming from his eyes.

"Young lady, welcome to Steinway."

Tommy stood across the street in the shadows of a Lexington Avenue doorway that evening and watched

Carrie and Lizzie alight from the omnibus, the Spaffords waving and calling out to them, "Until tomorrow!" He watched as they climbed the stone steps, and Lizzie pushed through the building's front door, then called out.

"Mrs. Maxwell . . ."

Carrie wheeled about, her gloved hand over her throat, and he rushed to assay her fear, stepping into the lamplight. "It is Tommy. Thomas Jameson."

She stared across at him, her eyes wide with disbelief and fright. "What are you doing here?"

"I wanted to see you . . . to speak with you."

"Why did you not join us for dinner?"

"Mrs. Spafford finds me abrasive and ill-mannered." He looked down at his boots, then up again. "She is right." He shook his head. "She was right."

Carrie lingered halfway through the doorway, indecision and confusion making her frown. He crossed the street and stood on the sidewalk, looking up at her.

"Walk with me." He held out a gloved hand, and she remained frozen on the step. He left his hand outstretched, loathe to retract it, willing to wait while she worked through the feelings that traveled across her face and held her firmly in place. After what seemed like minutes, she murmured something to Lizzie and closed the door. She gazed at him for a long moment, then her hand inched forward, and he smiled with relief when it slid into his. He drew her down the stairs and next to his side, and they began to walk.

"Do you like it here?"

She didn't answer immediately, and Tommy wondered if she'd heard the question, so intense was her concentration, her brow furrowed, her hand gripping his arm. They strolled in silence along the well-lit street until she voiced her own question.

"Why did you come?"

"I leave tomorrow for Europe." He saw that his news shocked her. Her lips parted, but she said nothing. "To find my father."

She turned to him then. "Your father? For what purpose?"

"To try to be the son he's always wanted."

She looked at him with surprise and something like hope. "And when will you return?"

"I don't know. Soon, if he will not welcome me."

"And if he does?"

"Then by spring. No later."

He watched her absorb these facts, bursting with the need to tell her about the transformation in his heart and life. But he knew with a certainty that he would have to demonstrate the change to her, or she would think it a ruse.

She was shivering a little, and he very reluctantly turned back toward her building, moving as slowly as possible along the sidewalk, delaying the moment when he would have to say good-bye. She stared straight ahead, and her next question came out on a frosty breath.

"And then, come spring . . . what will you do?"

251

Tommy brought them to a halt in front of her door and turned, forcing her to look straight at him. "I will come find you." She stared, searching his face. He let her search him, leaving his features wide open, physically encouraging her to trust that what she could see on his face was living in his heart.

When he saw that she had her answer, he held her away from him, gripping her upper arms, demanding a response to his own question.

"Will you be here, Carrie?" She looked away, and he squeezed her arms to force her eyes back to his. "Will you?"

She drew a short breath, leaned forward, and whispered, "Yes!"

And then she was running up the steps and through the door. And she never let him say good-bye.

CHAPTER 21

November 14, 1873

Spafford watched his wife closely as she read the telegram. The message from McDaid was brief, but its urgency was unmistakable. They had an offer for the land that had cost them so dearly, but the interested party would not complete the sale without Spafford present.

He could not decide if the timing could be better or worse. He did not want to send his family on this journey without him. Yet the land sale would relieve him—and McDaid and all of the partners—of nearly all their debt. He could travel throughout Europe without the cloud of financial worries hanging over him.

Anna's brow creased in concern, and she moved to close the door between their bedroom and the suite where the children slept. Then she sat at the dressing table, studying the words on the yellow paper.

Spafford knew his wife well enough to assume that she was worried about the lack of an escort. So he mentioned the four French pastors with whom they'd dined the previous evening, reminding her that they also traveled to France tomorrow, assuring her that both Weiss and Lorriaux were eager to offer their services as chaperones and protectors.

"Pastor Lorriaux has invited you to stay with his family in Bertry. He spoke very energetically of their regional specialties—a leek pie and dessert much like a waffle." He smiled.

Anna handed him the telegram. "You seem to have worked out all the details."

"I did not want to present you with unknowns and indecision, dearest." He studied her. "What are your thoughts?"

She sat down at the vanity and began to brush her hair as she contemplated the situation. "I think . . ." She carefully placed the brush onto the vanity and looked at his reflection. "I think it is ultimately your decision. You will know what's best."

He watched his wife open a jar of cream, rub some

into her palms, and smooth it over her cheeks. Her answer should have appeased him—it was exactly what he'd hoped for. But he could not shake the feeling that the outcome from this new plan would be far less than any of them had bargained for.

November 15

Winter vapor encased the North River, lending the SS *Ville du Havre* a ghostly, ominous appearance as the Spaffords stepped onto Pier 50. The fog was so thick, the ship had all lights up—green, red, and white globes glowing along the starboard side.

Anna felt the weather mirrored her spirits—taxing, gloomy, uncertain. She tried to keep her chin up as she walked the gangplank close behind Gates, a child gripping each hand. She'd had plenty of opportunity last night to alter this morning's outcome. But she hadn't taken it. She'd listened to her husband's reasoning and responded exactly as she'd learned to respond over the past two years—she'd acquiesced. And perhaps that was what found her so dismal this morning—the realization that nothing had really changed for either of them since she'd walked out of her life in October.

She squared her shoulders and tried to shake off her mood as a charming French steward bowed to their small party, then held an oil lamp before him, escorting them along the enshrouded deck. The size of the vessel was a mystery, as the fog was so dense they could see only as far as the lantern in the steward's hand. But the decks were wide and smooth and their footing exceptionally sure. Within moments the steward stopped at a pair of doors paneled in stained glass and announced, "*Le grandiose salon.*"

They stepped into a large and sumptuous room set for dinner. Long rows of tables glittered under the gas- and candlelight, the *Compagnie Général Transatlantique* insignia stamped onto fine porcelain and shining silver. Damask linens in intricate folds burst out of crystal glasses that appeared to Anna much too fragile to survive an ocean voyage. Bouquets of fresh flowers filled the air with a sweet, intoxicating smell. Encased in rich woodwork and bronze work, the elegant room had the effect on her that was intended—she looked forward to time spent here.

The steward led them further along the rail, stopping for a moment to present the library—a cozy room of nine hundred volumes, dark furnishings, and a smell of new leather. Then he turned and descended a grand staircase of carved oak that appeared from nowhere. Down, down they went through the fog until they emerged into the main cabin.

It was a splendid apartment, pierced by the mainmast painted a silvery white and dressed at the ceiling with a circle of crushed glass. The ship's designer had continued the theme, fitting the walls with circular-topped pilasters, separated by panels inlaid with mirrors and paintings of ancient oceanic mythology—

here was the mighty Poseidon and there, across from him, his son, Triton. Anna perceived the girls' interest from their bulging eyes and gaping mouths, and she envisioned many hours of study from books found in the little library.

Their staterooms were amidships, and the steward coaxed them to doors of white holly and brushed silver hardware. He opened one with a flourish to reveal a warm and spacious dwelling.

Their trunks had been called for that morning and now stood neatly against the delicate pink walls. Anna felt herself relax in the light and airy space, appreciating the feminine detail of damask silk hangings in French white and crimson satin stripes, the corresponding sofa of tufted velvet. As she turned about, admiring the little *chiffonier* and fixed lavatory, the steward stepped to a curtained wall, reached in, and pulled down a double bed. The children gasped in delight—this had been one of their favorite features of the Pullman sleeping car. Just as easily, he restored the bed, converting the space back into a sitting room.

Anna marveled at the luxurious rooms, wishing she could recall any detail of her family's crossing from Norway. But she had been just four years old. She would have liked to compare her experience on the *Norden* to what she anticipated it would be on the *Ville du Havre*. She made a mental note to find a Norwegian from that journey and make the comparison on her return home.

The tour continued on, the steward leading them the length and breadth of the great ship, pointing out the ladies' *boudoir,* the drawing room, the smoking room, and surrounding it all, yards and yards of promenade. They returned to the grand *saloon,* very much impressed with this triumph of opulence and art.

They were at their leisure while the fog, ever so slowly, burned away. By one o'clock the *Ville du Havre* began to reveal itself, and its size was remarkable. From the stern where they stood to the bow projecting over the harbor, the ship was one hundred and forty yards, its triple masts towering over them with furled canvas.

Maggie stared up at the mizzenmast, her arms out to the side, weaving as she gaped, and calling out, "It makes me dizzy, Mama."

Anna smiled. "Then look away, darling."

"But I love being dizzy."

At two o'clock the call was made for guests to depart. Anna searched across the crowded deck for Gates, but he was not to be found. A crowd had gathered on the pier, photographers poised to record the drama and ritual of the launch, friends and relatives waiting to wave their handkerchiefs with tears of sorrow or joy.

Just as Anna was about to send a steward in search of him, Gates appeared at her side.

"I have made a change."

Anna shook her head, confused. Gates drew her through the crowd and along the deck to the bow, asking her to hurry. He did not explain to her their mission as he begged the pardon of more than one passenger gathered along the rail, finally cutting across the ship to the portside. Then they were at the bow and descending into its main cabin.

This apartment was just as opulent but in a heavier, richer fashion. Spanish mahogany walls, sofas upholstered in bloodred frieze velvet and brocade, and a heavy mock Jacobean carpet gave it an old-world, masculine feel. Anna was intrigued but frustrated with the last-minute jaunt. She raised a brow at her husband as she caught her breath.

He stood near a gilded mirror in the shape of a compass. "I have asked the purser to change your rooms from amidships to these in the bow."

Anna stared at him. "What? Why?"

"I cannot explain it, other than that the location causes me unease. Please trust me on this, Anna." He turned and knocked on a paneled door.

"Come," called the male voice inside.

Gates turned the brass handle and led her into a lavish sitting room with seating in embossed crimson plush and a massive bronze-framed porthole . . . and Tommy Jameson. Gates gave her no time to protest.

"Mr. Jameson has very generously offered to exchange accommodations, and the room next door is available. I've made all the arrangements. By the time you are out of the harbor, your trunks will be moved, and all will be settled."

Anna was speechless. In less than twenty-four

hours, her husband had managed to alter every aspect of a trip they had planned together for weeks. She did not want to travel alone—even if four French pastors were at her disposal. She did not want to change staterooms—she loved the bright and open quality of the rooms amidships. And most significantly, she did not wish to be indebted, in any way, to Tommy Jameson. But she let none of this show on her features as she looked about the room, barely noting the four berths bunked in satinwood and hung with rich damask curtains.

The ship blew a long, loud whistle, and Gates sprang into action. He shook hands with Jameson, thanking him again for his trouble, then pulled Anna up the staircase and back along the deck.

They found their brood in the stern, and Gates had just enough time to make hurried good-byes, hugging and kissing his girls, shaking hands with the pastors, and holding Anna in a tight embrace, whispering his love for her. He tucked a folded paper inside her glove and vanished down the gangplank.

And then the top-hatted launcher triggered the mechanism to release the moorings, causing cheers and camera lenses to click in rapid succession. The water began to boil as the ship's engines whirred to life and the great floating hotel moved away from the dock, tugged along by a boat a fraction of its size.

Anna stood waving with her girls as they steamed away, the roofs and spires of New York rising before them, the brackish water churning around them, until the pier was nothing but a spot in the distance. And only then, while her children pointed to the white-sailed schooners and colorful ferry-boats and barges on the river, did she pull the slip of paper from her glove and read Gates' final words:

My heart is filled,
half with memory of your smile,
half with expectation of it.

She took a deep breath, filling her lungs with the crisp winter air. She could carry her disappointment across an ocean, or she could drop it into the harbor and embrace the coming adventure. It was a simple decision, really.

As they made their way into the Narrows, a steward approached her group with a tray of hot cocoa. They each took a mug, letting the steam warm their faces, savoring the rich chocolate. She looked at her happy little group and thought of her husband, even now on his way home. And she decided right then—it would cost her some pride, but she would meet his expectation. And she smiled.

CHAPTER 22

Chicago
November 16

The lights of Chicago blinked into view, the conductor began his series of whistle blasts, and Spafford could not shake the feeling of unease that had haunted him on deck yesterday.

It was only a matter of a week or two, and he would join his family and whisk them off to Paris for a whirlwind tour of museums and art galleries and out-of-the-way eateries. The alterations to their plans had worked out so perfectly, so elegantly, with the invitation to Bertry.

So why this worry?

He could only suspect that it was his wife's quiet consent to the change that bothered him. If she had said to him, "Do not go," if she had looked him straight in the eye, as she used to, and firmly argued against his return to Chicago, if she had told him she could not bear the journey alone . . . .

He stared out the window as they chugged over the north river and mentally winced. The reality was that even if she had done those things, he would still be on this train. The nature of their relationship had always been that he led and she followed. And her personal nature was one of obedience and discipline. He had the unpleasant feeling that when he'd been forced to choose between business and family, he'd disappointed her yet again, and she had let him.

He would write a letter tonight, gently exploring this aspect of their relationship, quietly encouraging that they both adjust their manner of communicating. And then he would have to push himself and his partners very hard. The sooner he closed this deal, the sooner he could be on his way to Anna.

Atlantic Ocean
November 16

Anna was impressed.

Not only had the French pastors provided the attendees with a lovely Sunday service, but they had done it in two languages. The statements and translations had been so fluid, they were almost musical. And with the gentle rocking of a ship in full sail on a placid sea and the sun sparkling through the glass-domed skylight, the effect had been otherworldly.

Feeling the first measure of well-being since the telegram had arrived and disrupted their plans, she convinced her family to linger in the main *saloon,* hoping to prolong the sensation. She invited Pastor Lorriaux to sit with her, and together they dissected the poetic significance of one of her favorite hymns.

"Mama, Moby Dick is outside."

Anna looked up from the hymnal in her lap and considered her daughter kneeling on the plush upholstery, her arms resting on the rosewood window

262

frame as she looked out to sea. What a curious statement, even from Maggie.

Not a moment later, a loud *crack!* like a rifleshot stopped all conversation, followed by the first mate's appearance at the door, calling out, "*Les baleines au bâbord!*"

Anna looked to the pastor for translation.

"Whales on the portside, *Madame!*"

The lingering patrons rushed to the deck. There in the water, running alongside their ship, was a pod of what Anna guessed were sperm whales—the very image of the fictional Moby Dick.

As the children squealed and pointed, the largest whale lifted its dark gray tail high into the air and slapped it down onto the water's surface, creating the gunshot noise that had startled them earlier. The children screamed in delight and clapped their hands over their ears, then pointed again as several whales sent forward showers of steaming breath through their blowholes.

Anna found herself both exhilarated by the sight and unhappy that Gates was not here to experience this extraordinary event with them. The girls would talk about seeing Moby Dick for years, and their father would be absent, again, from the memory.

"It's such a pity," Maggie sighed. And Anna wondered if the child was reading her mind. She tipped up her daughter's face. "What is a pity, my little bird?"

"That Mr. Melville is not with us. He would have so enjoyed seeing his captain's . . . nemesis."

Anna simply could not believe that a nine-year-old child had the first notion of what a nemesis was. She bent closer. "Maggie, are you reading *Moby Dick?*"

Maggie's eyes widened. "Oh no, Mama. It is too, too difficult for me." Anna nodded and released the child's chin, almost missing her next declaration. "Mr. Jameson is reading it to us."

Anna's jaw dropped, and she shot a questioning look at Nicolet, who nodded, rather sheepishly, she thought.

Maggie sighed. "I do so love to watch Mr. Jameson read."

Nicolet leaned in. "*Monsieur* Spafford gave the book to *Monsieur* Jameson at departure and asked that he read aloud only the parts that were . . . *correctes* . . . for children. It is part of their lessons."

Anna digested that piece of information with gritted teeth and could not decide who infuriated her more— her husband for secretly providing the source of entertainment, Tommy Jameson for carrying out the assignment, or Nicolet for going along with it. But why had Gates been so clandestine about it? She shook her head. She knew why. She would have opposed the idea from the start. So they wanted to read *Moby Dick* without her. So be it. They would find out soon enough that the man reading to them was just as self-centered, just as ungodly, as the book's captain chasing the great leviathan.

She cast her eyes over the rail, looking for anything like the white whale's markings. But in the time she had taken to stew over the maddening situation, the whales had gone. And so had her hard-won sense of well-being.

Chicago
November 18

Spafford sat in a corner of the Brevoort House dining room, attempting to wipe the smile of satisfaction from his face. But it was impossible.

Word was out in attorneys' circles that a certain well-respected teacher had grossly miscalculated when he'd preyed on one of his young female students. The girl had not only been compromised, she'd become pregnant and had been clever enough to lay a trap for her predator to salvage what was left of her future.

As she was a child of a wealthy urban family, the details were closely guarded. But Spafford had it from the highest sources in city government that the letch—the very profligate who had nearly destroyed Lizzie—was charged with criminal sexual assault, and that no respectable lawyer would plead the teacher's defense, and that justice would be done. He would finish out his life in prison.

He thought of the Lord's reply to Habakkuk when the prophet had cried out for justice. *"Though it tarry,"* the Lord had said, *"wait for it; because it will surely come . . . ."* Spafford considered that if he'd had more time, if he hadn't booked passage on a ship bound for France, he might have tampered with God's plan and rushed Lizzie's uncle to justice. And that could have been disastrous, for God knew what Spafford had not: evil would soon reveal itself.

He thought of all the times Moody had been faced with a difficult, if not impossible, situation. *"Put forth every effort you can,"* had been the preacher's standard advice. *"Then wait on the Lord."*

There was a lesson in this—Spafford was sure of it. He pulled the pen from his coat pocket and several sheets of hotel stationery from a side table and wrote in bold black strokes across the top—the date, the time, and that day's notable message: *Wait on the Lord.*

Atlantic Ocean
November 19

Anna closed the book and relaxed on a deck lounge. After three days of violent storms and dense fog, the weather had finally cleared and the afternoon sun soaked into her dark wool coat, consorting with the salty air to make her sleepy. The girls were otherwise occupied, and she took full advantage of the ship's library, the open air, and a moment's peace and rest.

She was just beginning to doze when a persistent shadow brought on a chill.

"Mrs. Spafford?"

She recognized that voice—that sarcastic, insensitive voice. She did not want to open her eyes. But she

266

knew he stood there, staring down at her like a fox eyeing a sleeping hen. She resisted the urge to sigh and looked up.

"Mr. Jameson."

He stood at the rail, blocking the sun, his cheeks pink from the crisp winter day. "I wonder if you would do me the honor of a turn about the deck?"

Anna raised an eyebrow. Such formality. It became him, but she would do him no honor. "I think not, Mr. Jameson." She stared up at him from her inferior position, dismissing him with her expression.

He gave no sign of taking his leave, and she was about to bid him "good day" when he indicated the lounge beside her. "Then I wonder if I might join you?"

She did sigh then. Clearly the man had something on his mind. He had never, not one time away from Gates, paid her such respect. She lifted a gloved hand quite reluctantly, motioned to the lounge, and looked out to sea.

He perched on the edge of the deck chair and removed his hat. Out of the corner of her eye she watched his magnificent hair curl and dance in the light breeze, then chided herself for thinking anything was excellent about this man. They sat in silence until she could tolerate his presence no more.

"You wish to tell me something, Mr. Jameson?"

He nodded, gazing down at the hat he turned around and around in his hands.

She stared at him, willing him to speak his mind

and leave her, but he sat there, irritatingly mute. "You wish to tell me something *today?*" The sarcasm in her voice surprised her. She despised that very trait in this man, and it appeared as if his mere proximity inflicted the mannerism onto her. She would not give in to it. She relaxed her features and tried a sociable tone.

"Is this in relation to Mrs. Maxwell?"

He looked up then. "Everything, of late, is related to Mrs. Maxwell." And his smile was a bit rueful and sad and lovely all at the same time.

Anna felt herself drawn into the smile and reacted with the cruelest response she could summon.

"She will not have you."

She expected a bold rejoinder to that, something with the same kind of belligerence and mockery she'd suffered through on too many occasions. But he met her gaze with eyes sparkling with unshed tears. He opened his mouth, pursed his lips, looked away for a moment, then tried again to speak.

"You are right." A look of sheer torment crossed his handsome face. "She will not have the dishonorable man I have become."

She was shocked at his admission. She had used that very word to describe him—to Gates, to Moody, and especially to Carrie. But she had never expected to hear it from his own lips.

"I have been a disappointment almost from birth . . . to my father, to myself." He looked directly at her. "I am going to Europe to find my father and ask his pardon."

Ah. Here, at last, was the truth of it. His father was his benefactor. The cad must be running out of money and was prepared to travel to Europe to grovel for more. But why was he speaking to *her* of such private matters? Was he penniless already? Had he expected Gates to sponsor him at sea? Well. Gates was not here, and Tommy Jameson was the last sort of person she would ever support. She would bring this matter to an immediate close.

"I cannot help you, Mr. Jameson."

He cocked his head in the way most men did when they were truly perplexed. She sighed and tried a more direct attack. "I have no funds to spare."

Anna watched him grasp her meaning, saw his disappointment in the way his lips pursed and his eyes cut away. She felt a small victory when he stood and replaced his hat, then a stab of dismay when he doffed it and sat again.

He looked at her with an intensity that was disturbing, that made her summon her coldest demeanor in defense. But she was unprepared for the gentleness in his voice when he addressed her.

"I know you think me a cad, Mrs. Spafford. And it never mattered—at least, I told myself it did not—what you or anyone thought of me . . . until I met Mrs. Maxwell." He frowned and shook his head. "No, it was before that. It was Moody and your husband taking an interest in me. Taking an interest in my . . . soul." He said the word with not a little awe, as if he had no privilege to speak of such divine matters.

She scrutinized him as he talked about Moody and Gates. His features, once so cynical and ruthless, seemed more innocent. He looked even more handsome, his eyes bluer, his entire countenance softer.

He is forgiven.

The idea stunned her, and her hand almost flew to her breast. It was as if she were seeing him for the first time. And yet . . .

This could only be a ruse. He was using her to gain favor with Carrie, with Gates. Oh, he was very good. But she would not be duped.

He paused in his narrative and leaned forward, his face open, like a child's. "I came to you today to ask your pardon, dear lady, for the dishonor I have shown you and your family and guests." He waited expectantly for her response.

She had the strangest urge to laugh aloud. For even if he were serious—even if he were not giving the greatest performance of his life—pardon was not so easily gained. Not with her.

She swung her legs over the side of the chair and stood in one graceful movement. Then she walked to the ship's rail and turned to face him. "I will not give you something you have not earned. Good day, Mr. Jameson." And she dismissed him with a frigid stare.

He looked at her with such sorrow and dismay— emotions she'd thought him incapable of feeling— that she almost gave him what he wanted. Almost. But in the end she held her silence.

He nodded and rose to his feet like a repentant

schoolboy, donned his hat, and whispered, "Good day."

As he walked away, Anna expected to feel righteous for holding such a man accountable for his transgressions. Instead, she caught a glimpse of her blackest nature—merciless, bitter, immovable. It should have been enough to make her call him back. But she did not.

She turned and leaned against the rail, staring out to sea, her heart echoing the sentiment of the apostle Paul so many centuries ago. *Oh, what a wretch am I . . .*

Anna returned to the *saloon* after dinner that night, the children tucked into bed with Nicolet nearby, and sought out one of the Frenchmen—Pastor Weiss—for an evening stroll on the deck. Her heart was heavy with the afternoon's revelation, and she sought counsel in a man her husband trusted and revered.

The stars were close and bright, studding the sky like diamonds. It was remarkable to her how the heavens appeared so much nearer on the open sea, how God seemed a breath away. They walked the deck, commenting on creation and its awesome beauty.

And then Anna told the pastor of the battle in her heart, mentioning no names or situations, just the darkness dwelling there. He listened with utmost patience, asking no questions, requiring no details. And when she finished, he responded in a voice full of reflection and void of accusation.

"It is a simple matter to ask God for forgiveness, no? Yet much more *difficile* to give to others." He shrugged in that wholly French manner. "It is the nature of man."

"I know this," she admitted, "and I have struggled against my feelings."

He nodded and they strolled in companionable silence until they came to the stern and the pastor turned to her.

"You know the story of the *fils prodigue*—what you call the Prodigal Son?"

Anna nodded.

"I find this story most . . . *séduisant* . . ." He searched for a better word at her confusion. "Ahm . . . *intrigant*—intriguing—because of the hearts of the three men."

She raised an inquisitive brow and he continued.

"The father is Father God, and He is perfect. And then we have the first son and the second son—both men with *extreme* flaws. But the lesson is not in the flaws. It is in the forgiveness, mm?"

She nodded, captivated by the Frenchman and his logic.

"The Prodigal risks everything and expects very little when he returns home. Yet when he is forgiven, he simply accepts it. He . . ." The pastor hugged himself. "He . . . *l'embrasse*—embraces—it, much like the father embraces him. And so it is more *probable* that the Prodigal will also forgive." He shook his head.

"But the first son . . . mm . . . he refuses to forgive because there is no justice, no *punition,* for his brother's sins. And so he is lost to the father just as the Prodigal was."

Pastor Weiss tucked Anna's hand back into his arm and pulled her along the portside rail.

"This is a lesson of *grande importance.* When you are faced with forgiveness, you must remind yourself, there are three hearts in this story: the father's and the two brothers'—the two sons'. And then you must ask, which heart is most like yours?"

Anna wanted to weep then, because the Frenchman had revealed to her in his generous way that she had the heart of the older brother. She had not forgiven Gates for abandoning her for business interests—not for the past two years and not for this voyage. She was making him earn his way into her favor, just as she expected Tommy Jameson to prove his worthiness.

And with that realization came another. She had never prayed for Mr. Jameson's salvation. Not once. And that shamed her to her core. While Moody and Gates had worked and watched and waited, she had relegated the man to hell. And now she was certain that her observation earlier in the day had been correct—Tommy Jameson *was* forgiven. And she had wanted to laugh at him.

Her only hope of reparation lay in the knowledge that she and Mr. Jameson were trapped together on a ship at sea. She would seek him out—if not tomorrow, then the next day, or the next. And they would speak of the willful nature of man's heart. And then she would throw wide her arms, like the father, and welcome him home.

November 21

Tommy peeked through the portside windows of the main *saloon,* quickly spotting the Spafford children with their French governess. He scanned the remaining occupants and released a sigh of relief. Mrs. Spafford—the very person he'd been avoiding for two days—was absent.

He clutched Melville's *Moby Dick* in his left hand and reached for the door's ornate bronze handle with his right. He regretted the lost afternoons of reading while he'd hidden out in his rooms. He missed Annie's encouraging smiles, Maggie's adoring gaze, Bessie's insistence that she "read" from his lap. He would need to make up for the lost time or they would never finish the book by landfall. He would start with—

"Mr. Jameson."

His hand released the bronze handle, and he almost winced at the sound of the voice that had mocked him so recently. He turned with great reluctance and looked into the serious and determined face of Anna Spafford. He was at a loss for an appropriate greeting, wondering instead how he'd ever thought he could avoid the lady for the remainder of their voyage.

She attempted a smile that came out like a grimace. "Might I speak with you?"

At his nod she turned toward the stern and led him across the deck to a small, beautifully carved door that he'd noticed once in passing. She opened it herself and preceded him into an elegant room lined with shelves against oak wainscoting and lit with ambient light that spilled through intricate stained-glass windows. She took a seat in one of the massive chairs, and he noted that she looked rather childlike, perched on the edge of the red leather cushion, the brass studs framing her delicate features.

Tommy walked to one of the shelves, pretending to admire the gold-lettered volumes, tracing his finger over the names of distinguished authors carved into the wood, all the while dreading the confrontation that was about to occur. After all, he had the evidence in his hand.

He'd been on the upper deck the day of the whale sighting and overheard Maggie's confession. Until that moment he'd thought Mrs. Spafford had agreed to the afternoon readings, even if reluctantly. But her phrasing and the ensuing silence had convinced him otherwise. Oh, why had Spafford put him in such a position?

"Please join me, Mr. Jameson."

He closed his eyes briefly, then made his way across the small library to a matching chair across from her. He noticed, as he sat, that a uniformed man stood outside the small door, his back against the colored glass.

She followed his glance. "I have asked a steward to make certain we are not interrupted, for I have a matter of grave importance to discuss with you."

He could not quite place her tone. It was filled with neither anger nor reproach. In fact, it was not unlike the inflection he'd heard her use with her children. But it unnerved him nonetheless.

She leaned forward and looked him full in the face. "I have done you a great dishonor, dear sir, and must beg your forgiveness. For you very kindly asked for mine, and I would not give it."

He was so stunned at her words that he sat back hard in his chair and heard a small *crack*. What? What was this? *She* begged *his* forgiveness? And what of *Moby Dick?* He shook his head, the myriad Scriptures he'd pored over flashing through his mind. *Confess your faults one to another . . . A brother offended is harder to be won than a strong city . . . Forgive us our debts, as we forgive our debtors.* And the one that had given him the most pause—*Unto him that smiteth thee on the one cheek offer also the other.*

Her gaze never wavered from his face as he struggled to form a reply. But the longer he remained silent, the more her mouth drooped in sadness until she finally opened it and spoke in a shaky voice.

"You may wish to think it over. But know this—I will not rest peaceably until you have given me pardon."

She stood then, and he suddenly found the strength to rise and hold out a hand to stop her.

"Please . . . please, dear lady. Stay awhile. I have much to say."

They sat again, and after a while, he began to talk, haltingly at first, unused to this kind of directness with anyone other than Moody. But he found in Anna Spafford a patient and compassionate ear.

Tommy told her about his childhood and the misery he and his father had brought on themselves. He spoke of Jimmy and the tragedy of war. He felt the tears sting his eyes and wondered if she thought less of a man for displaying such emotion. He showed her Moody's Bible, for he always carried it with him. They sat together, their knees almost touching, as he walked her down the biblical trail the preacher had laid for him. He told her about that day in the church, how he had wrestled with God and won . . . salvation. They spoke at some length about Carrie—her patience, her beauty, her conviction even in the face of ardent longing.

And then they forgave each other for their individual actions and misconceptions and loathing.

So intense was their discussion, they failed to notice the sun setting and the gaslights lighting. They looked at each other with surprise when the steward knocked and announced dinner.

Anna stood and offered him her hand. And as he took it, she quite formally invited him to dine with her family that evening. His heart swelled, and he said it would be an honor.

And as they made their way across the deck, enveloped in a spectacular sunset, he reflected that he

277

had lived too many years outside of such pure joy. He had read about it in the Psalms but only now grasped its true measure. Yes. *Blessed is he whose transgression is forgiven.*

The sea that night was like a sheet of glass, and their ship as steady as a carver's hand.

For once, the racks over their tables did not swing, the oil lamps did not sputter, and no water sloshed onto the damask tablecloth. The *saloon* windows remained uncovered—a rarity—and soon the diners were crossing to them, commenting on the brilliant star-studded sky.

The children had clapped with delight when Anna had arrived on the arm of their favorite reader and announced, "Mr. Jameson will be joining us this evening."

Maggie leaned over to her sister and whispered theatrically, "I adore Mr. Jameson! Is he not the most beautiful man?"

"Maggie!" Annie flushed at her sister's brashness, and Maggie simply shrugged.

"But he is."

Pastor Lorriaux continued his nightly French lesson with Anna, helping her order from the menu.

"Que voudriez-vous?" What would you like?

Anna shot him a mischievous look. *"Je voudrais un . . . café."*

"Please."

Anna grimaced. *"S'il vous plaît."*

"Tres bien!"

"Maman," Maggie interjected. "You must order *de la glace.*"

Anna raised a brow. "Must I?"

"Oui! It is ice cream!"

Anna smiled. "But perhaps I would prefer—" she scanned the menu—*"creme brûlée* instead."

Maggie clapped her hands in glee. *"Maman! You are a wonderful student!"* And she turned to her governess. *"N'est-ce pas, Nicolet?"*

Mr. Montague, a favorite at their table because of his impeccable dress and manners and delicious sense of humor, suggested a game in which everyone must make a flattering statement to Mrs. Spafford, but at least one of the words must be in French. He began. *"Madame Spafford, your gown is fit for le tribunal."* The court.

Anna looked around the table for help. "Tribes? It is a tribal gown?" Her companions looked away, biting their lips. She gave up, and Nicolet translated. Anna smiled demurely at Mr. Montague and thanked him for the compliment.

And then it was Maggie's turn, and then Annie's. Soon their table was engulfed in fits of laughter, with many a diner glancing their way. But they cared not.

After the last dish was cleared away and the children sent to bed under great protest, the adults lingered in the *saloon,* enjoying the amusements. They could not speak for the other guests on board, but at their table, stomachs swelled with sumptuous food, minds clicked with good humor, and hearts beat with peace and joy.

CHAPTER 23

Atlantic Ocean, off Newfoundland
November 23, 1873, 1:30 A.M.

The triple blast of a trumpet caused Anna to turn toward the wall, tucking the baby's warm little body into her side. What a long night it had been— Bessie feverish and Tanetta fussy, Anna walking Tanetta up and down the passageway, Nicolet tending Bessie, both still in their evening gowns, all of them exhausted.

But twenty minutes later, shouts and what sounded like two terrific claps of thunder had her fully awake, then clinging to the edge of the bunk as the ship pitched and rolled and shivered.

She waited until she could gain footing, listening intently through the porthole she'd cracked open an hour earlier. Impossible. She thought she'd heard *"collision"* shouted across the deck, and even she could translate that. She rolled from the bunk, thankful that she'd been too tired to remove her shoes, and looked into the fearful eyes of Annie.

"Mama?"

Anna cupped her eldest child's face and whispered, "I will just go see what it's about. Wake Nicolet, then gather the coats, hats, and gloves, and help your sisters into them . . . over their nightgowns."

She pulled her coat from the trunk and opened the

door. Sleepy and confused passengers, illumined only by the lights near the stairs, drifted into the dark hall, all in nightwear, calling, "What is the matter?" She turned to her daughter, already alert and gathering the items.

"Shoes, Annie. I shall return."

She closed the door and made her way up the stairs as calmly as her wildly beating heart allowed. What trial awaited them now? Would she never have a full night's rest? She emerged onto the deck, turned, and shrank back at the fantastic sight.

Under a clear and starlit sky, a great three-masted ship loomed up before her, all sails set, its bow projecting over the deck, protruding into their side amidships. Sailors shouted English and French commands back and forth as the *du Havre* began to tear free with a piercing shriek, wood splitting and water rushing furiously into the massive hole.

She stood paralyzed for critical moments, spellbound by the crush of events and sailors dashing about, until a hand touched her arm and a familiar voice gained her attention.

"Mrs. Spafford?" It was Mr. Montague, dressed for all the world like a man on his way to the opera. "Where are your children?"

The ship listed slightly, and she grabbed at his arm. The children. She turned and made to run down the stairs when he caught her, told her to wait, and convinced a passing steward to go belowdecks with them.

They raced down the stairs and into the crowded passageway. All elegance aside, Anna forced her way through the mass of people and around broken pieces of smashed cabins—ruins produced by the bow of one ship breaking free from another. Water poured in and passengers, wounded and imprisoned, cried for help. It occurred to her that Mr. Jameson could be trapped in there. A chill ran through her, but she could not stop.

The ship's surgeon passed them, shouting, *"C'est tout pour rien!"*

She looked at Montague. "What does he say?"

He shook his head. "It is all for nothing."

Anna gaped. "Is he mad?"

They reached the cabin and burst through the door, finding Nicolet and the children dressing peaceably, reciting the Lord's Prayer.

"Give us this day our daily bread," Annie was saying as she stuffed Bessie's arms into her little coat. Maggie stood dutifully beside Nicolet, holding her hand, reciting with fervor.

"And forgive us our debts, as we forgive our debtors."

Anna rushed to the trunk, entreating them to continue as she gathered papers, jewelry, and money. The valuables secured, she whirled about, snatched Tanetta from Nicolet, and placed her into Montague's arms, where the baby immediately became fascinated with his silk tie.

"And lead us not into temptation, but deliver us from evil."

She took Annie's right hand and placed it into the

282

steward's. Then she connected Maggie to Annie, Nicolet to Maggie, and Bessie to Nicolet, and drew up the rear.

"For thine is the kingdom, and the power, and the glory, for ever.

And on the "amen" Anna nodded, and Montague opened the door. Anna gripped Bessie's hand and squeezed. Annie looked back at her mother, a mixture of fear and excitement crossing her young face.

Anna tried for an encouraging smile and failed. She met each of her daughters' eyes and raised her clasped hand. "Do not let go.

On deck a frightful scene unfolded. Barely five minutes had passed, and all was chaos. Great flames burst out of the ventilator while half-dressed passengers fought sailors for seats on lifeboats that would surely swamp with the overcrowding.

And all the while the *du Havre* leaned to the portside, oscillating on the sea. The captain shouted orders in French to launch the longboats, and the crew worked with great diligence.

Groups of women huddled together, praying aloud, singing, and taking their last farewell of those near them. Anna wanted to shout at them for their hopelessness. They were in peril, yes, but they were not doomed. Another ship was within sight.

Maggie, however, thought it a splendid idea and implored, "Let us pray again!" And so they did.

"Our Father which art in heaven, hallowed be thy name . . ."

As the prayer ended, Montague handed Tanetta to her mother. "Some gentlemen and I will try to cut away a lifeboat." He smiled and rushed away.

But in another moment the mainmast, canvas sails flapping in the brisk wind, snapped and fell with an awful crash, pulling the mizzenmast with it, crushing Montague and the longboats ready to launch and any passenger in its terrible path.

And for the first time, Anna understood their fate.

The injured lay about the listing deck, calling, "Save me . . . save me . . ." Water poured into the gaping chasm. The ship shuddered. Men and women ran about screaming, "We are shipwrecked! God save us!" The *du Havre* was going down by the bow.

Anna gathered her children, pulling them against her, trying to shield their eyes from the terror around them.

"Mama . . ."

Anna looked down at Maggie, her dramatic and gifted child, and marveled at her composure.

"God will take care of us." And she said it with absolute conviction.

The bow broke free from the ship with a resounding crash, and people screamed. The cold seawater rushed onto the deck, drenching their feet and making the planks slippery. The captain's gig and whaleboat launched, and the captain began the call to evacuate.

"*Messieurs et mesdames!* This ship is heavily damaged and sinking! You must abandon ship *immédiatement!*"

284

Passengers protested, some working frantically with pocket-knives to free life buoys and boats stuck fast to the newly painted ship. Nearby a young woman of about twenty held her mother in a close embrace, saying, "Courage, dear Mama, a struggle of a few seconds and we shall enter heaven together."

The captain continued shouting orders. *"Faites attention!* You must step into the water! A rescue boat will come retrieve you!"

Anna lurched forward as Annie pulled away from the circle. "No! No one jumps! We will stay together!"

Annie turned to her mother, the serenity of an old soul in her eyes. "Don't be afraid, Mama. The sea is His and He made it."

And the sea rushed over the afterdeck, the tremendous force of the water parting the group. Annie hit the deck hard and let go of Maggie to reach for Bessie. Anna pitched forward, grabbing the hem of Maggie's nightgown, gripping Tanetta so tightly she screamed. Maggie reached for her mother, eyes wide, the seawater choking her. Anna bunched the fabric in her hand, bracing herself against the rail, looking frantically about for her other children. But the pull of the ocean was too strong, and with a terrible rip, Maggie slipped from her fingers.

And then Anna, too, was sucked into the whirlpool, descending into space, Tanetta pulled from her arms and into the black abyss.

The cold was intense and she almost gasped in

shock. The sea closed around her, the weight of her coat pulling at her. She recognized with cold certainty that she was drowning. She knew she only had to breathe in the salty water and suffer but a minute and had almost given in to the impulse when she found her head rising above the water.

Gasping and fighting her coat, she looked around wildly for her daughters, calling their names, her breath fogging around her.

"Maggie! Annie! Answer your mother! Bessie! Swim to me!"

A mighty shriek rent the air, and the *Ville du Havre,* lights still ablaze, disappeared into the agony of the Atlantic without reeling, going down bow first.

Anna was sucked under by the ship's tow, then was nearly horrified with surprise to find herself above water again, choking and bobbing on a piece of wreckage, which every minute! plunged with her under the waves. People drifted by, floating on life buoys, pieces of timber, yards, and casks. And one by one they all disappeared around her.

She called her children until she had no more voice, then gave in to the cold and faintness . . . and silence. Silence and the ominous dash of wave after wave.

CHAPTER 24

Chicago
December 2, 1873

The downtown office door burst open, and Spafford could see from the corner of his eye that McDaid stood there, about to interrupt. Spafford held up a hand for silence while he finished recording his thought on the intricate land contract, reread it, made a notation, then glanced at his partner.

All thoughts of real estate flew instantly from his mind. Never before had he seen such a look of terror on the man's face, not even when they'd run from their burning building the night of the Fire. He stood and spoke as one might to a panicked horse.

"What is it?"

McDaid's mouth worked, but no sound came out.

Spafford stepped from behind his desk. "Is it Dora?"

McDaid shook his head and remained mute.

Spafford switched tactics, hoping to startle the news from his friend and partner. "Speak, man!"

McDaid jumped and his eyes grew even wider as he stammered out the information. "Th-the . . . ship . . . It's a-all over t-town."

Spafford narrowed his eyes and cocked his head, confused. "Go on."

Tears sprang to the man's eyes, alarming Spafford

even more. McDaid swallowed convulsively, his voice coming out on a near whisper.

"The *Ville du Havre* . . . It went down in the Atlantic."

Spafford experienced a strange moment in which his vision went very clear and the room seemed to rotate like a child's spinning top. He watched McDaid's lips move, but no words made it to his ears. In fact, there was no sound at all, just the muffled thud of his own steady heartbeat. And then everything slowed to a crawl. He was telling his legs to run, but he could barely lift them. McDaid reached out a hand, and Spafford watched, fascinated, as his own arm rose up and knocked it away.

Then in a flash he was through the doorway and running down the street, running like he hadn't run since he was a young boy and a neighbor's dog had chased him home. He came face-to-face with a screaming horse and leapt onto the sidewalk filled with pedestrians. He dodged them left and right, vaguely aware of the spectacle he made—a gentleman on the tear.

The Tribune building was no more than two blocks away, and he barreled through the crowd until he came up against a wall of people surrounding the newspaper offices. An unnatural, unnerving hush emanated from the gathering as individuals and couples moved forward in a makeshift line and read the notices posted on the board. Every nerve was screaming at him to lunge through the crowd, trample people if he must. His hands came up, and his legs tensed to move when a single word, passed mouth to ear, stayed him: *Survivors.*

Spafford remained in line, breathing hard, staring straight ahead, outwardly controlled and dignified. A blast of winter air made him aware that he'd left the office in shirt-sleeves, and he began to shake from the cold and the unknown.

A woman at the front screamed and collapsed, her companion catching her and dragging her to the side. And Spafford stared straight ahead, his chest heaving, his eyes burning.

God is our refuge and strength, he chanted in his mind. *Our refuge and strength . . . a very present help in trouble. Therefore, we will not fear . . .* He inched ahead.

A rosy-cheeked man clutched the edge of the notice board, reading the bulletin again and again, shaking his head and sobbing. "My wife is dead! My daughter is saved, but my wife is dead!"

The crowd moved forward without a word, and Spafford picked up a new litany. *Why art thou cast down, oh my soul? And why art thou disquieted within me. Hope in God . . . hope in God . . . hope in God . . .*

He watched an older couple step up to the board. The man settled reading glasses on his nose with a shaking hand, his other arm wrapped tightly around his wife's shoulders. The man leaned into the board, scanning the information. And then he turned to his wife, his face filled with joy. "She lives!" They embraced, weeping, and the crowd pushed closer.

Be merciful . . . Spafford prayed. *Be merciful unto me, O Lord for I cry unto thee daily. Be merciful . . . merciful . . .*

A woman in mourning attire stepped to the board, read the information, quickly pulled the veil over her face, and slipped away.

Spafford was close enough to see that the posted information was a list—of survivors, he guessed. His heart pounded in his ears as he waited but a moment, and finally he stood before the board.

He ran his fingers over the glass, down the list, his heart rejoicing when the name appeared: Anna Spafford. *She lives! She lives!* His spirit echoed that of the older couple, then instantly plunged into fear. But what of his children? He traced the list again, looking for more names ending in Spafford. None. He traced the names again. Perhaps no children were listed. That was it! Only the adult of the party would—his mind clicked. But what of Tommy Jameson? And Nicolet? He searched the list again . . . and again . . . until a quiet, shaking voice behind him interrupted his frenzied search.

"Sir, may I please have a look?"

Spafford moved away from the board, confused, flushed with happiness and anxiety. Why was the list so short? There had been no more than twenty-five names posted. It was impossible. And what of the ship's crew? He shook his head as he hurried back toward his office. He would set his partners on a fact-finding mission. He would send a telegram to the ship's agent in New York.

He was back at his Madison Street office in a thrice, forming the words, devising a plan. He pulled on the handle of the street-level door and nearly collided with a delivery boy in the familiar double-breasted uniform of the Western Union Telegraph Company, twin rows of shiny brass buttons marching down his jacket. Ah, just the lad he needed to see. He steadied the messenger and was about to make a special request when he saw the stack of messages clasped in the boy's gloved hand. He tightened his grip.

"Did you just make a delivery?"

"Yes, sir."

"To whom?"

"H. G. Spafford, of Spafford, McDaid, and Wilson."

Spafford released the boy and raced down the hall to his office. Just inside the door stood McDaid, the yellow envelope with the Western Union insignia in his hand.

McDaid offered it to his partner and stood, word-lessly, as Spafford broke the seal with shaking hands. Inside would be a message from Anna, a message dictated to a telegraph operator an ocean away, a message Spafford both wanted and feared.

He removed the folded sheet and saw that it was dated December 2 from Cardiff, Wales. He slowly unfolded it and read the brief message. He stared, unbelieving that his adult life, the building and rebuilding of his family, had been reduced to two words.

And yet it had.

For there on the page, written in a stranger's fluid hand, was the exact summation of what in one stroke of fate had finally become of H. G. and Anna Spafford: *Saved. Alone.*

Spafford paced up and down the great hallway of his Lake View home, his footsteps matching the *tick* and *tock* of the grandfather clock. He could not seem to get his breath. He could not rest. He felt that if he should sit down, he would go mad.

Coates . . . dear Coates . . . He sat in the parlor, a steady friend, offering no answers, no cliched rationalizations for such an unspeakable tragedy. Just an hour before, as the clock had struck three in the morning, Spafford had marched to his friend's side, his throat rough from the emotion he suppressed, and barked out, "Do you remember? When Anna left me—do you remember what I said to you? I said, 'I am glad to trust the Lord when it will cost me something!' I was a fool!"

Coates had looked at him with eyes red from sorrow and simply said, "I remember."

And that was how the night had passed—equal bouts of rage and grief, of guilt and penitence, pacing from room to room, asking, asking, asking . . . What, dear God, had he done that he should pay such a price? Most of his forty-five years had been a walk down the disciplined and straightforward path of success—both worldly and spiritually. But in the space of two years, he'd lost nearly everything—his business in the Fire, his fortune in the real estate venture, his security in marriage, and now, every one of his children. All that he had left was a wife who might not forgive him and a God who would not speak to him.

It was God's silence that so terrified him now. Never before had he needed such assurance. And never had the Lord been so absent. Perhaps this was his punishment for abandoning his family in the interest of business—God simply removed them. And then removed himself. But his mind railed against that. No! God was merciful. God promised that neither tribulation nor distress, neither death nor life, nor height nor depth—nothing would be able to separate man from the love of Christ. Nothing. And yet, He was silent.

Spafford's stomach heaved again, and he tasted the bile in his throat. How would he ever recover from this? Would the dawn never come? Would the train never arrive to take him to the ship that would carry him to Paris? He walked the floors of his house until the sky began to lighten and he could not stay within the walls another moment.

His hand was on the knob when Coates called his name. He looked up and into the doctor's drawn face, grief and exhaustion showing the man's age like never before.

Coates spoke softly. "Where do you go?"

"Only to the yard. I must get out of this house."

The doctor nodded and reached for the overcoat, hat, and gloves Spafford had discarded so many hours ago and helped him on with them.

And then Spafford was crunching through snow sparkling with the mystical light between night and day. He walked to the gate, then followed it to the end of his property, then back. He watched the sun come up and reflect off the parlor windows. He saw the doctor standing there, watching the sunrise, watching him.

He turned and trudged to the stand of tall elm trees. A crude board was nailed to one of the trunks, and he brushed the snow from it. POST OFFICE was painted on it in faded black. He smiled a little and looked lower to find an old mailbox, the flag bent and raised. Curious, he opened the little door, reached in and withdrew a handmade envelope warped and stiff from the winter weather. On the outside was written in childish letters, *My House.* His heart ached anew with the knowledge that there would be no more make-believe, no more letters from his imaginative children.

He removed a glove and gently worked open the flap. Inside, on a torn sheet of drawing paper, was a little note dated November 11, 1873. *Good-bye, dear sweet Lake View,* it read. *I will never see you again. Maggie Spafford.*

He blinked, and then he was falling into the snow,

his breath coming in great gasps. But he couldn't breathe. Somewhere in the distance he heard Coates shouting. And then, mercifully, mercifully . . . blackness.

CHAPTER 25

December 5, 1873

There was no word for it. Spafford stared through the frosty glass of the train window, the snowy scenery of New England passing by in a blur, thinking . . . thinking . . .

When a child loses his parents, he becomes an orphan. And great concern and pity are heaped upon him. Charles Dickens made sure of that. And when a woman loses her husband, she becomes a widow—no, it was more definitive. She becomes *the* widow—the Widow Larrssen, the Widow O'Brien. And with a simple title, everyone knows her plight and pain. And when a man loses his wife, he becomes a widower—not for long, as he is inundated with female companionship to ease his solitariness.

But when a parent loses a child, there is no word for it. It is out of sync in the cycle of life and death. There is no understanding it, so man had found no method to describe it. It was a wordless, ruthless, raw agony that defied classification. It was perdition.

Through the fog of these thoughts, Spafford heard someone calling to him and turned his head to find a steward standing in the aisle. He was an older fellow, crisp in his uniform of wool and shiny buttons, and spoke with the lilt of an Irishman.

"'Tis the end o' the line, sir. Ye'll be welcome to transfer or take the ferry across, God willin'. The snow is comin' down somethin' fierce?'

Spafford pulled himself up, numb with the fatigue of sleepless nights and a long journey. He looked around the railcar—empty but for the two of them. The steward ushered him toward the exit, and helped him down the steep steps and onto the platform.

Spafford moved toward his trunk, then halted in the wooden terminal, paralyzed with memory. Maggie— pink-cheeked in her fur-trimmed coat, squealing for joy at the sight of the colorful ferries. Anna—gathering the children around her in the crowded terminal like a hen with her chicks.

"Where might ye be stayin', sir?"

It was the Irishman, patient and vigilant of his weary passenger. Spafford thought hard and mumbled an address.

"Ye'll be wantin' the ferry to Cortlandt Street, then. If ye have the three penny I'll book yer passage."

Spafford dug in his pocket for the fare and watched the steward traipse off to the dock. He spied a bench along the wall, summoned the strength from deep within, and pulled his trunk over to it.

The steward returned to the terminal, glanced about, and found his passenger slumped against the wall. He ambled over with two cups of coffee in hand

and offered one to Spafford, along with the ticket.

"I thought as ye might be wantin' a cup o' joe. 'Tis a cold night and a colder crossin'."

Spafford nodded his thanks and tried to relax on the frigid bench with the Irishman. He sipped his coffee—strong and very hot—and appreciated a man who could sit in companionable silence. After a time it occurred to him that this steward might have answers to the myriad questions racing through his brain day and night. Answers that would alter nothing of his circumstances but lay his mind to rest.

"You . . . you speak often to the sailors . . . the men on the pier?"

The steward smiled. "Aye, some of us come from the same village. We work hard durin' the day and regale each other over a pint at night."

"Tell me, then, about . . . the *Ville du Havre*."

The Irishman frowned and shook his head. "Oh, now, that would be a sorry tale for the tellin'."

Spafford stared hard at the steward, imploring him with his eyes to tell what he knew. He watched as a slow understanding filled the man's weathered face. The Irishman nodded, and his lilting voice softened the edge of harsh detail.

"Well then. The word come from Cardiff when the first survivors landed there."

Spafford reached instinctively for the telegram that never left his side, a telegram from Cardiff, Wales.

"They were seven days out, a heavy sea runnin' bitterly cold. 'Twas late . . . late . . . two in the mornin' and everyone abed. The *Lochearn*—a Scottish vessel—was goin' afore the wind with all sails set. Only God knows why, but she struck the *Havre* amid-ships, nearly tearin' her in two."

Spafford thought of the cabin assigned to his family amid-ships, how young Thomas had graciously switched with them and unknowingly traded his life.

"They're sayin' the *Lochearn* had a steel-plated bowsprit built to force her way through ice. They're sayin' the damage was so great, the *Havre* went down in twelve minutes." He shook his head sadly. "No time . . . no time a'tall for savin' lives."

He lapsed into deep thought, sipping his coffee, staring out into the wooden shed. Spafford let the information settle over him, his coffee forgotten. He took a deep breath.

"And the survivors?"

The Irishman sipped his coffee. " 'Twas them near the steerage stairs what made it to the deck and into the whaling boat or over the rail that survived. 'Twas them what could swim or hang on to the wreckage . . . what little there was." He let out a long breath.

"Ach . . . 'twas a great tragedy . . . and an unspeakable loss." And he leaned forward, resting his arms on his knees, cradling his cup, shaking his head.

Spafford felt like he'd been running uphill. His heart raced. His clothing clung to him, drenched in sweat. He did not think he could stand. The horrific images played again through his mind—Annie flailing in the water, Bessie grasping for something,

298

anything, to hold on to. Tanetta pulled down, down into the Atlantic. Maggie . . . Maggie . . . his breath caught, and he stifled a sob.

The Irishman turned his head at the sound, and regret was written all over his face. He let some time pass, then leaned back against the wall. When he spoke, the lilt was stronger than ever.

"When me pa died, I was but a lad and could not be consoled for the loss of him. Me poor ma put me to bed each night, herself just barely survivin'. 'There, now,' she'd say. 'Earth has no sorrows that heaven cannot heal.' Every night she told me that." He adjusted his steward's cap.

"But . . . 'twas a long while before I believed it."

They sat together—two men a long way from home, and one a long way from peace. A muffled horn and shouting voices carried through the snow and into the terminal, breaking the gentle silence.

"Well now. There'll be yer ferry." The steward set down his cup, took the trunk's handle, and dragged it to the dock like a man half his age. Spafford followed behind, feeling old and consumed.

The steward settled the trunk and tipped his hat. "God be with ye, sir."

Spafford stood on the dock, the heavy snow falling around him, and did not reply. God was somewhere, he knew. But not with him. Not anymore.

He'd walked the streets of New York City all day. Down Broadway he'd trudged with the fashionable crowd, past the grand theatres, oblivious to the Christmas garland and champagne sparkle and bitter cold.

He'd passed the great retail houses of the Stewarts and the Tiffanys and the Lords & Taylors, ignoring their Venetian facades and elaborate windows full of lavish ornaments and modish goods. He'd bustled along with the impatient, aggressive crowd, glad to be in a city full of people who did not know him, who'd jostled and pushed past him, who did not look upon him with their eyes full of sorrow and pity. He'd walked until his body was numb with cold and fatigue. And then he'd kept walking, letting the rhythmic roar of hundreds of people and carriages on the resonant pavement drown out the piercing wail of his heart and mind.

He'd turned on Fourteenth Street and stood in front of Steinway Hall in Union Square, imagining Lizzie at the piano, grateful for the school reports that indicated all was well with their new prodigy. A missing birth certificate and a letter from an influential judge had been the difference between an ill-fated journey and a life of potential for one young girl. He wondered how much time would pass before Lizzie realized God's hand in her deliverance.

He sighed, turned, and tramped back up Lexington Avenue until he'd found himself in front of Carrie's brick building. And there he'd remained while the sun set and the gaslights came on.

How would he tell her? He had no insight, no per-

300

sonal details of their loved ones' last moments. He had just a two-word telegram folded and tucked into his inside coat pocket, next to his heart. This kind of news, he finally decided, was best told with candor. He would follow Job's example. He would "speak in the anguish of my spirit . . ."

A familiar figure appeared on the next block—a fashionable young woman blending in with the early evening crowd, hunkered down in her silk scarf and heavy wool coat. It was Carrie, but she did not move with the same burst of energy he was accustomed to seeing in her. He studied her as she moved closer. She looked tired—no, she looked defeated. He hesitated in his mission. He did not want to add to her burdens, did not want to watch her brown eyes darken with pain. If he left now, he could slip away through the crowd. He could send her a note. He could—

She noticed him when she was still ten yards away. She slowed to a halt, the crowd continuing around her, and considered him without a trace of surprise. And he saw immediately that she knew.

Of course she knew. The news would have reached New York first, then Chicago. She would have rushed to the *New York Times'* office and checked the lists, just as he had. She would have stood with the anxious crowd in front of the bulletin boards, waiting her turn, and seen the same name, the only name, on the list.

She continued toward him, looking straight into his soul, and the depth of her empathy was magnificent. This was a woman who understood grief. This was a woman who had wavered on the edge of her own sanity and consciously stepped back, lifted her chin, and soldiered on.

She stopped before him, holding out her hand, and Spafford took it. She smiled ever so slightly.

"I hoped you would come."

He stared at her, at a loss now as to what to do or say. Carrie seemed to understand his indecision and squeezed his hand.

"Would you join me for supper, Mr. Spafford? Lizzie is at music lessons until eight, and I do so dislike dining alone."

He nodded and offered his arm, and Carrie led him across Thirteenth Street to Collier's Cafe. They stepped through the stone archway, shaking the snow from their boots and coats, and settled at a table for two near the front window. It was warm and peaceful in the little bistro, and after placing an order of coffee and bread and large bowls of lentil soup, Spafford felt his body relax for the first time in days.

Carrie looked past him at the falling snow and constant traffic and spoke in a quiet, contemplative voice.

"Mr. Jameson," she began and blinked a little as she said his name, "came to see me the night before the ship sailed. He was . . . a changed man."

Spafford knew they were both filled with a hope that could only be answered once they reached heaven. But he was eager to share with her his own impressions of Tommy Jameson.

"Last month, before we left Chicago, there was a letter . . . from Moody. I never read it, but it seemed to have made the difference."

She smiled and nodded.

The soup arrived and they busied themselves with it, Tommy's conversion hanging between them. Spafford ate little, dipping his spoon in and out of the steaming broth until he rested the handle on the edge of the bowl, overwhelmed with the need to tell Carrie about his last encounter with Jameson.

"The day the *du Havre* sailed, I felt—" He shook his head. "I don't know what to call it . . . an unease, I suppose, about the location of my family's staterooms. To this day, I cannot explain it. Thomas very generously offered to exchange his suite in the bow for our rooms amidships."

She studied him as he spoke, and he let all of his emotions run free across his face as he spelled out for her the significance of that detail.

"The *Lochearn* struck the *du Havre* exactly at 'his rooms."

Carrie's face blanched.

"Thomas traded his life . . . for Anna's."

Carrie bit her lip, and the tears spilled onto her pale cheeks. Spafford reached for her hand.

"I am sorry, Carrie." His voice broke. "Yet I am not."

She nodded and smiled. "Please do not mistake the cause of my tears, for I am so happy!"

He gaped at her, and she rushed to assure him. "Just

imagine it—imagine his beautiful face as he stood before the Lord and heard from the Savior the words he'd been longing to hear all his life."

She leaned forward and whispered them. "'Well done, Thomas! Well done.'"

Spafford scanned her wet and radiant face, and the truth of her attachment dawned on him.

"You loved him?"

She nodded. "I loved him."

"Did he know?"

"I think he did . . . I hope he did."

He thought of the unbridled promise in young love—the dreams, the wishing, the wanting—and considered it was no different than the emotions he had rekindled with his wife over the past month. And now those, too, might very well be gone. His heart began to race again at the depth of his loss, and he looked across the table, choking out his misery.

"How do you bear it?"

She considered him a moment, then blotted her wet cheeks and folded the napkin in her lap. And then she began.

"When Joseph died, I no longer wanted to live." She saw his surprise and rushed to assure him. "Oh, I was no danger to myself. Not in that way." She stared out the window at the passing horses, their harnesses jingling, the *clip-clop* of their hooves muffled by the snow.

"But I longed to pass from this life into the next. I would lie in bed, night after night, hoping I would pass in my sleep and wake up in heaven. I thought that maybe a person truly could die of a broken heart."

She paused and they sat in contemplative silence, Spafford remembering that tragic time and the constant vigil Anna had kept.

"Then Brother Moody came to visit. Dr. Coates had been coming every other day, and I could mark the week by his arrival. But this time Moody came with him. He was unusually quiet—so quiet it was discomfiting." She looked at Spafford with a slight smile. "You know how he is, so high-spirited, so *alive*."

Spafford gave the barest of nods.

"He sat by my bed, opened his old Bible, and quoted me promise after promise. And I believed not a word of it." She leaned forward, forcing Spafford to look her full in the face.

"But then he said something I will never forget. He closed that Bible and looked at me with those piercing eyes and said, 'Even despair will eventually run its course. What will you do, Carrie? What will you do with your life when you are ready again to live it?'

"He didn't wait for an answer, and I didn't have one. But that question rattled around and around in my head for days afterward. And when despair had run its course, just as he said, I had a plan. It was a small plan. And God took care of the rest."

The bill arrived and Spafford paid it, and then they

were crunching through the snow again, making the short trip to Carrie's rooms in comfortable quiet. He walked her up the steps and squeezed her hand, and returned to the street without a word.

He'd gone just a few steps when he heard Carrie call out, "Mr. Spafford—" He turned, and she looked at him with eyes that were both old with wisdom and bright with promise.

"I know you can hardly imagine it. But one day— not tomorrow, maybe not for a full year—but one day, you will be able to look up without the weight of rage and guilt and declare, 'It is well . . . it is well with my soul.'"

Spafford wound his way across Manhattan, then up West Street and along the wharf, Carrie's parting words ringing in his ears. He watched the dock workers load the heavy bales of cotton and barrels of wheat into the cargo hold of the *Guadeloupe*—the steamer that would take him to Paris, to Anna.

And the words still drummed against his breast.

And the next morning, when he stood back from the rail and felt the ship's engines spring to life and watched the crowd wave gaily as they pulled away from the pier, he looked across the Hudson River and felt the hand of the Lord on his shoulder. But he shrugged it away.

For four days Spafford had cried out to the Lord, just as Mary and Martha had cried out for Lazarus. And yes, in His own time, Jesus had come. But He had come too late.

CHAPTER 26

Atlantic Ocean
December 13, 1873

S pafford blinked hard as he stared down at the map. The captain's hand had returned to the coordinates—47 degrees latitude, 35 degrees longitude—the point they were now crossing and the best estimate of where the SS *Ville du Havre* had taken his children and two hundred twenty-two others to a watery grave. The valley of the shadow of death.

He felt the familiar grip on his throat and wondered if he'd ever be able to breathe normally again.

Come to me.

He looked up at the captain. The voice had not been Italian. It had been . . . could it have been . . . ?

Take my yoke . . . learn from me.

He shook his head, then turned and rushed off the bridge, down the stairs and onto the portside deck. He leaned against the rail, panting, uncaring anymore who might see him and what they might think.

He looked down, deep into the heart of the Atlantic, and everything in him cried, Why? What had he done? What had Anna done that they should suffer such . . . such . . . heartbreak?

But the Atlantic, as usual, was brutally silent.

He watched the waves crash against the side of the mighty ship as he choked on his anguish, his eyes watering from the effort to swallow, to breathe. He simply could not bear the pain anymore.

And then, the hand of the Lord was firmly on his shoulder. And this time he did not shrug it away. *Why did you leave me?* Spafford's heart cried out.

Never will I leave you.

His hands gripped the rail. *But you did! You did!*

Never will I forsake you.

He pushed away and began to pace up the deck. *Then tell me why! Why did you take them? Why must we suffer so?* The moment the questions rushed out, the answer hastened in—a verse in Romans: *We glory in tribulations also, knowing that tribulation worketh patience . . . and patience, experience . . . and experience, hope . . .*

Take my yoke.

But this was not the answer he wanted. It sounded more like a test—of his sanity, of his faith. He loved the Lord. He always had. Why must he stand like Abraham and willingly sacrifice his children to prove his love? What was the purpose? *Where was the glory in that?*

And he heard the voice of God, firm but gentle, whisper into his broken soul.

Who is on the throne?

Spafford sank to his knees in the bow, his ears ringing with the question, sobbing with grief and self-doubt and remorse. God was on the throne. And next to him was Christ, His only Son, who had died a merciless death that no one understood at the time so that he, Horatio

Gates Spafford, sinful, willful man, might believe.

God understood sacrifice. God understood grief.

And then, like a song, Carrie's parting words rose up against his despair. *"One day,"* she had said. *"One day, you will be able to look up without the weight of rage and guilt . . ."*

And he suddenly knew that he did not want to simply wait for that day. He did not want to walk this same deck tomorrow, shouting at the Lord and laying blame. So he lifted his eyes to heaven and, with supplication and thanksgiving, made his request known.

Please . . . please, Lord . . . Give me peace. He waited in the bow as the ship, and the ocean and everything around him grew mysteriously quiet. No music or laughter erupted from the main *saloon,* no sailors called out orders. Even the waves broke silently. And then he heard the still, small voice.

My peace passes all understanding . . .

Spafford swallowed his humanness—his pride, his aggression, his demand for answers—and agreed. *I know.*

And the breath of God blew over him like the sweetest fragrance on a summer wind. And the waves broke like music against the bow, rolling, chanting, "It is well . . . it is well." He stayed there in the bow of the mighty ship, glorying in the Lord.

Then little by little he felt the pull of words, of putting pen to paper. He stood and made his way to his stateroom on steady legs. He pulled some paper from his trunk—stationery from the Brevoort Hotel in Chicago, the same paper on which he'd boldly written, "Wait on the Lord." He chose a fresh sheet, sat at the little writing desk, and wrote at the top, "It Is Well With My Soul."

He paused, pen hovering, as a verse from Isaiah filled his mind. *For thus saith the Lord . . . I will extend peace to her like a river . . .* Peace like a river . . . And the words came with very little interruption. Just line after line pouring out of him in perfect rhyme and meter.

When peace like a river attendeth my way,
When sorrows like sea-billows roll,
Whatever my lot, Thou hast taught me to say:
"It is well, it is well with my soul."

Tho' Satan should buffet, tho' trials should come,
Let this blest assurance control,
That Christ hath regarded my helpless estate,
And hath shed His own blood for my soul.

My sin—oh, the bliss of this glorious thought!
My sin—not in part but the whole,
Is nailed to His cross and I bear it no more;
Praise the Lord, praise the Lord, oh, my soul!

And, Lord, haste the day when the faith shall be sight,
The clouds be rolled back as a scroll,
The trump shall resound, and the Lord shall descend—
"Even so—it is well with my soul."

For me, be it Christ, be it Christ hence to live,
If Jordan above me shall roll,
No pang shall be mine, for in death as in life
Thou shalt whisper Thy peace to my soul.

He laid down the pen and stared at the words written so quickly and with such assurance. His heart was still heavy with sorrow, his future with Anna still uncertain. But his soul . . . his soul was secure.

The struggle had been fierce, but the victory was complete.

CHAPTER 27

Paris
December 18, 1873

Anna stood resolutely in the bright sun and longed for rain.

She'd refused the offer of an umbrella to protect her skin. She'd refused the carriage that would take her to and from the dock in mild obscurity. She'd refused an armed escort. What she wanted was rain.

Not a driving rain that would soak her mourner's skirt and cement the dock's filth to her. No, just a steady, dark wetness that would cling to her clothing and hair and face. Because there were no more tears left in her. And what kind of mother stops crying for her dead children?

She wanted to let the rain pour down her cheeks and

say to the world, "See? See the moisture on my face? I still mourn. I am a good mother."

But for three days fat, woolly clouds in the brilliant blue sky had dogged her every step as she'd tread the cobblestone path to the western dock. Happy sun-soaked sea gulls mocked her silent request as they led her on the route from hotel to waterfront, racing overhead, calling, calling, calling.

So she stood resolutely in the sun, her face impassive, her eyes fixed on the ship in harbor. Crewmen tossed out lines and readied the gangplank. People from all walks of life milled about the shops and docks with a mixture of excitement and purpose.

The commoners interested her with their fresh faces, large gestures, and accents. Chambermaids loudly greeted dock workers. Shopkeepers noisily bossed around young boys. There was urgency to their lives.

She noticed less the upper class as they waited patiently, haughtily, in their carriages or on the cobblestone, a studied boredom on their faces. Some daintily pressed handkerchiefs to their noses to cover the stench of cargo, horses, and fish, mixed with unwashed bodies and clothing. She stationed herself somewhere in between the classes, feeling part of neither.

But, oh, to stand with the dock workers. To be so candid. To go about daily life with simplicity and less expectation from society. To publicly cry out to God in anger and despair—like the homeless after the

Fire—with no thought for social graces, no fear of retribution.

For long moments in the icy Atlantic, and for days afterward, she'd known the freedom of being simply Anna. When her throat was raw from choking on seawater and calling out to her drowning children, she was no longer Mrs. Horatio Gates Spafford, social icon. When she clung to the wreckage, her whole body numb, deciding to let go and join her children in the inky blackness, she was no longer a paragon of Christian faith. When she awoke on the *Tremontain*, feverish from exposure, reliving her children's last moments and her failure as their protector, she was no longer a tower of strength.

As the rescue ship had slowly made its way across the Atlantic and the horror of the experience had settled within her, she'd spoken to no one—not to the survivors, not to Pastor Weiss, not even to God. Especially not God. She'd explained nothing, asked for nothing, expected nothing. Nine days of nearly uninterrupted silence had allowed her a liberty of thought and action she had not known was possible.

But that time was a gift. She understood that perfectly. Simply being Anna was unacceptable to her station. Now the shipwreck had managed to add one more crushing title to her legacy: survivor. It was yet another mindless elevation in status in a culture that thrived on sensation and situation. Mindless, for to survive in body is one thing—the brain signals, the heart pumps, the lungs expand, the blood circulates.

But to endure in spirit . . . Ah, to endure.

At last the passengers began to slowly make their way down the gangplank, steadying their sea legs with each step. People surged around her, waving, shouting, but she did not move. A bottleneck formed at the foot of the walkway, increasing the crowd's anxiety. She anchored her feet and scanned the travelers for her husband.

She needed to memorize that first moment when he saw her. She would know in an instant whether their relationship was over or really just begun. There would be no middle ground in his expression, no uncertainty in his approach. He was a decisive man, and she counted on this trait to set the course for the rest of their lives.

And suddenly, there he was. He stood like an immovable statue, a stone's throw away at the end of the gangplank, gazing at her. He was impeccably groomed, as usual—his garments elegant and showing no signs of a difficult crossing, his boots polished and reflecting the December sun, his face tanned, she knew, from spending a good amount of time at the ship's rail looking down, looking out, asking why. He was beautiful in a way that transcended the heritage of facial features and assigned fashion.

He was beautiful because he was a changed man.

The features that were always, *always,* so smooth and sure were now a mixture of pain and—could it be?—uncertainty. His brow showed relief, but his chin, normally set in quiet determination, quivered. There was a question in his eyes, a longing that transformed him.

This was a man to whom she could say, "I will not go home. I will not live in a house bereft of children and laughter. I will not endlessly relate the drama of the shipwreck to curious visitors. I will not be strong."

This was a man to whom she could confide her deepest anxieties, who would understand the indignity of their children buried at sea in their nightgowns. She could tell him how she could not speak to the Lord through her rage and despair. And he would not judge her for it.

She took in the essence of this man she had known through fourteen years of friendship, courtship, and marriage and came to a wonderful realization. She loved this man. God loved this man.

As the knowledge struck her, the feeling started somewhere in her chest and spread outward through her body until her ears were ringing with it.

Hope.

Tragedy had knocked on their door before—losing their fortune to the Fire, losing their relationship through endless service, now losing their children in a mindless accident. Tragedy knocked, knocked, knocked. It could knock again. But they—Anna and Gates—would always find each other. They would always endure.

And then he was before her. "Anna . . ." he whis-

315

pered on a sob of untold grief. He seemed unable to speak more and simply went to his knees, circling her waist with his arms, weeping into her skirt like a child.

She placed her hands on his shoulders, feeling his anguish through layers of proper winter clothing. She heard the sea gulls again, calling, calling, calling, and her heart cautiously cracked open and cried out with them, *Lord, send us peace . . . send us peace . . . send us peace . . .*

EPILOGUE

Horatio Gates and Anna Spafford slowly put their lives back together. They eventually returned to Chicago and devoted themselves to working with the city's poor. Their work was satisfying, their marriage thrived, and they were soon blessed with three more children—Horatio Gates, Jr., Bertha, and Grace.

Then tragedy once again knocked on the Spaffords' door. Their only son contracted scarlet fever and died at the age of four. Their loss was significant, but their faith did not waver.

In fact, their church's negative Puritan belief—that sickness or sorrow was the result of sin—prompted the Spaffords to make another life-altering change. They sold most of their belongings, packed what remained, and began life anew in Jerusalem, Israel.

Their small group of twenty-five adults and children began caring for the sick and orphaned in the Old City. They opened a school and organized a soup kitchen but did not preach conversion to Christianity, hoping instead to win the hearts of their neighbors through service. Eventually their community formed into the American Colony—the subject of Swedish novelist Selma Lagerlof, who won a Nobel Prize for her work on *Jerusalem.*

On October 16, 1888, almost seven years after his arrival in Israel, Horatio Gates Spafford died of malaria in Jerusalem. He was fifty-nine years old. His

317

body rests in a mass grave outside the old city walls at the Joppa Gate. There, a large memorial stone records the names of those buried within—Horatio Gates Spafford topping the list.

Anna assumed leadership at the Colony for another thirty-five years, expanding the settlement's services from weaving and cattle farming to automobile sales and photography. She died in 1923 at the age of eighty-one.

Although the Spaffords had money, opportunity, and status, their lives were marked by a steady stream of tragedy—tragedy they chose to use as a catalyst to change lives.

It was in 1876 that Philip Bliss, a dear friend of the Spaffords, took the words written on a ship one cold December day and placed music around them. "It Is Well With My Soul" has become a song dearly loved, the world over, by people who search for hope and rest amidst suffering.

Center Point Publishing
600 Brooks Road • PO Box 1
Thorndike ME 04986-0001 USA

(207) 568-3717

US & Canada:
1 800 929-9108